SOMEONE'S WATCHING ME

SOMEONE'S WATCHING ME

ZOE ROSI

 THOMAS & MERCER

Text copyright © 2022 by Zoe Rosi
All rights reserved.

No part of this book may be reproduced, or stored in a retrieval system, or transmitted in any form or by any means, electronic, mechanical, photocopying, recording, or otherwise, without express written permission of the publisher.

Published by Thomas & Mercer, Seattle

www.apub.com

Amazon, the Amazon logo, and Thomas & Mercer are trademarks of Amazon.com, Inc., or its affiliates.

ISBN-13: 9781542037181
ISBN-10: 1542037182

Cover design by The Brewster Project

Printed in the United States of America

SOMEONE'S
WATCHING
ME

Chapter One

Light floods through the kitchen window, falling over our steaming mugs of coffee, the jug of milk on the table, the glinting cutlery. Alex bites into a piece of toast as he scrolls through today's headlines. I reach for the milk and pour some over my muesli. Gazing across the kitchen as I eat, I take in the vase of tulips on the counter, the overflowing fruit bowl, last night's laundry drying on the clothes horse.

'Can you pass the salt?' Alex asks, glancing at the salt shaker at my end of the table.

'Sure.' I pick it up and hand it to him.

'Thanks.'

Our fingertips brush against each other's as he takes it. I smile, feeling a frisson of electricity at his touch, at the blueness of his playful eyes. He smiles back before dusting his scrambled eggs.

It's funny, but even after three years, the spark between us hasn't faded. The novelty of being together hasn't worn off. Nor has the novelty that this is my life: living with a good man in a lovely, comfortable home, a place where I feel safe, happy and content. I still wake up some days, like today, and have these pinch-me moments, as though I must be dreaming.

I take another spoonful of my muesli.

A beeping sound pierces my thoughts.

I look up. The sound grows louder, accompanied by loud voices and the slamming of car doors.

'What's that?' I ask.

Alex shrugs, uninterested. But the beeping continues, and I find myself becoming irritated. Alex and I live on a quiet street in a suburb of south London. It's not a trendy area; in fact, hardly anyone's even heard of it, even Londoners. We have no exciting bars or interesting museums or well-known landmarks here, just rows of suburban streets centred around a few shops and a train station that links our little London village to the rest of the city. It's not an exciting area, but it's comfortable. It's nice. It's full of families and people who have lived here their whole lives, elderly residents who were born here and never left. It's not transient, like so many other parts of the city, with renters coming and going, living in high-rise blocks of flats. It's peaceful. We have hardly any crime. We keep our community tranquil, safe.

It's not the kind of street where vans beep loudly early in the morning, waking anyone who's not already up.

I get up. Alex looks up at me as I slip down the hall. I can practically feel him rolling his eyes, wishing I'd mind my own business, as I stop and look out of the hallway window. A man is standing by the fence of the house next door, a removal van parked jerkily on the street behind him. He must be our new neighbour. Strangely, he's looking right at me. Not even bothering to help the removal men who cross his front drive, carrying boxes into the house.

It's almost as though he's been waiting for me to appear. My skin prickles with unease, a strange chill flooding through me. I ignore it and smile brightly, raising my hand in a wave. But the man doesn't respond. Instead, he just stands there, staring at me with piercing eyes that flicker with an odd look, almost like excitement.

I smile again, awkwardly this time. And again, he doesn't react. He looks around my age, early thirties. He's tall and slim, with a pale, chiselled face and dark hair. He's dressed casually in jeans and a black top. He looks smart. An off-duty young professional.

A woman emerges from the van carrying a pot plant under her arm. She's wearing a cap and I can't quite make out her features, but she's slim, a brunette. She brushes her hand affectionately against the man's waist as she passes him, and heads into the house. She must be his partner. He smiles at her before returning his attention to me.

He carries on looking at me as two removal men navigate a bulky piece of furniture out of the van. They carefully carry it across the pavement and through the garden gate but the new neighbour ignores them. His attention seems fixed on me, unwavering. And then I realise that to him, I must look the same. I'm suddenly embarrassed and I feel heat rising to my cheeks.

'Becky?' Alex says.

I turn around, startled, to see Alex standing in the kitchen doorway.

'What's wrong? Are you okay?' he asks, no doubt clocking my disturbed expression.

'Yeah,' I reply with a forced smile. I walk away from the window, still feeling the lingering stare of the neighbour clinging to me like a shadow. Alex reaches out as I pass him.

'What happened?' he asks, his hand brushing against my hip.

'Oh, nothing.' I sit back down at the table.

I stare at my bowl of muesli, the now empty jug of milk on the table, the tulips on the counter. Strangely, everything feels a little different, unsettled, like the air pressure has shifted in the room, and the blissful bubble I was in five minutes ago is no longer quite the same.

'There are new neighbours.'

'Okay . . .' Alex laughs, looking perplexed.

'This guy, he was standing by his fence just *looking* at me,' I admit.

Alex raises an eyebrow.

'Well, he was probably just curious to see you,' he remarks.

'It wasn't like that. I waved at him. He just ignored me.'

'Really?' Alex asks.

'Yeah, it was a bit odd, but never mind,' I say, reaching for my spoon.

I want to say that it almost felt like the neighbour had been waiting for me, but I resist. It's the kind of comment that would lead Alex to remark that I watch too many true crime documentaries and read too many thrillers. And he's right. I do. My imagination can be overactive.

But Alex frowns. He knows something's up.

'I'm going to have a look,' he says.

'Alex, don't,' I protest, but it's too late. He's already pacing down the hall.

I peer around the doorway and see him stopping at the window.

'He's gone,' he says, glancing back at me. 'There's no one there. Just some removal men.'

'Okay, let's just forget about it then,' I reply, turning back to my breakfast.

I try to tell myself it was nothing, just a new neighbour appraising his new street, taking in the area. It was nothing to worry about. I'm just being paranoid. I guard my home, the beautiful, lovely home I've created with Alex, so fiercely sometimes that I'm seeing threats where there are none. I need to relax. To let go. I'm safe. It's okay.

Alex sits back down. I look over at him. He smiles.

I smile back as I dip my spoon into my muesli and try to eat. I want to return to the peaceful reality of our weekday morning rituals, although I have a weird feeling that the serenity and comfort I cherish so much has gone. I shudder at the thought. Of course it hasn't gone. Of course not.

Chapter Two

I wait in line at the café next door to the office, buying a coffee before work. As the barista turns to make my latte, I see one of my colleagues charge past outside, his lanyard bold and yellow around his neck. Mine is stashed somewhere in the bottom of my bag. I avoid wearing it in public as much as possible. I work for Cartwright and Brooks, one of London's leading estate agents, and we don't have the best reputation in the world. We're known for being pushy and cut-throat – not the sort of company I want to shout about working at.

I never set out to be an estate agent. In fact, if you'd told me ten years ago that I'd end up as one, I'd have laughed in your face. Not that I've ever really known what exactly I wanted to do, but when I studied Art History at university, I didn't think I'd end up selling houses. I assumed, after graduating, that I'd work for a gallery or as an artist's assistant or something like that, but I couldn't get an interview for that kind of job, let alone an offer. In the end, I landed a position as an admin assistant for Cartwright and Brooks. I figured it was just a stopgap until something better came along. But over time, I settled in. I discovered that despite the company's reputation, I liked it there. I liked the founder, Bill. He was a kind, decent man who was a mentor and friend to me before he retired. I developed a genuine interest in property, too, and I worked my way up. Eventually, I was given a job in the sales team, and I've progressed since then, going from an assistant to a fully-fledged senior sales negotiator.

I like my job, I really do. Some of my colleagues are all about the commission, but I genuinely love helping people find a home where they'll be happy. There's nothing quite like seeing someone's eyes light up when they find a place where they truly want to live. It was like that with me and Alex. When we saw our home, we just *knew*. It was where we were going to settle down and build our future. Home is everything to me and I'd been trying to find the perfect home my whole life. That's why, in a way, my job is a really good fit. I get to help other people find that sense of security and peace.

I probably value home more than your average person. Or at least think about it more. I was taken into foster care when I was five years old. My foster parents were good people, but despite their efforts, I never quite had that sense of security and belonging, that sense of home. Maybe it was the bedroom decorated with posters from kids who'd stayed there before me. Or the hand-me-down clothes and toys. Or the way that for the first year of me being in care, my foster dad, Alfie, kept calling me by another girl's name. Or maybe I don't feel like that house was my home because I hardly ever go back, and my foster parents are more like acquaintances these days than anything else. We catch up every now and again, but they're not exactly a shoulder to cry on.

I sigh and try to reframe my thoughts as the barista makes my drink. Home may not have come naturally to me, but it's my goal to create one for my children some day. A home full of love. Alex laughs at how much of a homebody I can be, spending Sunday afternoons baking or decorating each room with framed photographs and flowers, but I don't think he'll ever quite understand what all this means to someone like me. He grew up in a good,

6

loving family in a beautiful old house in Kent. They had a golden retriever. Sunday afternoon walks in the countryside. Cups of hot chocolate in the evenings, cosy nights in front of the TV. I had secrets, a past I wanted to forget, a home that never felt my own.

The barista hands me my latte. Tempted by the array of cakes on display, I decide to get a red velvet cupcake to have later, too. Alex would frown at such a treat. He sees cakes and biscuits and pretty much anything unhealthy as treats reserved for 'cheat days' only. I suppose it comes with the territory of being a personal trainer.

I swipe my card against the reader and thank the barista before heading outside. It's a nice morning, fresh and sunny. Clutching my coffee, with my cupcake in a pink paper bag wedged under my arm, I head to my office, reaching into my handbag to root around for my pass.

'Looks like you could do with an extra hand,' my colleague Susan says, approaching behind me, her pass at the ready.

'Oh, thanks!' I reply as she swipes us in and holds the door open for me.

I smile, although I instantly feel awkward. Susan unnerves me. She's always so polished and well presented, like a candidate on *The Apprentice*. Today, she's wearing a neat grey pencil skirt suit, a crisp white shirt and black stilettos, her hair pinned back into a neat chignon. Her look screams successful young professional. It's definitely a lot more corporate than the boho chic office vibe I tend to go for, featuring floral floaty dresses and ballet pumps, with a blazer thrown on top. Not to mention my corkscrew curls, which are near impossible to tame.

Sometimes I envy Susan's effortlessly polished and slick approach, but she's almost too slick. A bit cold. She joined the company six months ago on our trainee scheme and yet I hardly know anything about her. I invited her for after-work drinks once, just after she started, and she gave me a look like it was the most bizarre suggestion in the world. All I really know is that she regularly gets French manicures on her lunch break, has a boyfriend who plays for a Premier team, and uses the word 'perfect' a lot. She'll be talking to buyers on the phone and viewing times are always 'perfect'; houses are always 'perfect'; streets are 'perfect'. Everything is 'perfect'. It's probably easier to remain aloof at work, but I can't help feeling that such coldness is a bit sad, and kind of a waste of life.

Susan smiles as I pass her. She comes in after me, the office door closing behind us.

'Busy day?' I ask as we walk to our desks.

Susan and I may not be particularly close, but it would be rude not to make small talk. I take a sip of my coffee.

'Yeah, I've got a viewing later for the Mountview house,' she tells me, her expression impassive, admirably lacking in smugness.

The Mountview house is the most expensive property we have on our books. It's an incredible £5m eight-bedroom mansion with its own cinema, library, state-of-the-art gym, heated indoor pool and enormous garden. Susan's so new at the company that I didn't even realise she'd be allowed to do a viewing of such an important property, and I find myself feeling a little put out. I've worked in sales for years. I should be showing people around houses like Mountview.

But I shouldn't be jealous or bitter. It's not fair, and yet I am. Maybe Susan is on to something with her aloofness and cold attitude to work after all. Perhaps I should take a leaf out of her book. The truth is, I do wish I was doing a bit better at my job. It's been a little too long since I last made a sale and I'm getting somewhat worried, but I plaster a smile on to my face and try to be supportive of Susan nonetheless.

'Wow, how exciting!' I say.

'I'm not expecting much, but it'll be interesting!' Susan replies modestly.

'Well, good luck with it!' I say, stopping at my desk.

'Thanks, Becky,' Susan replies over her shoulder as she heads to her workstation.

She sets her handbag down and takes off her jacket.

I take another sip of my coffee before placing it down by my keyboard.

'Morning,' I say quietly to my colleagues Anita and Lucy, who are both on calls.

Lucy gives me a wave, but she's frowning, her receiver clamped to her ear, clearly having a difficult conversation. Anita smiles and mouths 'morning' back at me. Unlike me and Lucy, Anita doesn't have to deal with difficult property stuff. She works on the marketing side of things. We hit it off immediately when she joined the company a few years ago. We've been sitting next to each other ever since, sharing our love of stupid memes and bad reality TV.

I spend the morning catching up on emails. At around 11 a.m., Alex sends me a photo of the glittering pool at the gym, just as I'm opening the bag containing my cupcake.

Aqua-aerobics has been cancelled so I have the pool to myself!

He's added a few grinning emojis.

I smile. Only Alex could get so excited by an empty pool. A pool he sees every day.

I message back.

Wish I could join you.

I hit 'send'. The truth is that the last thing I feel like doing is aqua-aerobics. I'm still feeling quite rattled from my encounter with the new neighbour this morning. I think of his dark eyes and the intense way he just *looked* at me. I think of how it felt to see him standing there, like he'd been waiting for me, and suppress a shudder as I take my cupcake out of the bag.

Lucy dumps her phone down in the receiver and lets out a loud groan, distracting me from my troubling thoughts.

'What's up?' I ask as I take a bite.

'Tenants from hell. Grumpy landlords. The story of my life! You wouldn't believe these two. Honestly, they're the worst I've ever had,' Lucy says, before launching into a story about a landlord and tenant arguing over a broken boiler. Neither of them sounds like a particularly nice person and apparently they're threatening to sue each other.

Lucy has a new horror story every week, and each one seems to top the last. I do feel for her. My job can be quite frustrating, but I'd much rather work in sales than lettings. It tends to be less dramatic.

Anita starts telling a story about a nightmare tenant she dealt with at her old company who deliberately tampered with their boiler when they left, breaking it internally just to annoy the landlord. As she's talking, she strokes her baby bump. I don't think she even realises she's doing it, it's second nature to her these days. She's six months pregnant and she and her husband, Sam, can't wait. They're expecting a girl and they've already got a shortlist of names lined up. They're all flower names, like Daisy, Rose, Dahlia. I find the names a little twee, but each to their own.

Anita picks up baby clothes quite often in her lunch breaks from the Marks & Spencer down the road. I don't blame her. I went in there the other day to get some new towels and somehow ended up wandering into the kids' section. I lingered over the tiniest pair of baby trainers. They were so small that they just about fitted my thumb. They were adorable and I almost considered buying them, before it hit me that I don't even have a fertilised egg yet, let alone a baby on the way.

I find that ugly, thorny feeling rearing its head again. Jealousy. I want what Anita has so desperately. More desperately with each month that passes by. In the grand scheme of things, I know six months isn't very long, which is how long Alex and I have been trying. But I'm only thirty. I'm not that old and I naively assumed I'd get pregnant pretty much instantly. Ever since I started having sex, back in my university days, I've always been so careful about avoiding pregnancy, taking the pill, using condoms and ensuring I take the morning-after pill after any slip-ups.

But now that I've stopped using any contraception entirely, and started having more regular sex than ever, my period just keeps coming. Every month it arrives, like a blow, crushing my dreams of motherhood and sending me right back to square one, my dream of finally having a family slipping out of my grasp. This dream is another reason I wish I was doing better at work. I want to start saving, building for my future.

My phone rings, interrupting my thoughts.

Anita and Lucy are still discussing nightmare tenants. I toss my cupcake wrapper into the bin under my desk and turn to pick up the receiver.

'Hello, Cartwright and Brooks, Becky speaking, how can I help?' I answer automatically.

'Hi there,' a man replies. 'I'm calling about the house on Lake Street.'

I assume he's referring to a nice two-bed terrace house that came on to the market a few weeks ago.

'Ah yes, you'd like to arrange a viewing?' I ask brightly, pulling the property up on my system.

'No, not the two-bed. The detached house. I think it has' – he hesitates for a moment – 'six bedrooms.'

'Oh, right. Yes!' I reply, sitting upright, suddenly a lot more alert.

There's an enormous mansion for sale at the end of Lake Street that I'd all but forgotten about. It's on the market for £3m. It's up there with the Mountview mansion. It's huge, with a sprawling garden and conservatory, and it's been decorated beautifully. Yet it's on a quiet street a little too far out of central London to have been snapped up yet. It needs the right person.

I take down his details and his property situation. He's well spoken, his voice soft and slightly laboured, and I can tell he's from an older generation. He gives me his address, which I quickly look up – a huge town house in a good part of north London. Again, promising. He mentions that he's a hedge fund manager and property investor, looking to expand his portfolio. He seems almost too good to be true, and as I jot down his details I notice my hand beginning to shake, a nervous energy bubbling through me. It's odd. Why would I be intimidated by an elderly man wanting to view a house? And yet I am. Perhaps I'm still feeling shaken from this morning.

I make a conscious effort to still my hand and push my nervousness aside. I open my diary. I have a slot available at 4 p.m. He's probably too busy to take it at such short notice, but I suggest it anyway.

'Four p.m.? Let me check.' He pauses for a moment. 'Actually, 4 p.m. works. Shall I meet you there?'

'Definitely!' I reply.

I end the call and send over a confirmation email.

'Was that about the Lake Street mansion?' Wendy asks, not skipping a beat as she swivels her chair around to me.

'It was indeed,' I reply brightly, unable to keep the enthusiastic smile off my face.

'Hmm, nice!' Wendy replies.

Wendy isn't my biggest fan. Unlike most of the people in the sales team, I was hired by her predecessor, Bill, rather than her. I think she finds me, with my Art History degree and boho fashion sense, a bit tiresome. I once overheard her describe me in the office kitchen as 'arty' in a tone of disgust, as though it was the worst slur imaginable.

'Well, good luck with it!' Wendy says, with a polite smile.

'Thanks, Wendy,' I reply, hoping I clinch this sale.

I write Edward's name down in my diary. My hand is still shaking a little and I can't figure out why. I should be excited to be doing a viewing like this, and yet for some reason I feel uneasy. A sense of foreboding fills me as I look at Edward's name on the page.

Chapter Three

I arrive at the Lake Street mansion and park in the driveway. Pausing, I take in the house for a moment before getting out of my car. The lights are all off and the flowers in the pot plants by the front steps have shrivelled up. Someone's shoved some flyers into the letterbox but failed to push them the whole way through. The overall impression is of a house that's distinctly unoccupied.

I'm fifteen minutes early, which fortunately gives me a bit of time to make the house feel more lived-in and welcoming. I get out of my car and head straight for the wilted pot plants. I pick them up and carry them out of sight, tucking them behind a wall at the back where Edward won't see them.

Heading back to the front door, I grab the flyers wedged in the letterbox. I let myself in, but the door jams against a pile of letters, circulars and even more flyers. Sighing, I reach down, gathering the post. I leave the letters in a drawer in a bureau and head into the kitchen, where I deposit the junk mail into the recycling bin.

It's still light outside but I want the room to look its best, so I turn on the spotlights that are dotted all over the ceiling. The kitchen is pristine and stylishly staged. Not only has every room been furnished to an incredibly high standard, but there are added homely touches like copies of the *Economist*, *The Week* and *Harper's*

Bazaar on the kitchen counter, rustic cooking pots arranged neatly on the hob and a spice rack full of artisan spices.

Heading upstairs, I decide to flick on a few of the bedroom lights, too, ahead of Edward's arrival, to make it feel as homely as possible. It's a little chilly in the house and I find myself wishing I'd had a chance to get here earlier, giving me time to put the heating on, but Wendy doesn't approve of things like that. She likes us to stay in the office as much as possible, where she can keep an eye on us.

Edward should be here soon. I walk over to the dressing table and check my reflection. My face is pale. I can't seem to quell my sense of unease, a feeling that there's something not quite right about Edward and this viewing. Sighing, I reach into my bag and take out my make-up, applying a few dabs of blusher to my cheeks and a slick of lipstick. I pout in the mirror, admiring my fresher appearance.

A car slows outside. Could it be Edward? I dash back to the hallway and peer out of the window, but I can't see anyone on the street. Perhaps it was just someone passing by.

I go back downstairs and sit down on the sofa in the living room, gingerly, since I don't want to disturb the perfectly arranged cushions. I take the particulars for the property from my handbag and have a quick read through, reminding myself of all the relevant details so I'll be fully prepared for any questions.

I hear the rumble of an engine and get up, expecting the door-bell to ring any second, but then I hear the car retreating. I look at my watch. It's past four now. Edward's late. I wonder if I should give him a call, but decide to wait a bit longer.

I sit down again and turn my attention back to my file. But another five minutes passes and Edward's still not here. I start to feel irritated. He's probably stuck in traffic, but he could have at least let me know. It's basic manners.

I dial his number and stand up, pacing the room as his phone rings. I expect him to answer, but his phone goes to voicemail. Damn it. Wendy's going to be expecting me back at the office soon.

I leave a message, letting Edward know that I'm here, and then I hang up.

I'm growing agitated. I don't have time to waste on no-show viewings. I should have listened to my intuition – my gut feeling that something was off – and avoided this viewing entirely. I'm wondering whether to call Wendy and explain that I'm going to be late back when I hear someone honking outside.

That must be him! Although I don't really understand why he's honking. Can't he just get out of his car and come to the front door?

It doesn't matter, though, as long as he's here.

I head to the front door and pull it open, wedging it with an old brass doorstop.

I dash down the drive, looking out for a car, but all I see is someone speeding off down the road. There's no one else around. No one's waiting.

'Damn,' I spit, annoyed now.

I turn around and head back towards the house. I need to get my bag, turn all the lights off and lock up.

But as I walk back up the driveway, I hear the sound of a door slamming.

A few steps further and I see that the front door of the house is shut.

No way. I wedged it open with the doorstop.

I rush up to it, praying it's not properly shut, but it is. It's firmly closed. My bag and my car keys are inside. All I have with me is my phone.

'Damn!'

So much for having managed to get a really good viewing booked. Wendy's going to think I'm an idiot. I'm constantly having to rise above her prejudices about me and this will only reinforce her belief that I'm an 'arty' misfit who doesn't really belong in the industry. It doesn't help that a couple of months ago, I went to a viewing and took keys for the wrong property. Sometimes I can be a bit ditzy and I get the feeling Wendy holds every incident against me. Great. I let out a groan of frustration, louder than I mean to. I hope the neighbours can't hear me.

'Damn, damn, damn!' I spit once more.

What a total disaster. I must not have wedged the doorstop in place firmly enough.

I walk around the house, looking to see if there might be a window open, but I know I didn't open any. I sigh, giving up. I lean against a window sill and, swallowing my pride, I call the office. I'm pretty sure we have an extra set of keys, meaning one of my colleagues can come and let me in.

Susan answers the phone, sounding bright, upbeat and flawlessly professional. I wince. Susan's the last person I wanted to pick up.

I ask her to put me through to Anita. I'm hoping Anita can subtly come and save me and I won't have to admit to anyone else that I got locked out of the house. But Susan informs me that Anita's on the phone. I ask for Lucy, but Lucy's apparently on the phone too.

'Can I help?' Susan asks.

She sounds sweet and well intentioned, although I really don't feel like sharing my predicament with her.

'Um . . .' I hesitate.

'What is it?' Susan asks.

I sigh, feeling like a total fool. Susan's ten years younger than me and at the start of her career, and yet today she's doing a viewing of a mansion, and here I am, a senior member of the sales team who's managed to lock herself out of a property following a no-show. It's tragic. But then again, Susan must have screwed up at some point in her life too, despite seeming so poised and put together. Everyone has bad days, after all.

I take a deep breath and launch into what's happened.

'Oh no!' Susan says, sounding surprisingly sympathetic, making me feel like I made the right decision in telling her. 'Oh my goodness!' she gushes. 'You poor thing!'

'Thanks. I couldn't believe it. It's just one of those days!'

'Totally. That's terrible! Let me put you through to Wendy, I have to pop out for my viewing. She'll be able to help. Good luck!'

Wendy?! Wendy was the one person I was hoping wouldn't be roped into this mess.

Before I have a chance to object, Susan cuts me off and transfers me to Wendy's line. Wendy's phone starts ringing.

I make a mental note never to trust Susan again.

Wendy answers after a few rings, sounding busy and impatient, and, deeply embarrassed, I explain what's happened.

Wendy sighs dramatically. 'So I suppose you want me to come out and get you?'

'Well, if not you, maybe Anita could help?' I suggest.

'Anita's working.' Wendy huffs. 'I'll come.'

A second later, she hangs up.

Feeling completely humiliated, I look up from my phone, noticing something in the corner of my vision. A movement. A rustling of branches in the bushes alongside the front drive, as though they've been disturbed. My hairs suddenly stand on end, my skin prickling. I have the strangest sensation that I'm being watched, and yet I can't see anyone. But the feeling is hard to shake.

Thoughts of the call with Wendy are suddenly wiped from my mind as I frown and tentatively wander over to have a look. There

18

must be an innocent explanation. The area probably has a problem with foxes, like so many other parts of the city. Clapham is the worst. It's overrun with them, and rats.

I have a look around, but I can't see anything. No foxes. No rats. Not even a squirrel. I try to shake my paranoia. I must be watching too many horror films.

I turn back and perch against the window sill once more, hoping Wendy gets here soon. I don't want to be here alone for much longer.

Chapter Four

It takes me a while to calm down from the afternoon's events, including getting berated by Wendy.

She came and met me at the property, an extra set of keys jangling in her hand, and reminded me repeatedly how lucky it was that we had two sets. She followed me around the house while I turned off all the lights and got my bag, asking me over and over how I'd got myself into 'such a mess'. She insisted it must 'never happen again', like I plan to make a habit of getting locked outside properties. Wendy was clearly annoyed, but I got the feeling that on some level she was revelling in it too. I suspect in a way she felt quite validated, because I'd proved her right about me.

To help me unwind, Anita and Lucy suggested a drink after work at our local pub, The Albert. I take a sip of my wine, sighing. It's not just getting locked out of the house that's bothering me, it's a general feeling of unease. I've felt off-kilter all day. Ever since I looked into the dark, knowing eyes of the new neighbour, I've been on edge, and I can't quite figure out why. He's just a stranger, another face in a busy city, and yet it felt like something shifted inside me the moment I saw him.

'You know what Wendy's like,' Anita comments, swirling the ice in her orange juice with her straw.

'Yeah, I guess so,' I reply, pushing my darker feelings down.

'Don't let her get to you,' Lucy adds, taking a sip of her pint.

Like me, Lucy's drinking. Tonight, she's opted for her favourite: a pint of Guinness. Lucy's a few years younger than me and Anita. She has the same work hard, play hard attitude as some of the other people in the office, but she's more into going to gigs than having cocktails at City bars. She's single and she was doing online dating for a while, but recently she's been focusing on 'finding herself', which seems to involve a lot of meditation, self-help books and hiking at the weekends. I don't think her life is exactly where she wants it to be yet, but she's sweet natured and on a day like today, it helps to be around people like her.

'Did you hear Susan landed the Mountview sale?' says Lucy, rolling her eyes.

'Seriously?' Anita raises an eyebrow.

'I'm going to need another drink!' I feel a bit put out. I'd have loved to have scored that sale.

Anita and Lucy laugh.

'She's so new! It's pretty impressive,' Lucy says, taking another sip of her Guinness.

'Mm,' I murmur.

'You know what she's like though, right?' Anita says, leaning forward. She glances over her shoulder, checking for colleagues. 'I heard she can be a bit ruthless. Apparently, on the day of her interview, she "accidentally" knocked a coffee over another candidate to make them look bad. The candidate complained about her, but of course, Susan denied it. And she got the job, so I guess it worked.'

'No way!'

I'm shocked. Susan might be all glossy hair and slick sales talk, but it's hard to imagine her being actively calculating.

'Well, that's what I heard.' Anita shrugs. 'It might just be a rumour.'

'Yeah, maybe she just has butterfingers,' Lucy suggests, exaggeratedly wiggling her fingers.

'Maybe.' I laugh.

Anita strokes her baby bump, distracting me from thoughts of work.

'So, have you decided on a name yet?' I ask.

Anita and Lucy light up as we discuss possibilities. Jokingly, Lucy and I suggest that Becky and Lucy are lovely choices, but Anita insists she's torn between Poppy and Dahlia. Last week, she was set on calling the baby Rose.

'Maybe you just have to wait to see her before you decide,' says Lucy.

'She might look more like a Peony,' I suggest.

'Exactly, or you might look at her and think, "That's a Daffodil!"' Lucy jokes.

'Shut up, guys! I'm not calling my baby Daffodil!' Anita shakes her head in mock horror.

And then, all at once, I regret starting this conversation. I want to be happy for Anita, but those awful feelings are welling up again. I should be the one in her shoes, stroking my bump, and it's just not happening.

A large group of half-drunk office workers pour into the bar. As though on cue, the staff turn up the music and lower the lights, readying for the night-time clientele. Thursdays really are the new Fridays for corporate London.

'Guys, I think I'm going to have to call it a night,' Anita says, yawning.

'Yeah, I should head back too. I need to feed Jekyll and Hyde,' Lucy says, referring to the cats she lives with in her flat down the road. One is incredibly cute and affectionate and the other the complete opposite, hence their names.

'Yeah, let's go.' I take a final sip of my drink.

Thinking of pregnancy has made me want to see Alex. Thursday night is one of the few nights he's not busy training clients and I find myself hoping we can make the most of the evening.

'We should get a selfie!' Lucy suggests brightly. 'Once this one pops, it might be a while until we're out for drinks again!' She gestures towards Anita's belly.

Anita laughs. 'Good idea!'

Lucy gets her phone and holds it out as we all squeeze in, arms looping around each other's shoulders. We smile as Lucy takes half a dozen shots.

'That should be enough,' she says, and we pull apart.

Anita and I peer over Lucy's shoulder as she scrolls through the photos. They're really nice – we all look happy and relaxed, and the bar is one of those places with warm, flattering lighting. I ask Lucy to message me the best ones and she fires them over.

We gather our things and head out of the bar. I walk to my car and message Alex, telling him I'm setting off. I check out the pictures Lucy's sent and choose my favourite, deciding to upload it to Instagram. After the rough day I've had, the lovely picture makes me feel better.

Clicking on to Instagram, I upload the shot, adding the caption: 'What would I do without these two!' with a few love-heart emojis. A few likes come through instantly. I put my phone back in my bag and turn my key in the ignition.

My phone buzzes a few minutes later as I stop at traffic lights. I take a look. Alex has messaged saying he can't wait to see me. The feeling's mutual. I smile to myself and see I have another couple of Instagram notifications.

Lucy's liked the picture and so have a few other friends, but someone's left a comment. I expect it to be Lucy or Anita, saying

23

something about our night, but it's from an account I don't recognise with no profile picture.

@john09380974 You ugly fucking bitch

What the hell? A jolt of unease shoots through me as I stare at the message, my stomach twisting. Who would do that? Who would speak to me like that?

I barely use social media. My profile on Instagram is public but I only have a couple of hundred followers, mostly people I know personally – friends, colleagues, friends of friends. I post photos now and again, but I'm not exactly looking for attention on there. I've never been trolled before. And now this. A vicious, spiteful message coming from God knows where.

My mind races. Have I upset someone recently? Would someone want to hurt me? But I can't think of anyone. Everything's been fine. I don't have any enemies.

A car honks behind me, interrupting my thoughts. I look up to see an angry driver pointing at the lights, which have turned green. Damn.

I put my phone down and carry on driving, the cruel words of the troll echoing in my head.

Chapter Five

I park outside my house and immediately grab my phone. I check out the profile of @john09380974. I check his feed. He has no pictures and no followers. He only follows one person and that person turns out to be me.

I reread his comment.

@john09380974 You ugly fucking bitch

I look at the picture of me, Anita and Lucy again, wondering if there's something strange or off-putting about it. But it's just a normal photo, a nice shot of three friends. There's nothing offensive or provocative about it whatsoever. What the hell is this troll's problem?

I'm tempted to reply telling @john09380974 where to go, but instead I delete the comment and block him.

I throw my phone into my bag, feeling irritated. What's wrong with people? I get out of the car and head into my house.

I let myself in, feeling instantly calmer as I close the front door behind me, shutting out the world. Alex has tidied up and our front room looks and smells gorgeous. He's lit a few of my favourite scented candles, which twinkle away on the mantelpiece, emitting a lovely calming smell of vanilla and spice. He's put the fairy lights on and a few lamps, and the room looks pretty and inviting. The carpet's been freshly hoovered and there's even a bottle of wine on the coffee table and two glasses. One's full, which Alex must have poured for himself.

I take my coat off, feeling better as I take in the room.

'Alex?' I call out to him as I kick off my shoes.

'Hey babe,' he shouts back from the kitchen.

I head down the hall and find him stirring something on the hob. He looks up and smiles.

'Ooh, what's that?' I ask, approaching him from behind, slipping my hands around his waist.

I notice a recipe open on his phone by the hob, and a message popping up from his family WhatsApp group, 'Chadwick Chats'. His parents and his two brothers are always messaging in their group, catching up, sharing news and jokes and interesting articles. Commenting on life together. I'm not a Chadwick so I'm not in the group. I don't mind. It's a family thing, but I do envy it somewhat.

Alex turns to kiss me.

'It's a red pepper and cherry tomato sauce,' he says. 'I'm making a pasta bake.'

I smile. Alex has always liked to cook.

'Mmm, looks nice!' I say, even though at the moment it looks like lumpy goop.

'It should be good,' Alex replies as he carries on stirring.

His abs flex under his T-shirt as he stirs, and I feel a stab of desire for him.

'I'll get the wine from next door. Looking nice in there!' I comment.

'Thought you'd like it.' Alex smiles as I head next door.

I take the wine from the coffee table and pour myself a glass. I probably shouldn't drink too much on a work night, but I'm shaken from Wendy's telling-off. Something tells me she'd be glad of an excuse to get rid of me.

As I place the bottle back down, something catches my eye out of the living-room window. It's the new neighbour. He's carrying some bin bags to the end of his drive. He must be busy with getting unpacked and sorting his things. He's taller than I remember him from this morning and he's quite handsome in a dark, brooding kind of way. He looks lost in thought, frowning slightly, completely oblivious to me watching him as he dumps the bin bags and heads back into his house.

He looks ordinary now, unassuming. I think back to the way he made me feel this morning and the lingering unease I was left with all day. Did I overreact? I still don't quite know what to make of it.

I pick up my glass of wine and take a sip. It's a nice one. Rich and fruity. I carry the glasses into the kitchen, handing Alex's to him.

'Thanks,' he says, and carries on stirring the sauce.

I sit down at the kitchen table and let out a sigh.

'Long day?' Alex asks, glancing over.

'Kind of,' I reply, wondering where to start.

That troll @john09380974 is bothering me. Getting locked out of the Lake Street house is bothering me. Feeling watched as I stood outside is bothering me. The neighbour is bothering me. *Everything* is bothering me.

I groan, lowering my head on to the table.

I tell him about the viewing and getting locked out.

'I felt like someone was watching me,' I tell Alex.

He turns around from the hob and eyes me strangely. 'Really?'

'Yes! I felt like I was being watched and I could hear this rustling in the bushes,' I say.

'Rustling?' Alex replies. 'Are you sure it wasn't just a rat?'

27

I sigh. I can tell he thinks I'm being paranoid and overreacting. Just like he thought I was this morning.

'Maybe it was a rat.' I shrug. 'Maybe it was . . . It was still horrible though.'

I grumble about Wendy and my failure to get any kind of commission.

Alex turns around from stirring the sauce. 'Oh, babe. You'll get a sale. It was just a bad day.' He smiles sweetly.

'I suppose. And then this guy just left the rudest comment on my Instagram post,' I tell him, explaining the whole thing. 'He called me an ugly fucking bitch!' I show the picture to Alex, even though the comment is long gone.

'What an idiot,' Alex says. 'Ignore it. It's just some weird low life getting kicks from upsetting strangers on the internet. There are some pathetic people out there. Don't let it get to you.'

'I know,' I reply weakly, placing my phone on the kitchen table. 'It was just so vicious. This guy only followed one person as well. Me!'

'That's creepy,' Alex remarks, adding some dried herbs to his sauce.

'Yeah, it is,' I agree.

'Maybe it's some disgruntled client or someone using a fake account to try to get at you.'

I frown. It seems unlikely that a client would do something like that. Occasionally sales do fall through and emotions ride high. I can think of a few people whose sales haven't worked out in recent months. There was a business consultant who lost out on the sale of his flat when the buyer withdrew at the last minute. He wasn't particularly happy about that. And then there was a young woman who I helped find her dream home, she put in an offer, and then one of my colleagues accepted a higher offer on the same property and Wendy decided it was okay. I felt terrible and the poor woman was not happy. She ranted and raved, but I haven't heard from either of them for months. It would be a bit odd for them, or anyone else I've met through work, to go out of their way to set up an anonymous account to troll me with. I doubt they'd be able to find me anyway. My Instagram account doesn't even include my full name.

'I'd just ignore it,' Alex says. 'Whoever it is clearly needs to get a life.'

'I guess so,' I murmur.

'Oh, Becks,' Alex coos, removing the pan from the hob. He turns the heat off and comes over to me, sweeping some hair away from my face. 'You've had a rough day, haven't you?'

He places his finger under my chin and tilts my head up. Our eyes meet.

Alex really is gorgeous. I love his big blue eyes, his strong features, his ripped, muscular body, straining against the cotton of his T-shirt. He's my dream man. I never thought I'd have a boyfriend so good-looking and yet so kind, mature and sweet. He's always there for me, reassuring and strong, never failing to say the right thing, put things in perspective and calm me down.

He opens his arms, tilting his head to the side and inviting me in for a hug.

I smile and get up, slipping into his embrace.

Thoughts of that stupid troll disappear from my mind as Alex wraps his arms around me. I rest my head on his shoulder, breathing in his comforting smell before turning my head up to kiss him, closing my eyes as our lips meet.

'It'll be all right,' Alex says reassuringly, his eyes warm and tender as I pull away.

'Yeah.' I feel soothed by his touch, his words. 'I'm going to get changed.'

I head upstairs and close the bedroom door behind me before unzipping my dress. I turn to place it in the laundry basket and realise that I forgot to pull the curtains closed. I'm wandering over to the window to shut them when I see the new neighbour again, on the street outside by a van. It's not a removal van this time, but a battered old grey Transit. He opens the rear doors. It's darker outside now, the sun having fully set.

He turns around and I shrink behind the curtain. The light is on up here. If he looks up, he could see me. But he doesn't look up. He marches towards his house with a look of concentration etched on his face. He looks angry, preoccupied. I find myself oddly captivated and watch as he heads inside. Suddenly, I hear a woman's voice, shouting, and then a second later the neighbour reappears with a small dark-haired woman. He grabs her arm and marches her forcefully towards the van. I watch, in shock, unable to quite process what I'm seeing. The woman shouts again but the neighbour spits some words at her that I can't make out. Panic floods through me. The woman is clearly in distress. Is she the woman I saw moving in with him? I can't quite tell. She looks young, around my age, but it's too dark for me to see her properly and I can only really make out the back of her head, her messy hair, bundled into a ponytail. She staggers slightly, unable to walk properly because of the tight grip the neighbour has on her arm. This is not normal. My heart thuds and I glance around, looking for my phone to call the police, one eye scanning the room, the other on the scene outside. They reach the van. The neighbour attempts to force her into the back, but she resists. They tussle and then she pushes him off her and steps inside. The neighbour slams the doors shut.

I scan the bed and realise I left my phone downstairs. Damn. I look outside again. The neighbour is standing by the van, hands on his hips and breathing deeply. Then he turns and gets in, climbing on to the front seat. The engine revs up and he drives away.

I stand there, my palms sweating. I watch the van disappear down the street. I wish I had my phone so I could take a photo of it, catch the number plate, do something, but it disappears out of sight and I only manage to memorise a few digits.

I try to absorb what I just saw. Did the new neighbour really just manhandle a woman into the back of a van? She looked scared. Did I just witness domestic abuse? Should I call the police? I cross the room, wondering what to do.

I head downstairs and grab my phone from where I left it on the kitchen table. Alex's back is turned as he prepares dinner.

'What are you doing?' he asks, looking over with a bemused expression as he takes me in.

I realise I'm still only wearing my tights.

I'm about to tell him what I just saw. I'm about to blurt it out, but suddenly I clam up. I can't talk to Alex about that kind of thing. People getting thrown into vans. I know how close to home that would hit and I just know it would send my usually smiley boyfriend into a rare dark mood. I know from experience. There's one thing Alex can't deal with talking about. And that's Jacob.

When he was at university, up in Glasgow, one of his closest friends and housemates, Jacob, went missing after a night out. Alex and his friends had been partying at a nightclub and Jacob left early. Apparently, he'd had too much to drink and decided to head home alone. Their house was only a ten-minute walk away and they all assumed he'd be fine, slapping him on the back and telling him they'd see him later. But Jacob never made it home. Not that night. Not the next day. Never. There were reports made about him. Sightings. Leads that the police chased. Another student claimed he'd seen Jacob being bundled into the back of a car, but nothing ever came from the tip-offs and Jacob was never found.

Alex told me about it a few months after we started dating. I remember it vividly. His whole body tensed up as he recalled that night, his neck flushed with anxiety and his eyes filled with tears. He said it was like Jacob had just 'disappeared into thin air'. He confessed that for months he'd blamed himself. He'd been flirting with a girl at the club and he'd been distracted. He beat himself up, telling himself that he should never have let Jacob walk home alone. That he was a terrible friend and could have saved Jacob if he'd just left the club with him that night.

The guilt had got so bad that Alex had sunk into a deep depression. He'd stopped going out. He spent all his time alone. He didn't want to talk to anyone. He just about managed to finish his degree and then left Glasgow, trying to blot out the pain of what had happened. He had some therapy to cope with his feelings of guilt and grief, and eventually he moved on, as much as he could. I know what happened still hurts him, but he tries to deal with it better now. In fact, it's one of the reasons he's so positive and always tries to make the most of life. I think he feels he owes it to Jacob's memory. And he knows how finite life can be. One minute you can be going about your business, and the next you can be gone.

'I'm not doing anything!' I reply with a nervous laugh. 'Just remembered I needed to text someone!'

Alex frowns. 'Okay!' he replies, raising an eyebrow.

I smile awkwardly, ignoring his expression, and dash back upstairs.

Closing the bedroom door behind me, I punch my pin into my phone. My finger hovers over the keypad. Suddenly, I feel hesitant. Should I really call the police? Or am I overreacting? Should I get involved? I wander over to the bedroom window and peer out, as though I'll find proof of my neighbour's innocence or guilt. I look down at the spot where the van was parked. I think of the woman and the way that man threw her into the van. What if he and his partner have a weird relationship? Perhaps I should just leave it. Reporting your neighbour to the police is a big deal.

I pace the room, my palms sweating, trying to decide what to do. I want to call, but every time I'm about to, I back down. I wish I could run it past Alex, get his thoughts, but I can't. I can't go there with him. He'll be down for days.

I pull on a hoodie and jogging bottoms and stand by the window. My heart feels heavy with guilt as I think about the woman, wondering where she is now, what's happening. What if the neighbour's hurting her? I'd never forgive myself for not reaching out to the police.

I take a deep breath and dial again.

My phone rings twice before the operator answers.

'Emergency. Which service?'

'Um, police,' I say, my throat tight.

'Transferring you now,' the operator says.

My phone is slippery in my sweaty hand and there's a lump in my throat. Adrenaline floods through me: fear and unease.

'Hello, Met Police, what's your emergency?' the operator asks.

The words get stuck in my throat.

I lose my nerve and hang up.

I can't do it. I can't quite open that door. The last time I spoke to the police, things didn't go well for me. The last thing I want is to go back to the dark days of my past.

Instead of doing something rash, I'll wait, see if I hear anything else. I'll definitely call then.

I place my phone down and close the curtains, trying to shut out my fears and the threats that lurk outside.

Chapter Six

My alarm buzzes. I hit snooze and roll over, expecting to find Alex next to me, but his side of the bed is empty. He usually has Friday mornings off, but he must have a client today or else he's covering for a colleague and running one of their gym classes.

I sigh. I think back to last night. We had dinner and watched a film. I was feeling shaken after what I'd seen, but I kept my promise to leave Alex out of it. Alex commented a few times that I seemed 'quiet', but I brushed it off. The disastrous viewing made for an easy excuse.

Voices from outside interrupt my thoughts. Alex's voice. Ears pricked, I get up and go over to the bedroom window, where I spot him standing in his running gear, talking to the new neighbour. I feel an instant wave of unease and flinch, and yet looking at him now is like looking at a completely different person. He looks happy, relaxed. He's laughing and joking with Alex, clearly warming to him. He even pats Alex on the back.

What on earth?

Alex has a positive effect on people, that's just his personality, but I didn't expect him to evoke such a transformation in our neighbour. I look on, baffled and shocked as they chat, smiling, like old friends. As though neither of them has a care in the world.

Alex is being his usual bright, sociable self. He's a complete people person. He has this way about him. It's almost like he radiates good energy. It sounds cheesy but it's true. It's one of the reasons I was drawn to him back when he was my personal trainer at the gym. His enthusiasm for life is infectious. He brings out the best in the people around him, including me. Before I met him, I found it easy to wallow in painful memories for days on end, but Alex keeps me grounded and balanced. Funnily enough, he says I do the same for him, as though my tendency towards low moods is somehow a good thing.

The neighbour laughs loudly at something Alex has said. It's staggering. I feel protective of Alex, like I don't want him to be associating with this guy. I look down and there's more back-patting going on. The neighbour smiles affably and then suddenly he looks up, his eyes landing right on mine, as dark and penetrating as they were the first time I saw him.

I step away from the window, embarrassed that he saw me watching. Great. Now I look like a curtain-twitching busybody.

I head into the bathroom to have a shower. As I wash my hair, I feel shaken and disorientated. Nothing makes sense. Afterwards, I wrap myself in a towel and head back to the bedroom. My phone's flashing on the bedside table and I see I have a message from Alex.

Met the neighbour. His name's Max. A banker, works in the City. Nice guy!

I laugh, shaking my head.

Typical Alex. He really does see the best in everyone. I just hope Max the banker really is the nice guy that Alex seems to think he is.

Chapter Seven

I arrive at work and for once, I relish being in the office. It feels like a welcome return to normality after the incidents of last night. My anxiety is flushed away under the glow of the strip lights and seeing everyone, tapping at their computers and making calls, settles all the strange emotions that have been rattling around my head.

Wendy is already sitting at her desk. She glances over her shoulder at me as I cross the office. I give her a deliberately friendly smile, but she regards me blankly, her expression bored and impassive.

'Morning, Wendy,' I say brightly, determined not to let her get to me.

I miss the days of my old boss, Bill. I really do.

'Morning, Becky,' Wendy replies in a monotone before returning her attention to her monitor.

It might be a bit pathetic, but I dressed with Wendy in mind this morning. Instead of my usual floaty dresses, I'm wearing a suit. It's not my style at all, but I thought I'd make an effort to look a bit more corporate. I bought this suit for job interviews years ago, and it's tight and the waistband pinches, but I try to ignore that. My hair is pinned back into a neat bun too. Perhaps it's silly, but I want to look smart. I don't want to be seen as a hot mess who locks herself out of houses. Yesterday was mortifying. I tried to let it go after Lucy and Anita's pep talk in the pub, but just couldn't shake the feeling of shame as I was getting ready for work this morning. Maybe subconsciously I ended up dressing like Wendy and Susan, trying to channel my inner slick estate agent – like on some level it might make me feel more in control, as though a suit can somehow do that.

'Ooh, check you out!' Anita enthuses, giving me a once-over as I sit down at my desk. 'Looking good!' she remarks, before biting into a panini.

'Thanks!' I reply as I take off my jacket and drape it over the back of my chair. I feel immediately better to be relieved of it.

'I thought I'd try to look a bit more professional, you know?' I tell Anita quietly, glancing at Wendy with an eye roll as I turn on my computer.

'Thought I told you not to care about Wendy?' She tuts. 'You are professional. You don't need a suit to prove it!'

I shrug. 'I just thought it might help. I probably won't wear it again though,' I say as the trouser band digs into my stomach.

I must have been about a stone lighter when I bought this suit, but despite that, I do feel a bit bloated today. Could it be because I'm pregnant? Could there be a fertilised egg floating around inside me?

I could ask Anita what early pregnancy feels like exactly, but I can't bring myself to. I haven't told any of my friends that Alex and I are trying for a baby or admitted quite how much I want to be a mother. The only person who knows is Alex, and even he probably doesn't fully get it. I think that truly, it comes down to growing up in foster care and never quite having that sense of family. Anita grew up in a big, warm family. She knows I was fostered, but I'm almost worried that if I talk to her, I might crack up. The raw emotion might hit me and I fear I'd cry – I might end up sharing more of my past than I want to. I prefer to keep those days behind me. It's silly, though, because the longer I keep my desire to get pregnant to myself, the harder it's getting to tell anyone. I've built it up too much. I'll probably just have to blurt it out after a few drinks one night at The Albert.

'Becks, just be yourself,' Anita tells me as I turn on my computer.

'Yeah, I know.' I smile. 'Thanks.'

Anita's phone starts ringing. She sighs, placing her panini down before clearing her throat and picking up the receiver.

In theory, Anita's right. I should just be myself, but it's not that simple. Unlike me, Anita is one of those people who gets on with everyone at work and always looks effortlessly put together. She dresses well, nailing smart casual, and she has the most gorgeous, silky black bob that always seems to fall into place, framing her face perfectly. Even now, in a baggy maternity dress dusted in panini crumbs, Anita still looks sharp.

I never quite manage that level of polish. My wild, curly hair frizzes up at the slightest touch of moisture. Drizzle on the way to a viewing will guarantee that I arrive sporting a bird's nest. Alex used to joke when we first got together that I had the dress sense of Phoebe Buffay. I've always chosen to take that as a compliment, but messing up the viewing yesterday with such a rookie mistake has taken me back to my early days when I first started at the company, back when I still wanted to work at a gallery instead, and every day I felt like I was a square peg trying to fit into a round hole. It's silly, because I am good at my job, and I do enjoy it. My days of feeling like I don't belong should be long behind me.

I push my melancholy thoughts out of my mind and open up my emails, finding one from Wendy. It has the subject 'Review'.

Review? I feel a pang of nervousness. Am I up for some sort of appraisal? But I open the email and find a Google link, with a message.

> Edward Jones who wanted to view the Lake
> Street house yesterday left this review on our
> Google listing. I've reported it to Google to try
> and get it removed, but it doesn't look good.

What the hell? What's Wendy talking about?

I click the link. It takes me to a one-star Google review of our company. I read it with a feeling of dread.

> I had a viewing with sales agent Becky Nicholls
> yesterday. I arrived at the property, and from
> the end of the drive I could hear Becky on
> the phone to her company, complaining that
> she'd locked herself out of the house. She
> appeared to be very stressed out. I decided
> not to approach her as it was clear she'd got
> herself into a mess and I didn't want to make
> the situation worse. It's a shame as I was very
> interested in viewing the property, but given
> that my first impressions of the agency were
> not great, I'll be going elsewhere.

Oh no. What a terrible review.

I think back to yesterday. When I called Wendy, I was standing by the front door and don't remember seeing anyone walking by or hanging around outside. I'd checked the street just before the front door slammed on me, and it was completely empty. There were no cars coming and going. The street was quiet. Unless Edward arrived on foot.

I don't recall speaking loudly either. It's surprising that he heard me from the end of the drive, but he must have done. Maybe I was talking louder than I realised.

Rereading the review, I feel more and more deflated. No wonder Wendy was frosty when I said hello this morning.

I sigh. So much for having a good day.

Glancing over at Wendy, I see she's away from her desk. I reply to her email, expressing my concern over the review and apologising profusely for the situation. I ask if there's anything I can do to help with getting the review removed and apologise once more. Then I hit 'send' and hope for the best.

I try to get on with my work, but my thoughts keep drifting and I find myself getting increasingly wound up.

Edward's acted all high and mighty, and yet he's failed to mention that he was twenty minutes late for the viewing and didn't bother letting anyone know. If I hadn't grown tense waiting for him, I probably wouldn't have ended up running out of the house, looking for him and getting locked out.

And did he really have to jump on to Google to slander me? He could have phoned up and discussed the matter civilly, but instead he's targeting me in quite a pointed, vicious way. What if someone googles me and that review comes up? It won't look great next time I'm job-hunting. Did Edward really need to do that?

I start to wonder whether I should call him and try to sort it out.

I make a cup of tea, pondering it, and decide to go ahead. I'll call him. After all, what have I got to lose? He's already left a bad review; it can't get much worse.

I look up his number and punch it into my phone, cupping the receiver against my ear as it rings.

The phone rings four times before Edward suddenly picks up.

'Hello,' he says.

'Hi,' I reply. 'This is Becky from Cartwright and Brooks.'

I launch into a heartfelt apology, all the while secretly gritting my teeth. 'I'd really appreciate the chance to make it up to you if possible. I can assure you that I, and my colleagues, pride ourselves on our professionalism and incidents like yesterday are very rare indeed.'

I catch Anita looking at me. She pulls a face, and I can't help smiling.

'If you like, I could find another time to show you around the property. I'd really like another opportunity to. It's a beautiful home. And I can promise there will be no access issues this time. Would you like to arrange another viewing?' I suggest.

'I'm not sure,' Edward replies, sounding vaguely irritated, like he has better things to do than speak to a pushy estate agent. 'I'll think about it,' he adds.

'Of course. I'm happy to work around your availability,' I say, my desperation palpable. I really want to come out on the other side of this difficult situation.

'Okay, I'll let you know,' Edward says, his voice flat.

He doesn't sound interested at all. I should give up right now, but I think of something my old boss, Bill, used to say whenever someone was being rude or difficult: 'Most people aren't bad, they're just upset.' It's always reminded me to show sympathy and understanding when people are being a bit off.

'Of course,' I reply, when a thought hits me.

I'm hosting an open house viewing of a beautiful property not far from the Lake Street mansion tomorrow morning. It also has six bedrooms and a huge garden. I describe it to Edward, telling him about the event, since he might be more inclined to stop by at an open house than attend another one-to-one appointment. I do my best to describe the house in the best possible light and make the open house sound like an unmissable opportunity. I have a feeling Edward probably just wants to end the call, but it's worth a try nonetheless.

41

I finish my spiel and wait for him to say something. A moment's silence passes and I start to wonder whether the line's gone dead.

'Actually, yes, that sounds great. I'd like to come along,' Edward says, taking me by surprise.

'Right! Brilliant!' I reply, feeling invigorated.

I apologise once more and thank Edward for his time, telling him how much I'm looking forward to meeting him. I wish him a good day and hang up.

Smiling to myself, I take a sip of tea and prepare the confirmation email.

So much for letting a bad Google review ruin my day. It was just a minor setback that Wendy got far too worked up about. Hopefully Edward will delete the review now and I might even make a sale after all.

Thankfully, the rest of the morning passes uneventfully.

Anita and I head out for a late lunch and go for a wander around the shops. We stop in at a baby shop and Anita picks up a few things – a baby monitor, a rattle and some cute framed pictures for the nursery. I find myself daydreaming about what Alex and I could do with the spare room in our house. At the moment, we use it as a dumping ground for old junk. But the room would make a lovely nursery if we cleared it out. Maybe we could opt for a flower theme, like Anita and Sam's choice of a yellow sunflower vibe, or maybe we could go for something pretty and pink, or a blue and aquatic vibe.

'Earth to Becky,' Anita says.

I look up at her, coming back to reality. 'Sorry, I was miles away!'

'Yeah, I noticed!' Anita laughs.

She's holding a baby blanket in a shade of emerald green.

'Oh, that's gorgeous,' I comment, reaching out to touch it.

It's silky soft between my fingers. It feels like cashmere.

'Are you getting it?' I ask.

'Oh, no! I was just admiring it. It's way too expensive!' Anita places the blanket back down. 'This is pretty much all I can afford!' she says, gesturing at the stuff in her basket. 'Being a mum is already breaking the bank and she hasn't even arrived yet!'

I laugh as we head to the counter.

As Anita's paying, I glance at the stack of emerald blankets and make a mental note to come back later and buy one for her. It would make the perfect present for the baby.

Suddenly, I get a strange, uneasy feeling, like someone's looking my way. I glance towards the entrance of the shop and see a man outside, looking through the shop window right at me. He's older than me. Mid-fifties perhaps. He eyes me with a look of piercing intensity that makes my skin prickle. Who is he? And how long has he been staring at me? What does he want? I look back at him, my stomach churning, and then abruptly he looks away and turns, walking on. The passers-by continue to come and go on the street outside, and yet I feel rattled, shaken, almost dirty. There was menace in his eyes. Was he just some random creep? I definitely didn't recognise him.

'Becks?' Anita says.

I turn around to see her standing at the counter, looking over at me with a puzzled expression.

I smile and try to push the incident out of my mind.

It was probably nothing. Just an odd stranger.

I go over to her, telling myself that he wasn't looking at me. He must just have been admiring the window display. Surely it can't have been anything else?

Chapter Eight

I stay at the office an hour late, going the extra mile for tomorrow's open house. I email all the buyers, telling them how much I'm looking forward to showing them around the property. Then I reread the particulars of the house over and over again until I could practically recite them in my sleep.

Wendy and the accounts guy, Ryan, who often works late, are the only people still there by the time I leave.

'Right, I'm off,' I say as I turn off my computer and get up from my desk, feeling my back click as I straighten my spine.

'Feeling confident about tomorrow?' Wendy asks, a little patronisingly. Her question would be more suited to a newbie like Susan, but I let it go.

'Yes, very confident. It should go well!' I assert brightly.

I told her earlier that Edward was coming. She gave a small nod of approval in typical Wendy fashion.

'Good,' Wendy replies, looking back to her computer.

'Have a good weekend,' I say to both her and Ryan.

'Have a good one,' Ryan replies, smiling.

I smile back, even though Ryan's gaze lingers. He's a sweet guy, if a little intense.

I head outside. It's a nice evening. Warm enough to have dinner in a pub garden. Alex is working, though, training clients until after 10 p.m. It's a bit of a shame, but never mind. We got to spend the previous evening together, after all.

I get in my car and check my phone.

Lucy's messaged in the group chat we have with Anita. She's sent a screenshot of a new dating profile she's set up.

Back on the apps! Kill me now.

I laugh as I put my phone back in my bag. I turn my key in the ignition. Lucy's dating stories are amusing, but deep down, I feel a bit sorry for her. She's tried various apps: Tinder, Bumble, Hinge, Plenty of Fish, and yet she never seems to meet anyone nice. It's not her that's the problem. She's kind, funny, smart and attractive, but she only seems to encounter disrespectful men who want nothing from her except casual sex. She makes jokes about her terrible dates, turning negative experiences into comic anecdotes to be recounted over drinks at the pub, but the humour is starting to wear a little thin and I can tell she's ready for the real deal.

It makes me feel so lucky to have found Alex. I could so easily be in Lucy's shoes too. These things are just a matter of luck a lot of the time. Alex and I might never have met if that gym hadn't opened, and he hadn't got a job there and I hadn't randomly decided to join. It's not like I'd had much luck in relationships before I met him. I'd been single for years. I'd had a few boyfriends, but nothing particularly long-term or serious. Then when I met Alex, to my surprise I fell hard. Head over heels. He made me happier than I'd ever been before, than I ever even knew I could be. He's the first man I've ever truly loved. These days, I can't even imagine my life without him, without that companionship.

As I drive home, I find myself thinking how much better it would be if Lucy could meet someone in real life. Apps never seem to lead to anything good for her. Maybe it's because I've just said goodbye to him, but I think of Ryan, the accountant from work.

Ryan is quite attractive. He has nice eyes, big and brown, and he's tall and fit. I've sensed that he still has a slight soft spot for me since our office Christmas party kiss, but it's not like he's in love with me. He just gets bored and gives me a bit of attention every now and then. He had a girlfriend for a while, Cathy or Katie, I can't quite remember. But he's definitely single now. His relationship ended a while ago and he never mentions anyone new. He's not the coolest or most confident guy in the world, but he's nice, and from the stories Lucy tells of online dating, niceness is a rare quality.

As I pull on to my road, I wonder absently whether I should try to set Lucy and Ryan up, but my thoughts are interrupted when I see, in the distance, that someone's parked in my usual spot, right in front of the house. Our street has unallocated residents' parking all along the road, but there's an unwritten rule among neighbours that we don't park in front of each other's houses if we can avoid it. As I get closer, I see that the vehicle is the neighbour's van. The one I saw him bundle that woman into last night. I feel a chill as I take it in, and a fresh wave of guilt, wondering how his partner is. Wondering, yet again, if I should have done something more and got the police to come.

I slow down next to the van and get a closer look. It's battered, a piece of junk. I eye it, observing its peeling grey paintwork and collection of scratches and dents. It didn't look as bad last night in the dark. I barely noticed it until I saw what Max was doing. It's strange that he has an old van. It's an odd vehicle for a City banker to drive. Yet there's another car next to it: a much nicer-looking Audi. Perhaps that's the car Max uses more often.

I drive further up the road and find an empty space halfway down the street. I reverse into it and let out a sigh as I turn off the engine.

As I get closer to my house, I hear some music, a loud hammering baseline, scratchy guitars and the sound of screaming vocals. It's heavy metal. Who listens to heavy metal around here?

There are a lot of families with children of all ages, but there are no wild or rebellious teens. There haven't been any problems with crazy house parties or anything like that. The music gets louder as I approach my house and I realise that it's coming from Max's place.

It's so loud that it's almost as though the speakers have been placed right by the windows. It's blasting out. I stand in front of his house, taken aback.

The curtains in the front room and upstairs bedrooms are drawn so I have no idea what's going on in there. Is he having some kind of party?

I check the time on my phone. It's just after 7 p.m. It's a bit early for a party. I wonder whether I should knock on the door and tell him to keep the noise down, but I'm not in the mood for a confrontation, especially given the way I saw him behave last night. He scares me. And I'm tired after a long day, yet again.

'For goodness' sake,' I grumble to myself as I walk to my front door.

The screaming vocals tear out as I turn my key in the lock, making me feel even more irritated. I glance down the street, hoping one of the other neighbours might say something.

Even as I close the front door behind me, I can still hear the heavy metal. It's not as loud inside the house, but it's there: pounding bass and those horrible, strangled vocals.

Kicking off my shoes, I find myself wishing Max hadn't moved in. I wish the man who lived there before – Gerald – had never left. He was a pensioner who'd lived on this street all his life. The loudest he ever got was mowing the lawn in the summer. He used to chat about it with me over the garden fence, telling me how his roses were coming along. He was a lovely man, but he started to

47

get more and more confused, and eventually his family moved him into a care home.

Sighing, I take off my coat and head into the kitchen.

I pour myself a glass of water and look out of the window towards Max's house.

Our houses are detached, separated by a low fence. Our kitchen windows face each other, and I spot him sitting at his dining table with a laptop open in front of him and a look of concentration etched on his face, as though he's working. Despite the piercing cacophony, he looks perfectly calm and focused.

Puzzled, I take my water and head towards the living room.

I glance at the front door as I cross the hall. I'm feeling jumpy. Over the past few days, I've felt like I'm constantly looking over my shoulder. I walk to the door and make sure it's locked. I fasten it with the chain lock for good measure. I know I'm being paranoid, but it makes me feel a little better. A bit calmer.

I go into the living room and sit down on the sofa. I turn on the TV, flick through the channels and try to watch the news, but I can't concentrate. The metal music coming from next door is too distracting. I turn the volume up on the TV, but I'm unable to drown out the metal. It feels like it's reverberating through the walls, and I'm getting more and more wound up.

What kind of person moves into a small house on a suburban street and behaves like this? It's so unbelievably rude.

I should go over and say something, I really should. That's what the lettings people at work would suggest in this kind of situation. Knock on his door and politely ask him to turn the volume down, and yet I don't want to go over there on my own. I can't risk it. What if he loses his temper at me? What if he throws me into the back of his van too?

I sigh, trying to push the thought away. It feels crazy, irrational. And yet it snags at my mind. I still have no idea what happened to that woman. Dark thoughts flit through my mind. What if she's in a ditch somewhere? No. Surely not? I'm probably getting carried away. I knew I shouldn't have churned through that series on Ted Bundy last week.

I give up on the TV. I go upstairs and take my laptop from my bedside table, rooting around in my bedside drawer for my noise-cancelling headphones. I get into bed and turn my laptop on, putting on my headphones. Mercifully, the noise suddenly disappears.

My laptop loads up and I open a web browser, feeling a little guilty for what I'm about to do.

I log on to the true crime forum, truecrimefanatics.com, that I've been frequenting for over a decade. It's a weird corner of the internet, a place where true crime obsessives like myself gather to discuss serial killers and their crimes. Anonymous users pick apart everything from motive to modus operandi, analysing serial killers' childhoods, the nature of their crimes and how they got caught. I find it fascinating. What interests me most is the psychology behind killing, trying to understand what drives a person to commit the most unimaginable act.

Alex doesn't get it at all. He thinks it's strange and morbid that I have these interests. Before we got together, I'd spend hours feeding my obsession. I read so many books, biographies of serial killers like Ted Bundy, John Wayne Gacy and Jeffrey Dahmer. I'd watch true crime documentaries and film adaptations of serial killers' lives. And I'd come on to this forum, sometimes on a daily basis, to chat to other people who shared my interests. But Alex would always change the subject if I mentioned such things. He didn't like watching serial killer films with me. And I could tell he didn't approve of the shelves full of true crime books in my old room. I knew it unsettled him.

When we moved in together, I didn't even bother unpacking my box of true crime books. I didn't want to upset Alex or bring him down. They're in the spare room now and I haven't bought any new ones. I know Alex wouldn't want to see them cluttering up our shared space. If I feel like reading one these days, I download it on my Kindle.

Alex doesn't know about the forum, and I don't plan on mentioning it to him. He'd find it strange if he knew I was part of an online community of true crime obsessives. He wouldn't understand. Every couple has secrets, whether they admit it to themselves or not. There are certain parts of me and my past that I keep from Alex. Things I've been through that I'm not sure he'd understand. We're close, I love him deeply and I know he loves me too, but our pasts are so different. I feel bad, but I've told lies to cover up some of my secrets. I've told Alex, and everyone I know in fact, that I don't remember anything from my first home, the one I was born into, that I was rescued from when I was five years old. But that's not quite true. I do remember. But I could never tell Alex about those days. I told him my parents were just too young, too immature to care for me. The truth would be too much for him. I don't want to drive him away. Just because I had a difficult start in life, it doesn't mean I can't have a happy future. I don't want to be tainted by my past.

I check out the latest post on the forum. It's about the Zodiac Killer and I wade into the discussion. The Zodiac Killer is one of my personal favourites in terms of his cryptic nature and his ciphers. I scroll through posts, commenting and catching up. I make a few cups of tea, wade in on various threads and before I know it, Alex is at the bedroom door. I glance at the time on my laptop: it's 10.20 p.m.

I was so wrapped up in the forum that I lost track of time.

I pull my headphones down, the sound of the metal music instantly returning, making me wince.

'Hey,' I say as Alex comes over to the bed.

I quickly click out of the forum and on to Facebook.

'Hey,' he replies, sounding weary.

He looks tired. His hair is mussed up and his T-shirt crumpled. He flops down on to the bed, lying next to me.

'You okay?' I ask, reaching out to him.

He leans in for a kiss. 'Yeah, three clients in a row, back to back, and I led two classes. Body pump and spin. Knackered.'

'Aw,' I murmur.

I'm about to ask if he's eaten when a roaring scream tears out from next door.

'For God's sake,' I grumble. 'He's been at this for hours! I got home at seven o'clock and he was blasting out this godawful music. I've been here with my headphones on, trying to block it out.'

'It's pretty bad,' Alex agrees.

'I know. Who listens to metal?' I grimace. 'It's deafening.'

'It is loud.' Alex winces. 'Maybe he's having a house-warming party.'

'I don't think so. I saw him sitting at his kitchen table with his laptop open. He looked like he was working or something. He seemed to be alone.'

Alex turns to me, propping himself up on his elbow.

'Hmm, strange,' he says, frowning.

'I know!' I put my laptop down and lie next to him. 'Imagine moving into a house and blasting out metal like that. Does he want everyone to hate him?'

'Maybe he's just had a really bad day and he needs to let off some steam?' Alex suggests.

I roll my eyes. One of the things I love about Alex is his kindness and compassion, but it can be frustrating. Sometimes he looks for reasons to excuse people's behaviour when really, they're simply being unreasonable.

'If Max needs to let off steam, then he should do it like a normal person and not upset everyone on the street.'

Screeching vocals boom through the wall, and Alex squirms.

'Yeah.' He sighs. 'You're right.' He sits up. 'I'll go over and have a word with him.'

I feel a little bad given how tired he looks and how unwilling I've been to do anything about the situation.

'Are you sure? You're tired.'

'Yeah, I am, but it's not like I'm going to get much rest with that racket,' Alex comments as he gets up. 'I'll go over.'

'Okay.' I reach over and squeeze his hand. 'Love you.'

Alex smiles, a lopsided, lazy smile. 'Love you too,' he says, before heading out of the room.

I close my laptop and put it on the bedside table. I hear Alex bounding down the stairs, but as he reaches the hall, the music stops. Silence returns.

'Alex?' I call out.

He comes back up.

'Ha! He's stopped.' Alex grins.

'Brilliant!' I enthuse. 'About time!'

'I'm glad I don't have to deal with that,' Alex says, lying back down on the bed.

I think back to seeing Alex and Max this morning and the text he sent after, calling Max 'nice'. I feel a prickle of unease over holding back what I saw. I'd love to tell Alex, to get it off my chest, but I can't bring myself to. The words are stuck in my throat. I'm too afraid of his reaction.

I sigh and cuddle up next to him. 'So what's Max like then, given you two had a chat?' I ask.

'He seems all right. He said he's moved from Canary Wharf, wanted somewhere bigger.' Alex reaches for my glass of water and takes a sip.

'Did you meet his partner?' I ask.

Alex frowns, looking my way. 'What partner? He's living alone. I'm pretty sure he's single.'

'Single?' I echo, confused.

'Yeah, single!' Alex repeats, raising an eyebrow.

I laugh. 'It's just, there was a woman here when he moved in. They were together. She was carrying stuff into the house. I assumed she was his partner.'

Alex shrugs. 'Maybe he just had a friend helping him?'

'Hmm, maybe.' I'm unconvinced.

I assumed the woman I saw Max with was his partner and they were having some kind of falling-out. But if he's single, then who was she? Was she a woman he'd only just met? What did he do to her? What if he's some kind of predator? The thought makes my chest feel tight.

'He definitely told me he was single!' Alex pauses, as though casting his mind back. 'He said something about having the "whole place to himself".' He does air quotes.

'Right, okay. I guess he must be,' I reply. 'So what's brought him to this area then?' Our part of town doesn't tend to attract City bachelors.

'A change of scenery.' Alex shrugs. 'And like I said, he wanted more space than what he could get in Canary Wharf.' He looks at me. 'You're very interested in Max!' he teases.

'Oh, come on!' I scoff.

Alex laughs. 'He said he might want training,' he says.

'Oh, really?'

'Yeah, he said something about wanting to build up strength. I gave him my number. Maybe he'll call. I don't know.' Alex yawns.

'Fair enough,' I reply, although I'm not particularly thrilled by the prospect of Alex spending time with Max.

He's creepy. He's potentially dangerous. And it's not like Alex needs any more clients. He's already out all the time, and we're making enough money. But I know he wouldn't turn Max down if he wanted training. He'd feel rude. And it would be easy for them both to fit in sessions with Max living so close.

'I'm going to have a shower,' Alex says, getting up and stretching, making his spine crack.

'Okay,' I reply as he heads to the bathroom.

I stare into space as I hear Alex turn the shower on.

I gaze at the ceiling, replaying what I saw last night and this morning. I'm pretty sure that Max is bad news and it makes me feel tainted, down. All I've ever wanted is a happy, peaceful place to call home, and now a weird stranger is here. A disturbing presence. Right next door.

My stomach rumbles and I'm distracted from my thoughts. I've hardly eaten all day apart from a bag of crisps at lunchtime. I get up and head downstairs to make a quick dinner. I can't stay up too late. I need to get an early night before my open house tomorrow.

I walk into the kitchen and grab a microwave meal from the freezer. I pop it in and while it's heating, I look over towards Max's place. He's still sitting at his kitchen table with his laptop open in front of him. He's sipping from a can of beer, lost in thought, oblivious to me. I close the kitchen curtains. The microwave pings, and I yelp, jumping out of my skin.

I laugh, shaking my head, as I take out my meal.

Chapter Nine

I look out of my bedroom window as I sip a cup of coffee. The sun is shining, the sky clear blue.

Perfect. Good weather bodes well for my open house. Houses always look nicer in the sun, and the one I'm selling, with its conservatory and huge sprawling garden, is going to sell itself in this weather. There's nothing like grey skies and torrential downpours to ruin viewings.

I choose one of my favourite dresses to wear. A pretty but smart tea dress. I put it on, feeling good as I look at my reflection in the mirror. I look nice. I look like me again, rather than trying to be something I'm not.

I don't know what I was thinking yesterday with that suit. Anita and Lucy were right. I shouldn't let Wendy and her bad moods affect me. I have fourteen prospective buyers booked to view a £3m house today. A sale is pretty much guaranteed, and the commission will be huge. Wendy should realise that stuff like that matters far more than Google reviews.

I don't have time for breakfast, but I bought some biscuits to serve at the open house so I'll have a few of those later. I place my coffee mug in the dishwasher and steal a glance towards Max's house. The neighbour before Max used to have a blind, giving him privacy, but I can't see it. I think Max has removed it. It's almost as though he wants to be observed. He's left his computer on his kitchen table with a couple of discarded beer cans next to it. He must have sat there all evening, in front of his laptop, drinking. I shake off the thought. Max's personal life is none of my business.

I grab my bag and head outside. It really is a lovely day, fresh with a gentle breeze.

For a moment, as I scan the street, I wonder where my car is, before remembering that I parked down the road. The battered old van that was in my spot last night has gone, thankfully. Hopefully it won't return, and I can park in my usual spot when I get back.

I walk down the street towards my car. The cool, refreshing breeze makes me feel optimistic – as well as a neighbour's cute cat prowling along a garden wall. I stop to pet it and it meows adorably, rubbing its head against my hand. I leave it meowing on the wall and carry on walking. But as I approach my car, my stomach drops.

My tyres are flat. Slashed. The rubber is completely torn, and my car is resting flat against the concrete.

'No! No way!' I exclaim, horrified.

I walk around my car and find that both of my front tyres are completely deflated.

'Who did this?' I cry out to no one in particular.

Panicking, I look around at the surrounding houses. Nice, well-maintained homes with neat front gardens and cars parked outside.

And yet someone's slashed my tyres. Who would do that?

I check the other cars nearby, but they're all fine. It's only my tyres that have been obliterated.

I stand there, wondering what to do. Maybe I should call the police. There might be some gang targeting cars, causing damage. Our street isn't too far from some rough areas. There was a spate of muggings a few years ago, which was unsettling for a while. Life's been good here recently though.

I check the time on my phone. It's 10.15 a.m. I'm running a bit late, and my open house is in just forty-five minutes. What am I going to do?

I grab my phone and try calling Alex, hoping he might be free and can come and get me, but I know it's unlikely. He's probably with clients or leading classes and he never answers his phone when he's doing that. He never even looks at it.

His phone rings but it goes to voicemail. Great. I try again, but the same thing happens. Damn it. My hands shake with stress as I hang up.

I try to think if there's anyone else I could call, but Anita lives on the other side of London and it would take her too long to get here. Lucy doesn't have a car. And I don't have any other friends who I feel I could ask. I'm going to have to take a taxi or a bus. But it's not like I can hail a taxi. There are no London cabs out here. If I was in central London, it wouldn't be a problem, but they don't roam the streets this far out. I could get an Uber, but I've never downloaded the app. I drive everywhere and if I'm not driving, I use the overground and the Tube or I get Alex to pick me up. A bus would take too long. It would probably snake around a million backstreets before eventually arriving somewhere vaguely near to where I need to be. I simply don't have the time.

I place my bag on the bonnet of my car, glancing sadly inside. I just want to be behind the wheel and on my way, but no. Some idiot had to ruin everything. I remember the shopping bags of biscuits I left on the back seat that I'd been planning to serve at the open house. I retrieve them and place the carrier bag on my bonnet too.

I take a deep breath and look up taxi apps in the app store.

I find one and click on the install button, trying to stay calm as the app downloads. I enter my details and link my account to my PayPal, cursing under my breath at the amount of time it's taking.

I really hope the buyers are late.

I enter my destination into the app and request a ride.

The app tells me it's searching for a driver. I tap my foot against the pavement, wanting to cry with frustration as the seconds tick by.

'Come on, you stupid thing,' I shout at my phone.

'Morning!' a man's voice says.

I turn around and see Max. I flinch, shocked. He regards me with a friendly, bemused smile. He's wearing a long-sleeved running top, shorts and trainers, and he's a little bit out of breath, like he's just been for a jog. I feel instantly tense.

'Morning,' I reply, trying to quell my nerves. I smile politely even though Max is the last person I feel like speaking to.

'Everything okay?' Max asks with a strained smile, clearly picking up on my bad mood.

'Yes. I'm just having some issues. Someone slashed my tyres and I'm trying to get a cab,' I explain.

Max's face falls. 'Oh, right . . .' He looks down at my car tyres, his eyes widening. 'That's terrible.'

'Yeah,' I grumble.

He kneels down to get a closer look.

I feel my whole body go rigid. I don't need this. I really don't. Can't he just carry on with his run? I look down at his broad shoulders and muscular arms. He's clearly pretty strong. No wonder the woman he was with couldn't free herself from his grip.

I want to say something, confront him.

'You should check your tyres,' I suggest, thinking of the van I saw him driving last night.

'Oh, my car's fine,' he replies.

Car?

'The Audi?' I ask, recalling the other car that's been parked outside.

58

'Yes.' Max glances up at me.

I feel like mentioning the van but, unnerved by his gaze, I decide against it.

I glance down at the app. It's finally allocated me a driver, thank God. It says the driver is seven minutes away.

I watch the progress of the driver on the map. He's a few miles away, which isn't ideal, but at least he's en route. I check the time. It's 10.25 a.m. now. I might just be able to make it to the open house in time.

I force myself to take a deep breath. I want to rant and rave. I feel like screaming, but I need to calm down. I need to accept this situation and stay controlled. I need to be poised and professional for my clients. I can let off steam later.

'Are you sure your tyres got slashed?' he asks, looking up at me from his crouching position.

'Well, yeah! They didn't do that to themselves,' I snap.

Max looks suddenly shocked, affronted by my tone.

'Sorry,' I say, even though I'm not particularly sorry. 'I'm really stressed out.'

Max smiles. 'No problem. It's just there's some glass by your tyres. I thought maybe it was that,' he says, gesturing at some broken glass on the road.

I bend down and take a closer look. He's right. There's broken glass scattered around my tyres. It looks like shards from smashed beer bottles around my two front wheels.

'No way,' I mutter, thinking back to yesterday.

Did I not see this glass as I parked? I must have missed it. I must have been so wrapped up thinking about Lucy and her love life or whatever else was going on in my mind that I drove right into the space without noticing.

'This should have been cleared up. That's really unfair for you,' Max says sympathetically as he stands up.

He looks genuinely concerned and sorry for me, and I feel myself softening ever so slightly towards him. Maybe he isn't so bad. Maybe what I saw the other night wasn't all that extreme. Perhaps I've been overthinking it.

'Yeah, it's unfortunate, but never mind.' I sigh. 'Anyway, I'm Becky. I live at number 40, next door to you. You've already met my boyfriend, Alex, but I haven't had a chance to introduce myself.'

I extend my hand.

He smiles and shakes it.

'Hi, Becky, good to meet you. I'm Max.'

His handshake is firm and the expression in his eyes is sincere, if a little intense.

It's odd, but I have a strange feeling, as I take his hand, that I know him from somewhere. It's as though I've seen him before, but I can't quite put my finger on where.

It's quite disconcerting. I almost want to say something. Pick apart our histories, see if our paths have crossed at some point. Maybe we went to the same university, up in Leeds. Maybe we sat together in lectures, and I've totally forgotten him. Or perhaps he's from the same place as me. Maybe he grew up in Cambridgeshire too. Or I could know him locally. Could it be that I saw him at a party once or one of my friends dated him? I wrack my brains, but I can't figure it out.

My thoughts are interrupted by the sound of a car honking behind me.

I turn to see that a black car has pulled up. It must be my driver. I glance down at the app, which shows he's arrived.

'Sorry, my lift's here. I have to go,' I explain to Max. 'I'll speak to you another time.'

Max smiles. 'No worries. I hope your day gets better.'

'Thanks,' I reply, before gathering my bags and getting into the car.

Max breaks into a jog, disappearing down the road. My driver confirms my destination and we set off.

Despite the stress of the morning, as we drive I start to feel a bit better. Max seemed fairly polite and balanced, which makes me think that maybe I did overreact to what I saw. He didn't seem threatening or scary, but then I guess you never know. If true crime forums have taught me anything, it's that you can never really tell.

My driver stops at traffic lights. I check out my surroundings. He's gone past the exit to the dual carriageway, which means he's heading in completely the wrong direction. 'Excuse me!' I pipe up.

I lean forward and tell him which road we should be taking.

'There's traffic that way,' my driver says. 'A huge jam. I checked.'

'What?' I groan, exasperated. 'So what are we going to do?'

'We'll have to take a detour,' he explains. 'It's either that or getting stuck in traffic.'

I glance at the time on my phone. It's 10.35 a.m. now. People are going to be arriving at my open house soon.

I tap my foot against the floor as I look out of the window, urging the journey to go quicker, but the car crawls along and every traffic light seems to turn red as we approach. I feel completely on edge as I watch the minutes pass on my phone. I had everything planned for this morning. Everything was in order and now it's all going awry.

I reach into my bag and take out my make-up mirror. I check my reflection. I dust my nose with some powder and try to calm down.

So I'm going to be late. It's not ideal, but it's not the end of the world. I'll just apologise to the buyers, explain that there was traffic and carry on with the viewing. It's a shame I didn't have time to get the house ready, but hopefully the buyers will have been caught up in the traffic too, and will be running late like I am.

My driver starts weaving through the labyrinthine streets around a shopping centre.

I draw in a deep breath but it's raggedy. With each winding street, I'm getting more and more wound up. I check the time. It's now 10.50 a.m. Great. I'm definitely going to be late. Some of the buyers might even have arrived already. They could be standing, waiting outside the property, and here I am in the middle of a shopping centre miles away.

'Please, just get me there urgently,' I beg the driver, my voice shaky, pleading.

'I will, don't worry,' my driver replies casually.

Don't worry! That's easy for him to say. Wendy will have a field day if I screw up this open house.

'Look, I just really need to get to Wellington Road. How far away are we now?' I ask.

My driver shrugs. 'Ten minutes.'

'You said ten minutes ten minutes ago!' I snap, unable to keep my cool any longer.

I slump back into my seat and try to accept my situation. I'm going to be late now, that's just a fact. I need to inform the buyers, even though the thought makes me cringe. Buyers get to be late. They're late all the time, but estate agents have to be punctual. We don't get the luxury of running late.

I draft an apologetic text that I'm about to send to the buyers when one of them calls me, asking where I am. It just so happens to be the most intimidating of all the people coming to view the house today. Regina Yates – a top barrister and experienced property investor with a portfolio of dozens of flats and houses across London. She's extremely wealthy and pretty scary.

'There are six of us out here!' Regina tells me, laughing dryly. 'We've been getting to know each other!'

I laugh politely too, although I'm not exactly part of the joke. 'I'm so sorry to keep you waiting, Regina. There's terrible traffic, not that that's an excuse. I'll be with you all very soon. I can't wait to show you the house!'

I keep the slashed tyres incident to myself. I don't want Regina thinking I live in the ghetto.

'Well, we can't wait to see it!' Regina remarks, with an edge to her voice.

'I'm not far. I'll see you very soon!' I say enthusiastically, before hanging up.

Finally, my driver takes a turning and I start to recognise my surroundings. We're in the right area now, not too far from Wellington Road.

It's 11.07 a.m. I'm definitely going to be at least another five or ten minutes late, but it could be worse.

Finally, we arrive at Wellington Road. I spot the group of buyers waiting for me outside the property. I cringe at the sight. A couple more have arrived. There are eight of them. I'm embarrassed to be rocking up in a taxi like this. At least a few people haven't got here yet and won't witness my lateness.

Of the buyers who are waiting, most are on their phones, leaning against the wall, apart from Regina's husband, who scowls at nothing in particular while sucking on a cigarette.

I ask my driver to drop me off a few houses down, not wanting the buyers to see me getting out of his car.

'No spaces,' my driver says, peering down the road. 'I'll stop here.'

He pulls up right in front of the house.

'Right.' I sigh as all the buyers turn to look. 'Well, thanks.' I grab my bags and get out.

'See you,' my driver says as I shut the door and rush over to the buyers.

They eye me warily, clearly unimpressed by my late arrival.

'Oh, you made it!' Regina says sarcastically, looking up from her phone.

I smile politely, refusing to let her get to me. 'I did! I'm so sorry about that. I got stuck in traffic,' I say, looking around the group, hoping they accept my apology.

They all look a bit tense, but they seem to relax a little as I beckon them to follow me up the drive.

I try to gather my composure and launch into my spiel about the house, trying to remember all the particulars I memorised yesterday, waxing lyrical about the Edwardian building and the year it was built.

I open the front door and let the buyers in. They filter into the hallway and begin making all the right noises. I carry on telling them about the house, detailing the square footage of the front rooms and the recent renovations that have been carried out, but they've started wandering around of their own accord, exploring, and no one pays any attention.

I head into the kitchen and unload my shopping bag. I lay out a few plates of biscuits as a couple come in. The man grabs a biscuit, smiling at me.

'Wow!' says his wife, taking in the kitchen.

'Isn't it beautiful?' I enthuse, telling them about the chef-grade stove, built-in fridge and freezer and marble worktops.

'It's stunning,' the woman replies, wandering through.

A few more buyers come in to check it out too. They all seem impressed. It's a beautiful kitchen, after all. I gush about the high-end features as they walk through, opening and closing cupboards and checking out the appliances.

They venture from the kitchen to the adjoining dining area, which leads on to the conservatory.

I follow, making a few comments about the 'airy, spacious open-plan design' of the space, which seem to go right over everyone's heads. I'm beginning to feel like they'd be better off if I just kept quiet and let them explore without my commentary.

'Oh my God!' Regina's husband suddenly says in a shocked, almost disgusted voice.

I frown, looking over to see him peering out through the conservatory windows towards the back garden.

'Yuck! Filthy!' Regina comments.

My heart sinks. What now?

I rush over and see that the beautiful landscaped garden is covered in rubbish, as though a bin bag or several bin bags have been upturned all over the lawn. The garden's covered in everything from rotten fruit and vegetables to discarded food wrappers to used tissues and empty wine bottles. It's a complete mess.

'Oh no,' I utter, completely shocked.

I was at this house just a few weeks ago doing a one-to-one viewing with a buyer and the garden was immaculate. How is it now completely covered in trash?

'That's revolting!' Regina cups her hand over her mouth like she's about to be sick. She nudges her husband. 'Look, there's a sanitary towel,' she says, pointing across the garden.

Everyone, including myself, peers out, and she's right. A sanitary towel, soaked in blood, lies proudly by a bed of begonias.

'I'm leaving!' Regina declares.

She turns and walks out, not even glancing in my direction. Her husband shoots me a scathing look as he follows.

'I . . . I . . .' I stammer, not knowing what to say.

I'm speechless. Nothing like this has ever happened on a viewing before. I would never willingly show buyers around a house with the garden in such a state.

'I don't know what happened. It'll be cleaned,' I mumble, flummoxed, but a few more buyers turn to leave.

'I'm sorry, but that's just put me off,' one woman says, shuddering as she takes her husband by the hand and walks away.

Only one couple is left.

'It was probably foxes,' says a woman with kind eyes, giving me a sympathetic smile. 'They must have raided the bins.'

'Proper midnight feast!' her partner adds, with a laugh.

I smile weakly. She's right, it probably was foxes. They are everywhere in London.

And yet I feel so embarrassed. I feel personally responsible, like I trashed the garden. First I show up late for the viewing and then I show a load of wealthy, important buyers a house that's covered in rubbish, including used sanitary products. It's mortifying. If this gets back to Wendy . . . What if she comes down on me? What if I lose my job? I need a job if I'm going to have a family. My palms bead with sweat at the thought. How is everything going so wrong? It feels like I'm losing my grip; my sense of control over my life is slipping. Just a few weeks ago, everything was fine and now it feels like it's just one thing after another.

'Would you, erm, like to see the rest of the house?' I suggest, although I'd rather the ground just swallowed me up.

The woman glances at her partner.

'Sure!' she says, but I can tell from her weak smile and the pity in her eyes that she's not interested any more. She's just trying to be polite.

Nevertheless, we go through the motions and I show them the rest of the house. They leave, telling me they'll 'think about it'.

I'm pretty sure I'll never hear from them again.

I walk back into the kitchen in a daze. I find myself washing my hands, feeling dirty from the sight of the garden alone. I dry them on a kitchen towel and grab a biscuit, comfort eating it. Then another.

I wander back into the conservatory and appraise the mess in the garden once more. I spot a used nappy that I'd missed, too. Regina's right, the garden is disgusting.

Yet there are still five people due to come and view the house. A few couples and that guy, Edward. I'm going to have to clean the garden myself before they arrive. I really don't want to. There's so much rubbish everywhere. I shouldn't have to wander around someone else's garden clearing up their trash. And I especially don't want to have to deal with nappies and sanitary towels, but I know I have no choice. I can't risk the other buyers coming along and seeing the garden in its current state.

Sighing, I root around in the kitchen drawers, hoping to find some rubber gloves and bin bags. Luckily there are some, and I head outside.

I hold my breath as I pick up everything from mouldy courgettes to crisp wrappers to the nappy and sanitary towel. I try not to look at them too closely as I throw them into the bag. It takes less time than I expected to gather everything. I tie the bag up tightly. I can feel hot tears building behind my eyes, but I push the emotion away. I don't have time to cry. I can't afford to break down now. And yet, nothing feels fair. It's like the walls are closing in.

I look around. The garden still looks a bit messy. It's a bit trampled and grotty-looking. It's not exactly pristine, but it's fine. It's passable.

A little breathless, I look around for a bin, but there isn't one.

I wander back through the house, clutching the bag and hoping the buyers don't arrive right at this moment, finding me with a pair of rubber gloves on, lugging a bin bag around. I find a wheelie bin out front and leave the bin bag inside before quickly heading back to take off my rubber gloves and wash my hands.

As I lather the soap, I find myself wondering how the foxes managed to drag so much rubbish from the bin out at the front to the back garden. There were no bins at the back. It doesn't make sense.

Unless the vendor popped home and left a bag of rubbish out back, forgetting to put it in the bin. That must have been what happened.

The doorbell rings as I'm drying my hands. Right. My final chance to get a sale.

I check my reflection in the door of the stainless-steel fridge. I look tired and worn out already, but I plaster on my brightest smile and head to the front door, praying I can salvage this terrible day.

Chapter Ten

I pour myself a large glass of wine.

Today has been the day from hell.

A few more couples came to view the house in the end. One woman – a retired teacher – seemed fairly interested and she and her husband said they'd give it some thought and get back to me, but I noticed them exchange a few bemused looks as I showed them around. I was trying to keep my cool, but I felt frazzled and drained, and I think it showed.

The other couple's viewing took all of five minutes. They declared the house 'too small' after seeing the living room and kitchen, and promptly left. I'm definitely not going to be hearing from them.

I waited around for a while, wondering if Edward would show up. I called him a few times, not wanting us to miss each other again like last time, but he didn't answer. I sent him a text, telling him I'd wait until 1.30 p.m., but he didn't reply. I left a voicemail too, but he didn't call back. In the end, I waited at the house until 2 p.m. just in case he showed up, and then left. He was clearly a time-waster. I take a sip of wine as I think of him, shaking my head.

I ordered another Uber after the open house. There was no traffic on the way back and the journey took just ten minutes. When I got home, I called the AA to sort out my car. They sent a tow truck to take it to the garage, who quoted me £250 to replace the tyres. I think I'll be able to claim it back on my insurance, but it's still frustrating. I'll have to get Alex to give me a lift to work on Monday morning.

To cheer myself up, I went to the Chinese takeaway down the road and bought some food for a night in with Alex, since he tends to have Saturday nights free. I figured some comfort food and a trashy film would make me feel better, but Alex texted five minutes ago, telling me Max had called and wanted a training session and he wouldn't be back until 8 p.m., by which time his sweet and sour pork will be congealed and disgusting.

I decide to eat on my own. I sit down at the kitchen table and open up the takeaway boxes. I bite off the corner of a piece of prawn toast, washing it down with a few sips of wine.

The prawn toast makes me feel quite a lot better and I have a few more slices before tucking into my chicken chow mein, which I drizzle with soy sauce.

The food and wine are just what I need and I start to relax. I message Anita about my terrible day. She immediately replies.

A soiled nappy on the lawn? YUCK!!

I take another sip of wine and fire back a response.

I know!

What a nightmare! It'll probably be one of those things that's hell at the time but that you'll look back on and laugh.

I smile. She's right. I picture us in The Albert in a few weeks' time, maybe with Lucy and a couple of others from work. I'll probably be telling the story and making a joke out of it by then. Even if it does feel mortifying now.

I finish eating and top up my wine glass before heading next door to the living room. I decide to log on to the true crime forum and maybe even watch one of the serial killer documentaries Alex hates. I may as well, since he's not here to object. I put Netflix on and choose a documentary featuring interviews with killers on death row. It looks right up my street.

It's dark outside and I get up and close the curtains. I flick on the fairy lights and drink my wine as I watch a serial killer try to explain his heinous crimes to an interviewer sitting across from him in his high-security jail.

As I'm watching, I flick through the latest posts on the forum on my phone.

As usual, I lose myself in my weird hobby and time flies.

I forget about the stresses of my day. I forget about Alex being busy with Max. I feel strangely relaxed, my mind completely engaged in trying to understand this twisted killer and the workings of his warped mind. I've always been fascinated by what drives a person to the edge. It's the ultimate human drama to take a life and I find the psychology behind it so intriguing. My own problems and issues pale into insignificance compared to this man and his dark and morbid life.

'Becky?'

I look over from the TV to see Alex standing in the doorway in his gym uniform.

I quickly pick up the remote and hit the pause button, embarrassed. I'd been planning to turn the documentary off before Alex got home.

'Another serial killer show?' Alex asks, raising an eyebrow. 'You're not getting into all that stuff again, are you?'

I feel a prickle of irritation. Why can't he just accept that I find true crime interesting? It's not like I'm committing murders myself.

'Leave it, Alex,' I mutter. 'I've had the day from hell.' I take another sip of wine.

'Another one?' Alex remarks.

'Yes, another one.'

He sits down next to me, and I tell him everything, from the slashed tyres to the disastrous open house.

'Whoa!' Alex remarks. 'That really is the day from hell.' He reaches over and takes my hand, giving it a squeeze. 'When do you get your car back?'

'Monday or Tuesday.'

'Okay.' He nods. 'What a pain. Come here.'

He opens his arms wide, drawing me in for a hug. I put my glass of wine down on the coffee table and snuggle into his arms, breathing in his comforting, familiar smell.

I realise that all I've done is vent about my day without having asked Alex one question about his. I feel a twinge of guilt.

'So how was your day?' I ask.

'It was good. I met up with Max. We had our first session,' Alex tells me with a bright smile.

'Right,' I say, not sure how to respond.

'Yeah. We did some basic cardio and weightlifting. He's in good shape. He deadlifted 100 kilos. Good stamina too,' Alex tells me.

'Hmm,' I murmur.

I tell Alex about running into Max this morning.

'He's cool,' Alex comments.

I smile, trying to be positive even though I still feel uneasy.

'We have quite a lot in common, actually. He did the London Marathon last year. He's done it three years in a row,' Alex carries on.

'What time did he get?' I ask, knowing Alex would have asked, or at least wanted to ask.

'Three hours and forty minutes,' Alex replies. 'Beat him by five minutes! We probably ran past each other.'

I laugh.

'And he's into Britpop too. And history. Wars and stuff. We got talking about all sorts,' Alex says, grinning.

Unlike some of the other personal trainers at the gym, Alex has a geeky side. Before he got into fitness, he worked as an archivist in the history section of a library in central London. He's always been into history. He churns through books on everything from the Napoleonic Wars to the invasion of Iraq, not that he'd admit it to his workmates.

'So Max is into military history too?' I ask, a little taken aback.

'Yeah! He was early for our session and when I arrived, he was sitting in reception reading a book on Churchill!' Alex tells me.

'Seriously?' I try to picture Max with a tome on Churchill in the gym reception. It's hardly an ideal environment for reading. The gym blasts the latest pounding upbeat pop songs and there are always people hanging around talking.

'I know, it surprised me too! We got talking about it. I haven't met anyone into that stuff since uni,' Alex says, still smiling.

'Right!' I smile back, despite feeling unsettled.

It's one thing that Max and Alex are spending time together, given what I know about Max, but it seems that they're getting along on a level that's more than just trainer and client. More like friends. How close are they going to get? It's a troubling thought. And it doesn't feel normal or natural that Max would have so much in common with Alex, right down to military history and books on Churchill. There's something weird about it. I feel confused, discombobulated, like I don't quite know what's going on.

I reach out and lace my fingers through Alex's.

'So are you going to train with Max often then?' I ask, my voice a little hesitant.

'Yeah, twice a week! He really wants to work on his strength. I think he wants to get ripped!' Alex tells me cheerfully.

'Great,' I say, as enthusiastically as I can.

For the first time, Alex seems to pick up on my tone. 'What's up?' he asks.

'Nothing,' I reply, brushing it off. 'I got some Chinese for you. It's in the kitchen. It might be a bit gross now though.'

Alex smiles. 'It'll be fine. You're the best! I'm starving.'

He leans in for a kiss before getting up and heading to the kitchen.

I pick up the remote and click out of the documentary. I was enjoying it, but I'll find something lighter for me and Alex to watch together. Something more positive would probably be good for me now. It might help take away the squirming, queasy feeling in the pit of my stomach.

Chapter Eleven

'It'll be okay,' Alex assures me, reaching across and placing his hand on my thigh as we stop at the traffic lights on the way to work.

I smile, placing my hand on his.

I'm dreading having to tell Wendy about the open house on Saturday. It's been on my mind all weekend, even though Alex and I did our best to enjoy ourselves. He had Sunday off and the weather was lovely, so we drove out of London and went for a riverside walk, stopping at a nice old country pub for Sunday lunch.

It helped to get out of the city, but it's Monday morning now and as we drive into town, I can't escape the stresses of work and of not having my car.

The lights turn green and Alex lets go of my hand, steering around a roundabout. As we near Alex's gym, I see a woman who looks like she's in her early twenties standing outside, tapping on her phone, a gym bag at her feet.

She's strikingly pretty, even in gym gear with her hair tied back and hardly any make-up on. She has an amazing figure, big eyes and long dark hair. She looks like she could be a model.

I feel a little insecure as I take her in. Sometimes it's not easy having a boyfriend who works in an environment full of people flexing in Lycra. A lot of Alex's workmates are single. They seem to go from woman to woman and regularly use the gym to meet people. A few of them even offer women they like the look of free personal training sessions in the hope that they might get to sleep with them. Apparently, it often works.

Alex tells me this stuff in a mocking, disapproving way, but the stories do make me feel a bit paranoid. I remind myself that Alex isn't like that. He's a good boyfriend. He'd never cheat.

'Tara's here already,' Alex says as he waves out of the window at the woman, who looks up from her phone and waves back.

We stop at another set of traffic lights. Alex taps his fingers against the steering wheel, frowning.

'Can I drop you off here?' he asks, turning to me. 'Tara's my client. She thinks I'm coming now. If I drive you to work, then drive back, I'll take another ten minutes and she'll be standing around waiting.'

Ten minutes seems a bit of an exaggeration since my office is only around the corner, but I can see that it would be rude to keep his client waiting given she's seen him now. I glance over. She's looking our way, her gym bag on her shoulder.

'Sure,' I reply.

Alex smiles. He leans in for a kiss and I feel relieved. I haven't got anything to worry about. I shouldn't feel threatened by attractive women. If Alex was a cheater, he wouldn't kiss me right in front of his client. He's not remotely the type to stray. I'm just on edge.

I reach for the door handle. 'See you later. Thanks for the lift.'

'Okay, see you later,' Alex replies as I hop out of the car.

I close the door behind me as the lights go green. Alex pulls into the gym car park and I walk down the road towards work.

I arrive early. Fortunately, Wendy isn't in yet. In fact, only Ryan is here. We exchange pleasantries as I turn on my computer and log into my inbox. He doesn't pry about my weekend too much this time. Probably because several of our other colleagues are sitting nearby.

I see I have an email from Wendy. My stomach drops as I read the subject line: Issues with viewing.

Oh no.

I open it. It's a forwarded message from Regina, detailing all the problems with the open house on Saturday. Regina states that I arrived 'nearly an hour late', which is an exaggeration. She goes on to state that I looked 'wild-eyed and frazzled', speculating that I might have 'had a long night'. She then describes the state of the garden with capital letters for added effect. 'A horrifying mess with rubbish strewn everywhere, including SOILED NAPPIES AND WORSE!'

Regina concludes her message stating:

> I've been investing in property for thirty years now and I've dealt with a lot of estate agents. This was without doubt the most unprofessional viewing I've ever encountered, and I would like to request that you remove me and my husband from your mailing list with immediate effect as we will not be doing business with a company that represents itself in this way.

Ouch.

I stare at the email, aghast. A chilly, quivering sensation flows through my veins as I reread it. It's like my blood is running cold, a rising panic building within.

'Are you okay?' Ryan asks.

'What?' I look over and see him eyeing me with concern.

'I asked if you're okay? You don't look it!' Ryan remarks.

'I'm fine!' I reply, my voice shrill.

I smile weakly and get up. I feel like I need to scream, or cry, or wail. I need to be alone, without Ryan watching me.

I dash to the toilets, my face crumpling the moment I walk through the door.

I lock myself in a cubicle. I close the toilet lid and sit down. The icy feeling in my veins is still there.

Regina couldn't have been any more scathing. She was vicious. She made out that I was an idiot. And that line about never having had an experience like it in the thirty years she's been investing in property . . . it makes me sound like a complete liability.

First Edward's Google review and now this. Wendy's going to lap this up. Now she has solid evidence to prove what she's already believed about me for years – that I'm incompetent, useless and I don't belong in this industry.

It all feels so unfair. I've done three or four viewings with Regina in the past that all went swimmingly. I was on time, professional, the houses were immaculate. Can she not appreciate that sometimes unfortunate things just happen? Can she not appreciate that I might have been having a bad day?

Apparently not. Apparently, she had to jump right into her emails and send a vicious message attacking me to my boss.

I lower my head in my hands and try to resist the urge to cry. Everything feels too much, but I can't break down. I'm not going to cry. I'm not. I need to pull myself together and explain to Wendy what happened on Saturday, and swallow my pride and apologise to Regina. I need to try to turn the terrible incidents of the last few days around.

I emerge from the cubicle and check my reflection. I can see the stress in my eyes. My forehead is creased. I run my fingertips across it, smoothing out the lines. I force a smile and try to suppress the weary, defeated look on my face.

I brace myself and head back into the office.

Wendy and a few others have now arrived. Wendy's sitting at her desk, looking like she's already deep in concentration, even though she can only have been here for five minutes.

As I approach, she turns, registering me with a look of disdain.

'Hi, Wendy,' I say, making a conscious effort to maintain my poise. 'I saw your email. Could we have a word?'

'Yes,' Wendy replies curtly. 'Let's go to the boardroom.'

'Sure,' I say, following her.

I've always found it irritating how Wendy refers to our relatively small meeting room as 'the boardroom' as though she's Alan Sugar. Even now, as she marches across the office in her pinstripe suit and stilettos, leaving me one step behind, I find her almost theatrical with her over-the-top authoritative style.

She pushes open the door and we head inside.

She sits down and gestures for me to sit opposite her, all the while regarding me with a cold, withering gaze.

'So, do you want to tell me what happened on Saturday?' Wendy asks.

'Of course.' I launch into an explanation, telling her everything from the slashed tyres to the foxes raiding the bins, apologising profusely.

I expect Wendy to realise that I wasn't at fault and that it was just an unfortunate day. I expect her expression to soften, but it doesn't. She simply eyes me with an impassive, cold stare.

'It won't happen again, I promise you that,' I insist.

'Well, the thing is, Becky . . .' Wendy sighs. 'You said that last week when you locked yourself out of a house, leaving a buyer out on the street and causing the company to get a one-star review.'

Her words cut into me. 'Yes, but again, that was unfortunate. I'd put the doorstop under the door but—'

Wendy holds up her hand to silence me.

'I don't want to hear it,' she snaps, her eyes switching from impassive to angry. 'I don't want to hear your excuses. You have a duty to this company to behave professionally at viewings. That involves making the necessary preparations, like leaving home early enough to avoid any potential issues that might make you late. It means making sure you always have time to check a property thoroughly before showing it to buyers. It means taking your keys with you if you step outside a house, even for a second, to make sure you can't possibly get locked out. It means behaving in a way that people expect of a leading London estate agent. Your behaviour over the past week has fallen very short and it's brought the reputation of the whole company down.'

I feel my cheeks burn with shame. I shrink into my seat, mortified.

'Do you know how many people Regina knows? It's not just Regina you've turned away from our company. It's her friends, her colleagues, her family. It's anyone she chooses to tell about her experience with us. Word gets around.' Wendy shakes her head.

She has a point. Regina is the kind of person who's likely to tell other people about Saturday. She's probably already ranted and raved about the viewing to anyone who will listen. And Wendy's right, no one will book a viewing with us after hearing that story. We have potentially lost out on buyers.

'I should have left home earlier on Saturday. You're right, I messed up,' I admit. 'I'm so sorry, Wendy.'

Wendy sighs dramatically. 'Just make sure it never happens again, Becky,' she says, her eyes stern.

She holds my gaze for a moment and her words hang in the air between us. I can feel the implication in them. If I mess up again, there will be consequences.

'Understood. I guarantee it won't happen again,' I insist.

'Good,' says Wendy. 'Now let's get back to work.'

She gets up and leaves the meeting room without another word.

I follow, feeling two inches tall.

As I walk back through the office, my cheeks still burning, I see Susan looking in my direction with a smirk on her face, as though she's taking pleasure in my struggles. The moment she catches me looking, she quickly looks away to focus on her screen instead, and yet her expression makes me feel even more troubled. I thought Susan was a hard-working, corporate go-getter, but maybe Anita was right about her. Maybe she does have a mean streak.

She tenses up as I walk past her desk, her shoulders stiff as she stares fixedly at her screen. I consider saying something, but I'm too drained from the exchange with Wendy. I head on towards my desk.

A sparkly yellow envelope placed in front of my monitor distracts me from the unsettling thoughts rattling around my head.

'You're invited to my baby shower,' Anita trills as I pick it up.

'Oh!' I enthuse, smiling.

I open the letter and pull out a bright yellow invitation to a 'day of celebration' at the end of next week.

'Aw, thanks Anita!' I go over and give her a hug. 'I can't wait!'

She beams. 'Sorry for the short notice. But you can make it, right?' she says.

'Of course I can make it. I wouldn't miss it!'

'Great!' Anita replies.

I sit back down at my desk, feeling a bit better. So, Wendy and Susan aren't my biggest fans, but not everyone in the office hates me. In fact, a few people, like Anita, really care.

Chapter Twelve

I have some time to kill after work, since Alex is training a client. I decide to wander around town to clear my head after a stressful day spent working especially hard, knowing Wendy was keeping an eye on me. It's a nice evening and it feels good to be walking away from work, passing strangers and getting away from office politics.

I consider going to a coffee shop, but I spot that the baby shop Anita and I went to the other day is open, an eye-catching display of cots and teddy bears in its window.

I head inside and try to find that green blanket Anita liked.

There's one left and I pick it up, feeling the lovely fabric between my fingers. It's so incredibly soft. I locate the label and check what it's made from. Lamb and merino wool. I turn over the price tag. It's £120. Expensive for a blanket. And I am having to fork out £250 for new tyres for my car.

I feel hesitant. Should I buy it? Or should I find something cheaper? I glance around the shop, taking in the brightly coloured baby toys and teddy bears, but nothing leaps out at me quite like this blanket. And Anita did really like it. It would make the perfect gift.

Screw it. I head to the till. Anita's one of my closest friends. If I'm ever going to splash out, now is the time.

The cashier offers to gift-wrap the blanket, enfolding it in tissue paper and placing it in a pretty gift box.

I hand her my card, trying to push down my money worries. It doesn't help that I haven't made a house sale for a while. I definitely need to rectify that, not just for my finances but for my standing at work.

The cashier hands me the bag and I head outside. I check the time. I still have forty-five minutes to kill until Alex will be ready. I decide to head to a new café that recently opened down the road. It's a cute one I've seen on Instagram quite a lot, with flower walls, vintage teapots and colourful, over-the-top cakes, and I've been meaning to check it out.

I walk to the café, the bag swinging at my side. Being out and about, taking some time to myself, really is helpful. So I'm going through a bit of a rough time at work. It's not the end of the world. I have so much to be grateful for. I have good friends like Anita. I have Alex and our future together to look forward to. The prospect of a child. There are so many great, exciting things happening in my life. This is just a glitch that will pass.

The café is just as pretty in real life as it appears online, painted pink and gold. I head inside, taking in the walls covered in artificial flowers and the groups of friends chatting over tea and cake. I join the queue by the counter and admire the decadent cakes: huge delicious-looking slices of chocolate cake, carrot cake, Victoria sponge, as well as brownies, cookies and all kinds of pastries.

My turn in the queue arrives and I order a cup of tea and a slice of Victoria sponge, unable to resist the temptation. The barista, who wears a vintage 1950s apron, makes my tea. I turn around and watch a couple of teenagers taking photos together in front of a flower wall, shots that will no doubt be on their Instagram feeds later. The barista hands me my tray and I look around for a place to sit. The café's busy, but I spot a spare seat by the window.

I head over.

I take a bite of my cake. It's delicious. It looks cute on a pink-patterned plate, next to my matching teapot, and I take a picture and upload it to my Instagram stories, tagging the café like I'm some kind of influencer.

I realise I have a missed call from my foster mum, Linda. I contemplate calling her back as I take another bite, but I'm not quite in the right mood.

Linda and I have never been naturally close. I sometimes wondered if on some level she was scared of me when I was younger. I didn't come from a good family and I used to worry that maybe Linda didn't want to hug me too tightly or get too close in case she picked up some of my darkness, some of my tainted past. Of course, I never said anything. I've always maintained the lie that I don't remember anything about my real parents and the terrible things that happened. I was told what had happened, but I pretended I didn't know and that I didn't see it. It gave me a sense of distance from my parents. It made me feel separate, clean. It still does. I don't tell anyone anything.

Alfie wasn't much of a hugger either. He was always somewhat distant. He worked long hours in construction. But when I did see him, he was funny, always cracking jokes. He never took life too seriously. I liked that about him. But I didn't feel I could go to him for advice or fatherly wisdom. I was always aware that Linda and Alfie had other kids to look after. They were constantly on the phone to the council, making beds and preparing a place at the table for a new child.

I liked chatting to the other children that lived with us. Some stayed for years, like me, and we got close. Often, they felt more like family than Linda and Alfie did, because we needed each other. The feeling of need was mutual, a little desperate. They craved hugs like I did. They wanted that closeness. I was best friends with one girl, Nadia, who stayed in the home for a while, but she moved to Spain a few years ago and we don't speak as often any more.

I sigh and put my phone down. I make a mental note to call Linda this weekend when I'm feeling a bit more relaxed. I should probably speak to her soon. It's been a while. Definitely more than a month. I should probably visit them soon too. They still foster and have other kids staying with them, so I don't go back too often. I don't like to impose. They're busy and they need the beds for the children they look after.

I turn my attention to my cake. As I sip my tea, I absently watch people coming and going on the street outside. Other office workers are heading home, waiting for buses or picking up dinner on the way back.

I finish the cake and push my plate aside. I watch a woman walking the most adorable poodle.

I'm watching the poodle trot away into the distance when I spot a man standing at a bus stop down the road. He's looking directly at me, and I feel a strange chill when I see him. He's wearing a dark coat with his hood pulled up and sunglasses on, even though the sun's setting and it's overcast now. He's leaning against the bus stop, half obscured by it, but he's definitely looking my way. I can tell. I can feel his gaze on me, like a physical force.

It's not the man I saw the other day, at the baby shop with Anita. It's someone else. Someone taller, leaner, probably younger. What the hell? Is this some new London thing? Men wandering the streets trying to frighten women? It wouldn't surprise me, giving how much crime there is in the city these days. I think of Max and that woman. I squint, trying to make the man out in more detail. Could it be Max? The figure looks about the same height. But no. Max is weird, but why would he do that? He seemed okay with me at the weekend. He might have made me feel uneasy, but I can't see why he'd follow me. That would be something else. And yet the thought is disturbing, and I shudder.

I look back at the figure, hoping he'll turn away, embarrassed, and I can forget about the whole incident, write it off as nothing, but he doesn't. He doesn't move. He stays focused on me. I don't think I've seen him before, but he's too far away to make out properly. Is he someone I know? Someone who's trying to look obscure? The thought is strange, unsettling. His eyes are still on mine and I look away, my skin prickling. There are so many weird men around. Why can't this guy just mind his own business and let me drink my tea in peace? What does he want from me? Why would some man have chosen me? Decided to target me?

I try to act like I'm not bothered. I don't want that man thinking I'm scared. That might encourage him. It's probably exactly what he wants. I turn my attention to my phone instead. I scroll on Instagram. Anita has posted a picture of her and Sam in a field of sunflowers with a caption about her baby shower. I hit 'like' and post a comment about how excited I am. Lucy has posted a picture of her cats, Jekyll and Hyde. Her feed is mostly pictures of her cats these days. She jokes that she's a mad cat lady, poking fun at herself and writing captions about silly things the cats have done. It can be funny, but sometimes I find Lucy's humour a bit too self-deprecating. It's like she's making fun of herself before someone else does. I think that secretly, she wants more than this solitary life, but it's almost as though she's stopped trying.

I think about Ryan again. He and Lucy are both single. They both like cats. I go on to his feed. It's mostly pictures from his hikes, but there are a couple of his cat too. He and Lucy should really go on a date. I'm sure Ryan would be interested. What's not to like? Lucy's lovely. It might help him move on from his crush on me too. Lucy is a much better match for him. He might even have a soft spot for her already, but no idea how to go about making a move. Perhaps they both need a little nudge.

I message Anita, sharing my thoughts.

While I'm messaging, I glance up and see that the strange man is still standing at the bus stop. He's looking into the traffic, but as though sensing my attention returning to him, he looks my way. We stare at each other. I try again to make him out, but I can't see him properly in the waning evening light. And yet I can feel him looking at me from behind his sunglasses. I feel irritated. Why does this keep happening to me? One after the next; a constant sense of feeling watched, harassed.

I stir the dregs of my tea and try to shake it off. I'm not going to let some weird man get to me.

I look back down at my phone and see that Anita has messaged.

Why don't we do after work drinks at The Albert on Friday night?

Alex is always working on Friday nights. I think back to the weekend just gone, when I gorged on Chinese food and watched a documentary about serial killers. Going to the pub definitely sounds preferable. I send a reply.

Yes! We can get Ryan and Lucy to come. Get them together!

My phone buzzes. Good idea!

I look up from the message. The guy has gone. Finally. He's disappeared. I look up and down the street, but I can't see him. He must have got bored and moved along. I shudder again. What a creep.

I breathe a sigh of relief and message Anita about our plans for Friday.

Chapter Thirteen

My week may not have got off to the best start, but thankfully, no more drama ensued.

I collected my car from the garage on Tuesday lunchtime, and despite having to spend an hour on the phone to my insurance company, they agreed to cover the cost of my new tyres. Things have improved at work too.

I was shaken from the conversation with Wendy for a day or so and felt lost and off my stride, but by Wednesday I'd pulled myself together and got my fighting spirit back. I signed up a new vendor with a beautiful property in Dulwich – a spacious two-bedroom top-floor flat in an old Edwardian conversion. I immediately called every buyer who I thought might possibly be interested and managed to organise some viewings on Thursday morning before the listing was due to go live. Only three people could make it at such short notice, but one of them put in an offer on the spot. The offer was at asking price and the vendors accepted. Everyone was happy and even Wendy gave me a begrudging 'Good work'.

I also asked the seller if she could leave a Google review, which she did. It was five stars and praised my 'friendly demeanour and efficient, professional approach'. Ha. Have that, Wendy!

I feel back to my old self again as I lean across the bar in The Albert and ask the barman for two glasses of Pinot Grigio, an orange juice and two pints of Guinness.

True to our word, Anita and I organised Friday night after-work drinks. We sent an email round to Lucy and Ryan and a few others in the office who we thought might want to come. Ryan and Lucy both agreed, as well as Sophie, who works on reception.

Anita and I exchanged glances as we found a table, both of us carefully side-stepping chairs to try to get Ryan and Lucy to sit next to each other. I don't think they noticed, and it worked. Ryan got the first round in, then Lucy and Ryan got chatting about work, where they grew up and even their cats. They seem to be hitting it off. They even both drink Guinness.

The barman places the drinks on a tray in front of me. I thank him and head back to our table.

I sit down, sandwiched between Anita and Ryan, and pick up my Pinot Grigio.

I'm about to turn to Anita when I feel Ryan nudge me.

'So, Becky, how are things with you these days?' he asks. 'Aside from all that rubbish with Wendy. You should totally ignore her, by the way!'

'Oh, I know!' I laugh, a little taken aback. 'Things are good. I managed to get a sale yesterday.'

'Yeah, I heard. Nice one,' Ryan replies. 'So, what else is new?'

'Oh, not much,' I reply, toying with the stem of my wine glass.

Ryan smiles, eyeing me as though expecting more, but I'm not quite sure what to say.

What is new for me? I'm living in a lovely house with the man of my dreams, and I never thought I'd have it this good. And yet nothing new is happening exactly. It's not like I'm pregnant yet. It's not like Alex and I are engaged. Those things will come in time, but so far, we're just doing our thing. To me, it feels like my life is moving forward, but to anyone else, it probably seems as though nothing's changing at all.

'I'm just, you know, trying to do well at work. Trying to get by with Wendy in charge!' I say, deflecting the focus away from my personal life.

'I know the feeling,' Ryan grumbles.

I smile, although I can't help wondering how Ryan knows the feeling. He's probably the most innocuous person in the office. He doesn't deal with properties at all and most of the time he flies under the radar, avoiding any office drama. He crunches numbers and prepares accounts statements, and seems to spend most days sitting quietly at his desk with his headphones in.

We chat a bit about work. Ryan tells me about the latest accounting system upgrade he's been working on, in a little more detail than is necessary for a Friday night. This is not going as planned. Ryan's halfway through his second drink and rather than flirting with Lucy, he's talking to me about spreadsheets.

I try to change the subject, asking about his latest hike, since I know how much Lucy enjoys country walks.

'Oh yes. I'm still hiking whenever I can!' Ryan says enthusiastically.

He starts telling me about a trip he took to Scotland where he climbed mountains in the Highlands. I sip my wine, trying to think of a way I can involve Lucy in the conversation, but she's got her back turned to us and is having an animated conversation with Sophie and Anita. She seems completely oblivious to Ryan.

He tells me about the altitude he reached on his latest trek, and I find my brain switching off. Instead, I take in his features. He is attractive. He has lovely big brown eyes, and full, almost pouty, lips. I've hardly looked at him since I met Alex, but I definitely used to have a soft spot for him. He can be a little bit boring, but he's a good guy. Lucy could do a lot worse, and yet she doesn't seem interested at all.

Ryan has quite a lot to say about the Scottish Highlands and I finish off my glass of wine as I nod and listen. I feel a bit tipsy when I place my empty glass on the table.

'Another round?' Ryan suggests.

'Oh, I'm okay,' I reply, but Ryan insists it's his turn and heads to the bar, ordering another round of drinks for everyone.

I pop to the bathroom and by the time I'm back, Ryan has placed a tray of drinks down with a large glass of Pinot Grigio for me. I take it, but I tell myself I'm not going to drink much more. If I do, I won't be able to drive home.

I thank Ryan and clink my glass against his, saying, 'Cheers.'

Anita turns to me and asks me about a property I'm selling. I can tell she's trying to save me from more conversation about mountains and I lean forward to answer her, turning my back ever so subtly on Ryan.

He turns to Lucy and begins chatting with her and Sophie.

'Thank you,' I say, under my breath.

'You were looking a bit bored there!' Anita whispers.

'Well, there's only so much I need to know about the Scottish Highlands,' I comment.

As Anita and I chat, Ryan, Lucy and Sophie seem to be getting on well. Stupidly, I drink my wine, meaning I won't be able to drive. Anita finishes her third orange juice and starts yawning, looking visibly tired.

'It's past my bedtime!' she says, looking at her watch.

I check the time on my phone and see that it's 10.30 p.m.

'Pregnancy is exhausting,' Anita comments.

I smile sympathetically.

'I'd better go, guys,' Anita says, getting up from her seat with effort.

We hug her and say goodbye.

I consider whether to go home myself, but Lucy and Sophie bring me into their conversation and I'm tipsy enough that I don't feel like leaving the pub just yet.

We're all a little drunk and we chat about work, cracking jokes about silly office stuff.

Lucy gets a message from a friend offering her a lift home and says her goodbyes, with Sophie heading off with her.

I look down at my phone, trying to decide what to do. I could see if Alex would come and pick me up, but I feel bad since he works such long hours on Fridays. I consider using the taxi app again, but I'm not particularly keen after my experience last time.

I decide to get the train, seeing as the station is around the corner from the pub.

'Tonight's been good,' Ryan says, as I search for train times on my phone.

I look up and see him smiling warmly at me.

'Yeah, it's been fun.'

'We should do this kind of thing more often,' he suggests.

'Um, yeah,' I reply, a little flatly, looking back down at my phone.

I feel light-headed and I'm annoyed with myself for drinking too much. I parked my car next to the pub and it's frustrating to have to leave it there overnight. I spot that there's a train leaving in fifteen minutes.

Ryan takes a deep swig of his pint and places his glass back on the table. His pupils are dilated.

'We get on, don't we?' he says.

He leans a little too close, smiling soppily at me.

'Yeah, we get on!' I laugh, slightly uneasily. I edge away from him.

'I've always thought that,' Ryan says in a lower, almost husky voice. 'We just click, don't we?'

I raise an eyebrow sceptically, but Ryan doesn't seem to notice as he reaches for his beer. I'm not sure how Ryan has got it into his head that we click. Since when have I been into hiking and spreadsheets and all the things he likes? We barely speak apart from a bit of office chit-chat here and there.

'And you are pretty,' he comments, placing his hand on my thigh.

'Ryan!' I shriek, slapping his hand away. 'What are you doing? I'm with Alex!' I pull back from him, rattled.

'Oh.' Ryan looks shocked. 'I thought you guys weren't together any more. Or that you were going through a rough patch or something.'

'What?' I exclaim. 'Why would you think that?'

'I just . . . I guess . . .' he stammers, looking confused. 'You didn't mention him.'

I shake my head in disbelief. 'Just because I didn't mention Alex in passing conversation doesn't mean we're not together. Honestly, Ryan! You shouldn't jump to conclusions like that.'

'Okay,' Ryan mutters. 'Fine.' He looks across the crowded pub, pouting indignantly.

I roll my eyes. I need to get out of here. I put my phone in my bag and move to get up, but Ryan grabs my wrist and pulls me back down.

'Come on. Don't pretend that night didn't mean anything to you,' he snarls.

'Get off me!' I wrench my wrist from his grip.

I stand up again, but he gets hold of my wrist again and yanks me back into my seat. He eyes me imploringly. He looks desperate.

'I know it meant something to you too,' he says.

'What night?' I ask, baffled.

'What night?!' Ryan retorts disbelievingly.

I eye him blankly. Surely, surely, he's not talking about that kiss at the Christmas party over three years ago?

'You know what night,' he says.

He leans closer, placing his hand on my leg once more.

I push his hand away. If he wasn't a colleague, I'd slap him.

'Don't do that, Ryan!'

I'm revolted. I move to get up.

'We had a connection,' Ryan whines. 'I think about you all the time.'

His eyes are pleading, and I can tell, despite how strange this all is, that he means it. He's been harbouring a crush on me. He must have been ever since that party years ago. My heart sinks, filling with dread.

'Are you serious, Ryan? We had a drunken kiss.'

'It wasn't just a drunken kiss,' Ryan insists, his eyes clouding over with something darker.

I eye him, lost for words, completely taken aback. 'It wasn't some epic love affair!'

Ryan's mouth drops open. He gawps at me. 'We'd been flirting for months. It was . . .' He pauses, searching for the right word. 'It was special.'

I check the time on my phone. My train's leaving in eight minutes.

'Ryan, it was just a kiss, okay? It was years ago. You were seeing someone afterwards. I don't understand!'

'Cathy?' He raises an eyebrow.

'Yeah, Cathy. That woman you were seeing,' I say, vaguely recalling Ryan mentioning her.

'Cathy meant nothing to me. I only got with her to make you jealous,' he says.

I'm shocked as his words sink in. I barely gave our kiss a second's thought and yet Ryan's been obsessing over it for years.

My mind races. He looks so distraught. How did I get him so wrong? How did I not notice his growing obsession with me? Perhaps I should have spoken to him ages ago and nipped this in the bud.

'Look, Ryan, I'm sorry that you thought our kiss meant something more than it did, but I'm with Alex. I have been for three years now,' I say.

Ryan shakes his head. He looks crestfallen. He reaches for his pint.

'Ryan, I need to go to the station. My train's leaving in five minutes.'

Ryan doesn't respond. He doesn't even look at me. He just knocks back the rest of his pint.

I get up, pulling my bag on to my shoulder. Ryan looks ahead like I'm not even here.

'Right. Well, I'm off,' I say.

Ryan looks up at me and his expression is one I haven't seen from him before. He looks scornful, hateful, so hostile that it unnerves me instantly. I didn't think he had that side to him. I've always thought he was a nice, normal guy.

Yet I feel like I'm seeing him through new eyes, and I don't know him at all. He looks mean and bitter, glaring at me, sitting on his own at a table covered in empty glasses.

'See you later, then,' I mumble, flummoxed.

Ryan rolls his eyes. He gets up, checks his pocket for his wallet and marches off to the bar without so much as a second glance at me.

I turn around and leave, feeling shaken. I head out of the pub in a daze and walk to the station. I replay what just happened in my mind. I think back to the chats I've had with Ryan in the office, the friendly throwaway conversations. Did he think they were deep and meaningful? Did he misinterpret my friendliness for flirtation?

95

It's hard to believe he could have misread everything so drastically. And it's not like I've hidden my feelings for Alex. When we first started dating, I'd come into work telling the girls openly about our amazing dates. Alex used to send me flowers at work and I'd be totally smitten all afternoon. I think of all the Monday mornings when I've told colleagues about the things we did at the weekend. What was Ryan thinking? Did he think it was all just an act? A way to make him jealous? It's so creepy to think that for so many years he's been clinging to the memory of one stupid kiss. Maybe he was just waiting for things to go wrong with Alex so he could seize his opportunity to try and get together with me.

I arrive at the station with a minute to go before my train arrives. I feel miserable. I sit down on an empty bench and look blankly at the train tracks.

Tonight was meant to be a fun night, but it's gone so badly wrong. I just wanted to help Lucy, but now there's a weird situation between me and Ryan that I'm going to have to navigate at work and even more awkwardness that I don't need in the office.

Sighing, I get my phone from my bag. Alex has messaged a few times, asking when I'll be back. He's even sent a photo of our bedroom, with the bed surrounded by candles and rose petals scattered over the sheets.

What on earth? Rose petals?! We normally only do stuff like that on birthdays or Valentine's Day, not on a regular Friday night.

I send him a text.

Feeling romantic?!

The train arrives and I get on.
Alex replies: I am indeed!

The train sets off and even though the carriage smells stale and some passengers have left drink cans and kebab wrappers on the floor, I find myself smiling soppily. As usual, Alex makes everything better. He makes life sparkle even in the worst moments.

What's prompted this then?

Alex starts typing a reply.

I gaze out of the window as the train pulls out further, away from the pub. I think of Ryan on his own in there and try to have some compassion. I do feel somewhat sorry for him, even if his behaviour is irritating. He's not a bad person. I think he's just a bit lonely. A bit shy and introverted.

When I flirted with him at the office party and we kissed, it never occurred to me that it would be such a big deal for him, but I guess it was. He mustn't get much attention. He probably doesn't realise he's an attractive guy. I guess he doesn't put himself out there, spending too much time in his head instead. I should have thought twice about kissing someone from work. There was always the risk that it could lead to complications.

My phone buzzes. Nothing in particular. I just felt like having a nice night in together.

I smile to myself. I really did luck out with Alex.

I write a reply back. I'm ten minutes away. I can't wait to see you xxx

I hit send. It's true. I can't wait to see him. I can't wait to walk through the front door and into his arms. I want to breathe in his familiar smell and look into his beautiful eyes and feel the rest of the world fade away like it always does when we're together.

Chapter Fourteen

I wake up with a smile on my face as sunlight pours through the gap between the curtains. I'm still in a blissed-out state from last night.

Alex's romantic surprise was just as good as I'd imagined, if not better.

I roll over, wanting to snuggle up in his arms, but he's gone. I look at my alarm clock. It's 9.10 a.m. He's busy training clients. I'll never understand people who want to train early on a Saturday morning, but each to their own, I suppose.

I sit up and take my phone from my bedside table.

I'm surprised to see that I have twelve WhatsApp messages and thirteen Instagram notifications.

I open the messages. Two are from Alex.

Alex: You looked so beautiful asleep this morning xx

Alex: Going to come home for lunch. See you around 1? Xx

The other ten are from Ryan. Ryan? What the hell?

Ryan: I've seen the way you look at me, Becky. I know this isn't all one-sided.

Ryan: Don't you feel that spark when we're together? You must feel it. We have a connection. Don't deny it.

Ryan: Do you really have no feelings for me? I don't believe it. I just don't. Answer me.

Ryan: Stop ignoring me Becky.

Ryan: BECKY?!!

There are more, escalating in desperation and drunkenness. Ryan must have stayed at the pub for ages. The last messages he sent were at nearly 3 a.m.

Ryan: Pleosde domt ihnore me Becky. I realy thinj wed be good tohgtethr. Calll me

Ryan: Your special becku. I thinl I migtr love yoo

For goodness' sake. I cringe as I take them in. Ryan's going to be mortified when he sees these. He's probably sleeping right now. I wish I could delete them from both our messaging histories. He probably doesn't remember sending half of them and it would spare us the embarrassment of having to discuss this on Monday morning.

I got the feeling last night that he was much lonelier than I'd realised, and I was willing to be understanding over the way he behaved, even if it did make me uncomfortable, but these messages are too much. Saying he might love me. It's ridiculous. And all that stuff about us having a spark and how we'd be good together. It's totally inappropriate given I told him in no uncertain terms that I'm with Alex. Being drunk isn't an excuse. I'm going to have to say something and make him aware that this is not okay.

But before I do, I click on to Instagram, curious as to why I have thirteen notifications. It's not like I uploaded a photo last night.

I open the app and my heart sinks. They're all from Ryan. He's liked nine of my posts and left three comments.

I click on the first. It's a comment left underneath a selfie I took at home about a year ago. I'd done my hair and I liked my make-up.

@Ryan_rogers232 you're so stunning xxx

Cringing, I click on the next one. It's a shot of me at the wedding of a friend from university, standing outside the church in the sunshine, smiling at the camera.

> @Ryan_rogers232 wish I could have been your
> plus one

Oh my God.

I physically shudder. What was he thinking? I check the time he left the comment. It was posted six hours ago, well after 3 a.m. He must have been smashed.

I'm not even sure I can face reading the final comment, but I brace myself and click on it. It's been left under a photo of me and Alex lying on a beach in Spain.

> @Ryan_rogers232 you could do better xxx

Unbelievable. Fuming, I screenshot the comments and send them to Anita. It's one thing that Ryan said some intense, inappropriate stuff in the pub, but spamming my Instagram page with creepy comments and insulting my boyfriend is a step too far.

Anita doesn't appear online. She must be busy.

I get up and pace around the room, irritated. How could Ryan behave so idiotically? I thought he was better than that. He's a grown man, for goodness' sake. Yet he's behaving like a stupid teenager. How on earth are we going to face each other on Monday?

Just when I thought things were beginning to go well for me again at work, Ryan has to ruin it by being a complete fool.

I slump back down on the bed. I scroll through Ryan's messages again. They're so embarrassing. I go on to Instagram to delete the comments, but as I click into the app, the sound of heavy metal blasts through my bedroom wall.

It reverberates heavily, making the bed vibrate. It's even louder than it was last time and even more unbearable. The vocals are even more piercing and hellish.

What the hell does Max think he's doing? How dare he blast his music like that on a Saturday morning with absolutely no regard for others? Does he not care that there are elderly people living on this road? And what about the rest of us? What about people who just want a lie-in and a relaxing Saturday morning? We don't want to have to endure his metal. He's being beyond disrespectful. It's almost like he's tormenting me.

I groan in despair. It's such a horrible sound. It feels like the kind of thing that could be played in a torture chamber to torment someone. Who would listen to this for pleasure? I cover my ears, trying to block out the nightmarish screech of the vocals.

'Shut up!' I find myself screaming. 'Turn it off!'

But like my hammering fists, my screams are drowned out.

I march out of the bedroom and cross the hallway. I head into the bathroom and close the door, but the difference is negligible. The music is still booming.

Hands shaking with anger, I message Alex.

Max is playing metal again. REALLY loudly this time.

I hit send and wait a few moments, but Alex doesn't reply. He must be busy with clients.

I cover my ears again, but the screaming vocals are too unbearable. Suddenly, I flip. I shouldn't have to be doing this. I shouldn't be hiding in my bathroom on a Saturday morning with my hands clamped over my ears because of the selfish whims of my neighbour. I shouldn't have to tolerate this at all. No one on the street should.

I don't care that Max unnerves me. I don't care any more about creating awkwardness or neighbourly tensions. I just need him to stop.

I decide to go over there and say something. Max needs to realise that there are certain ways you behave on a street like this. There are limits to what your neighbours should be expected to put up with, and he has gone too far.

I storm back into the bedroom and take off my pyjamas. I pull on some leggings and a jumper and tie my hair back. I shove my feet into a pair of trainers and grab my keys.

I head out of the house and march over to Max's.

The music is even louder outside. It's pouring out into the street, an unbearable cacophony.

I approach Max's front door and press the buzzer hard three times, making sure he won't miss the sound. My palms sweat as I wait for him to answer. I tap my foot, feeling anxious. But Max doesn't answer. I press it again three times and midway through the third ring, the door bursts open and there he is, standing in the doorway, scowling.

'What?' he asks, his voice cold and cutting.

His whole demeanour is completely different to the other day when we discussed my car tyres. He looks tired and unkempt. His hair's greasy, like he hasn't washed it for days. His complexion is sallow and his skin looks unclean. He's wearing a pair of old jogging bottoms and a baggy old top. There are stains on both. He looks awful. But his personal hygiene is none of my business.

'You need to turn your music down,' I tell him loudly, making sure he hears me over the screeching vocals.

'Why?' he asks.

I roll my eyes, feeling a fresh wave of frustration bubbling up inside me.

'Because it's totally inconsiderate to blast your music this loudly on a Saturday morning!' I bark.

He shrugs and starts closing the door.

Gawping, I push back against it. 'You can't do this. I'll call the council,' I insist. 'I'm going to tell Alex about this.'

Max laughs. 'You do that,' he sneers, plastering on a fake smile before closing the door in my face.

I stand there, looking blankly at his front door in shock. How dare he be so rude? How dare he shut his door in my face like that?

I consider ringing the doorbell again, but I'm not sure it's worth it. It's not like Max seems to care and I'm only going to end up screaming at him if he answers.

My skin prickling with anger, I turn and am walking back down his drive when the music is turned up even louder.

No way.

Right, that's it. I turn around and go back to his front door. I press the buzzer long and hard. Once, twice, three times, four times, but there's no answer.

Hands shaking with anger, I get my phone out of my pocket and message Alex, telling him exactly what Max is doing. I send a voice note recording the noise.

I press Max's buzzer one more time, but predictably, he ignores it.

Groaning, I turn around and storm back to my house, the horrendous sound of booming metal overwhelming my brain. I can barely think straight.

As I head inside, I'm still fuming. I try to call the council to make a report about Max and his noise disturbance, but the office is closed. I hang up, annoyed, and make an online complaint instead.

I cry out with frustration as Max's music pounds through the walls. My only hope now is that the other neighbours kick up a fuss too, or that Alex comes home and tells Max what's what.

In the meantime, I'm going to need my noise-cancelling headphones. I find them and put them on, but the music's so loud that I can still hear it. Sighing, with tears in my eyes, I head into the living room, closing the door and slumping on to the sofa.

Chapter Fifteen

I try to busy myself with work while I wait for Alex to come home. I sit on the sofa with my laptop open and do some admin, clearing my inbox and processing some paperwork for my latest sale. I shouldn't be working on a Saturday, but it's a good distraction from Max and his horrific music.

It works to a degree, although every time the screeching vocals blast through my headphones, I find myself yet again questioning Max and what he's doing around here. There's something not right about the whole thing. There's something that doesn't add up. It's not just the incident with that woman. I can't understand why a City guy would want to live out here, blasting metal and being deliberately provocative on a quiet street. It doesn't make sense that he looks like he hasn't washed for days and yet claims to have this high-flying slick career. I feel like he's lying, like he's not who he says he is. I want to google him and try to verify his identity with a LinkedIn profile or a Facebook page or some kind of online presence, but I don't know his surname. I could find out from Alex later.

I make a coffee and defrost a pain au chocolat, but I still feel tired and low. I've always loved living on this street. I love our house and I've never taken it for granted. I know that I'm lucky to have found a place where I feel I belong, a place to call home. And yet now, with Max here, my home, my nest, suddenly doesn't feel like such a happy place any more. It's been compromised.

I don't want to overreact, and I'd like to have faith that things will get better, but I think of the way Max scowled at me, the way he slammed the door in my face, and I'm not sure they will at all.

I'm midway through replying to an email when the reverberations and music bleeding through my headphones suddenly stop. I take my headphones off. The music's gone. Finally. I breathe a sigh of relief.

I get up and head into the kitchen. I peer out of the window towards Max's house. His kitchen is empty. It looks clean too, unlike the other day when beer cans littered the dining table.

I get the feeling someone's looking at me and glance up. Max is standing in a room above his kitchen, looking down at me, watching.

Our eyes meet, but he does nothing. He just stares back at me like he's been waiting to see me. Like he did the first time I saw him, the day he moved in. I shudder. It's like he's trying to scare me. What does he want from me? Is he a predator? Again, I find myself thinking of the woman I saw him with, the one he bundled into his van. I wish I knew she was okay. But what if she's not? What if Max is after me? What if I'm next?

A chill runs down my spine. I shrink away from the window, out of sight.

Chapter Sixteen

Spooked, I double lock the front door, fasten the chain lock and go around the house, checking every window is sealed and locked shut. Then I get into bed and wrap myself up in a blanket. But I can't get warm enough. I feel jittery.

I scroll on my phone, trying to distract myself with pictures on Instagram. But it doesn't work. I'm still feeling strange when Alex returns home, startling me. I forgot he was coming back so soon.

'Becks?' he shouts out as the chain lock rattles.

I get out of bed and head downstairs.

'Why've you put the chain lock on?' Alex asks through the gap in the door.

I take off the lock and let him in. I shrug.

Alex appraises me. 'What's wrong?'

'I was just feeling weird,' I say as he comes in and places his gym bag down in the hallway. He kicks off his trainers.

He smells sweaty and I can tell he's done a workout after training his clients today. He prefers to shower at home rather than at the gym, where he risks having to have awkward small talk with clients in the changing rooms.

'I need a shower,' he says, heading upstairs.

I follow him.

'Can we talk for a minute?' I ask, pulling him into the bedroom.

'Sure,' Alex says. He pulls off his T-shirt and throws it into the laundry basket.

I perch on the side of the bed, feeling glum.

'So, what's up?' Alex asks, eyeing me with concern.

'It's Max. Did you see my messages?'

'Oh yeah, he was playing his music again,' Alex replies, sounding unfazed. He sits down next to me.

'Yeah, that metal music he was blasting out the other day. He did it again. Even louder this time,' I tell him. I decide to leave out the strange look he gave me. I'm not sure it's something I should share.

Alex laughs. 'Max really does have the worst music taste.' He tuts, rolling his eyes indulgently.

He lies down on the bed, smiling. A flicker of irritation pulses through me.

'Stop acting like he's just some lovable rogue, Alex,' I snap. 'He's been blasting out that music for hours. He doesn't care about anyone! Not the elderly people living here, not the kids. No one. It's sociopathic!'

Alex's eyes widen. 'Whoa, don't shout at me over it. It wasn't me!'

'I'm not shouting,' I insist, even though I realise I have raised my voice. I try to take it down a notch, although I'm still annoyed. 'You could take what Max is doing seriously rather than acting like he's just got rubbish music taste and it's not a big deal.'

Alex sighs.

'It was incredibly loud. It's like he's doing it to deliberately annoy people,' I tell him.

'I doubt that. He's probably just not aware of how loud it is or how much it's upsetting you,' Alex suggests.

'He is aware! I made him aware,' I say, wishing Alex would stop being so forgiving.

'You did what?' Alex replies.

'I went over there. I asked him to turn it down, but he was so rude to me. He slammed the door in my face,' I tell him, shuddering at the memory.

'Oh, God,' Alex groans.

'What do you mean, "Oh, God"?' I ask, offended.

'Max is my client. Now things are going to be awkward,' Alex grumbles.

'I can't believe this,' I exclaim. 'You're more worried about things being awkward between you and Max during your sessions than you are about him being really rude to me.'

'I'm not. It's just these things happen when you have neighbours living so close. I'm not saying Max's music isn't annoying but sometimes you just have to deal with stuff. We've been lucky so far, but there's bound to be someone who annoys you when you live on streets like this.'

In a way, I get where he's coming from. I hear stories of tenants from hell all the time at work and Alex is right, we have been very lucky with our neighbours so far, but that doesn't mean we should turn a blind eye to Max's behaviour.

'It's not just about the music, Alex. It's about Max's whole attitude. He was incredibly rude to me and I really don't like him,' I say.

As the words come out, I realise just how much I've been wanting to admit my true feelings out loud. It's a relief to get it off my chest. I really don't like Max and I'm tired of pretending otherwise.

'He's weird. He creeps me out,' I confess.

'What do you mean, he "creeps you out"?' Alex asks.

I want to tell him everything but I stop myself. I take a deep breath and decide to go ahead and open up about Max standing at his window staring at me.

'It's like he does it to freak me out. I don't get what his problem is,' I say, thinking back to Max's dark eyes and the intense look in them as he stood at his upstairs window, just looking down at me.

Alex reaches for my hand and strokes the back of it with his thumb. 'Why would he want to freak you out? Maybe he was just looking out of his window and you guys made eye contact and it was awkward for both of you.'

I yank my hand away. 'You don't get it,' I huff. 'Max is deliberately weird to me.'

'But you said you thought he was nice the other day,' Alex reminds me. 'When your tyres went flat.'

I sigh, wishing I hadn't fallen for Max's nice guy act that day. 'He was nice for five minutes and I wanted to believe he was a good guy, okay? But he's not. He's odd. He's creepy.'

Alex doesn't respond. He just gazes up at the bedroom ceiling.

A silence passes between us.

'Don't you care?' I demand.

'I do care,' Alex insists. 'But I've trained Max a few times now and I just don't get it. He's cool. He's funny. I don't see him as this creepy guy you're making him out to be.'

'Fine, whatever.'

I get up off the bed and leave the room. In a spasm of rage, I slam the door behind me. I feel a twinge of shame as it crashes closed. Alex and I rarely argue. We never lose our tempers with each other, and I hate arguing with him, but it feels like he's siding with Max.

It's like he has so much in common with Max that he won't take my word for it that there's something off about him. Alex and I usually see eye to eye, but it's as though Max has pulled the wool over his eyes. It's confusing. Part of me thinks I'm overreacting. What if Max isn't this scary, threatening presence I've made him out to be? What if I'm getting carried away? What if I blew the incident with that woman and the van way out of proportion? Am I becoming fixated on Max? Obsessed?

I wander back into the kitchen and look across towards Max's. His kitchen's empty and I don't know why I'm even looking over. Nothing is making sense any more.

Chapter Seventeen

I pace around the house in frustration. I get a glass of water and look out of the kitchen window again, half expecting Max to be staring down at me like he was earlier, but I can't see him.

I feel wound up, tense and claustrophobic in a way I've never felt at home before.

I take my jacket from the pegs by the door and zip it up over my hoodie. Then I grab my keys and phone and head outside. I need to clear my head.

As I walk out on to the street, it occurs to me that Max's van is gone. It hasn't been parked outside for a few days now. I find myself wondering where it is. Perhaps he parked it around the corner on one of the other streets with unallocated parking. Who knows?

It's a grey day. The clouds are heavy and it looks like it might rain, but I don't care. It's been a while since I went for a walk on my own with no particular destination in mind. I pass down a few streets until I arrive at an old country manor house now turned into a local library. I walk around it and find a garden at the back, open to the public. It's a Victorian-style garden with a stone fountain, a trimmed lawn and pretty flower beds flanked with benches. A little gem that's been here all this time that I hadn't even been aware of.

I sit down on one of the benches and gaze around the garden, taking in a cobweb adorning the nearby fountain and an elderly couple walking their dog. But my observations are quickly tarnished by worries about Max.

I feel sad and defeated. I've always loved living here, more than Alex realises. I love this community. I love how safe I feel. I like how I can just wander around and find somewhere like this lovely garden. I love the life Alex and I have been building here. I love it more than anything. Never in a million years did I think I'd have it so good. Alex will never understand quite how much our life means to me, and that's my fault because there are things I haven't told him. Memories from my first home I've kept to myself.

Alex doesn't realise what I've been through. He has no idea about some of the dark skeletons in my closet. I just want to be happy and content. And maybe I've clung to that need too hard, crushingly hard, so much so that I'm imagining threats where there aren't any. Perhaps I'm just convincing myself Max is out to get me when really, I'm unravelling. Maybe all my recent stress has got the better of me.

My phone buzzes. I wonder if the council might have got back to me over my noise report, but it's just a random spam message. I probably won't hear back from them for weeks.

Anita hasn't replied yet. It's 12.30 p.m. now. I look at the screenshots I sent her of the messages from Ryan and feel a fresh wave of embarrassment over the whole thing. He'll likely be awake by now. He's probably deleted those ridiculous comments he left on my Instagram pictures.

I go on to Instagram to check and see that Alex has uploaded some new pictures to his page. I'm surprised. He hardly ever bothers with social media. He's always saying that he should do more, but he rarely gets around to it. I check out the pictures. There's one of him suspended in mid-air, showing off in the weightlifting area of the gym. He really is incredibly fit.

There's another shot of him and that girl from the other day, Tara. She's doing some stretches with Alex guiding her. She really is attractive, her long ponytail flowing over her shoulder. Alex has captioned the picture with a comment about the personal training services he offers. Clearly, he's trying to be promotional. I think of that ruse Alex told me about, how his workmates offer women they fancy training sessions to try to seduce them, and I feel a twinge of worry. Alex isn't doing that, is he? But I recall the way he kissed me in the car right in front of Tara. No. Of course he's not doing that. He loves me.

The next shot is of a hideous-looking breakfast Alex must have knocked up when I was at work, featuring fried eggs, onions and a gigantic mound of spinach. He's added a caption about the importance of getting enough protein when training.

There's another new photo too. It's of him and Max at the gym, grinning at the camera, arms around each other's shoulders like old chums. Max looks like a completely different person in this picture. Beaming, laid-back, he's unrecognisable as the version of him I know: the scowling presence, the creepy figure at the window glaring at me. His whole demeanour seems so vastly different that I feel even more rattled.

No wonder Alex likes Max so much if he sees this happy, fun version of him and they get on this well. I check the likes and comments on the picture, but I can't find any linking back to an account that might belong to Max. I search in Alex's friends list too, but Max isn't there. He must not be on Instagram.

I take in Alex's profile, scrolling through it to check there are no other photos I've missed. His bio reads: South London Personal Trainer, marathon runner. Helping you reach your health & fitness goals. A thought occurs to me. Alex's gym encourages all trainers to include personal facts about themselves on the gym website. The idea is that it makes them come across as friendly and relatable. I go to the website and click on Alex's profile.

History graduate turned personal trainer. I've taken my passion for military history and turned it into a military mindset towards getting fit!

His profile goes on to list the services he offers and his personal motto: Go hard or go home!

I remember him sitting at the kitchen table writing that profile and how hard he cringed.

I google Alex's name and scroll through the results that come up. His profile page on the gym site appears first, but there's also his Instagram account, a few articles from the local press about fundraising initiatives the gym has undertaken with his name briefly mentioned, and his Twitter account. I click on to it.

I hardly ever go on Alex's Twitter page. Neither of us uses Twitter much. In fact, Alex's last tweet was two years ago. It was a retweet about an exhibition at the London War Museum. He's retweeted quite a few historians and left a comment for the author of a biography on Churchill, telling him how much he enjoyed his book. I realise the book he's complimenting is the same one Max was reading that time he was waiting for Alex in the gym reception.

The rest of Alex's tweets are about running, the London Marathon and his love for Oasis, with several retweets of Liam Gallagher's posts.

It occurs to me that all the interests Alex has mentioned publicly are ones that Max apparently shares: marathons, history, Britpop. Could Max have looked Alex up and emulated his interests? It does seem a bit too coincidental that he'd like all the same things, even down to having read that book on Churchill. And it's not like Max wasted any time at all hiring Alex as his trainer.

I look across the flower beds, absently watching as a bird flies off from a tree branch.

I feel a nervous, ominous feeling trickling through me as it dawns on me that Max might have targeted Alex, going out of his way to pursue him, deliberately trying to forge a connection. It seems obvious to me now as I go through Alex's online posts. But why would Max do that?

As I gaze across the overcast garden, I'm dogged by the question: who is Max? And what does he want?

Chapter Eighteen

When I get home, I hear the shower and the radio on in the bathroom.

My stomach rumbles and I head into the kitchen to make some lunch. I take some cheese and salad from the fridge and prepare a sandwich. I fill the kettle and make a cup of tea before heading into the living room, where I can be alone.

I close the door and sit down on the sofa, gazing out of the window at the quiet street as I take a bite of my sandwich, barely noticing the taste. I still feel tense and preoccupied. I can't stop thinking about Max and what a strange and destructive presence he's becoming in my life.

I place my plate on the coffee table. My laptop is still on the sofa and I turn it back on. I go on to Google and start typing in words relating to Max. It's tricky without his surname, but I try to find him regardless.

Max, Sydenham

Max, Canary Wharf

Max, banker, hedge fund

Nothing comes up.

I need to know his surname. Alex must know it since Max has been paying him, but I doubt he would want to tell me. He already seems to think I've got Max completely wrong.

I'm sure I'll find out Max's full name eventually. It's only a matter of time until a package is left here for him. But who knows how long it'll be?

Alex comes out of the bathroom upstairs. He turns the radio off. I reach for my mug of tea and carry on trying to find Max online.

Max, London Marathon

Max, Athletics Gym

Nothing comes up. Of course it doesn't. My searches are far too vague.

I drink the last of my tea and head into the kitchen to make another cup, leaving my laptop and my stupid internet searches behind.

As the kettle boils, I hear the front door snap shut. Alex has left. I look at the time on the oven. It's 4.35 p.m. Alex usually heads out at around 6 p.m. on Saturdays. He's either had something come up or he's trying to avoid me.

I drop a teabag into my mug, feeling disappointed.

I hate falling out with Alex. Neither of us likes conflict. Alex is particularly sensitive over it. He can't stand arguments or drama. Anita often tells me about the blazing rows she has with Sam, dramatic fallings-outs that lead to equally dramatic making up. They've been together for nearly ten years. It seems to just be the way they get along. But Alex and I aren't like that. We never raise our voices. Me slamming the bedroom door is about as dramatic as we've got for years. Whenever we fall out, we tend to do what we're doing now. We retreat into ourselves for a little bit, calm down separately, and then patch things up once we've had time to cool off.

It's annoying that Alex has been so blindsided by Max, but I don't feel quite as angry about it as I did earlier. It seems fairly clear to me, from my Google research, joining the dots, that Max has deliberately manipulated Alex, mimicking his interests to get close to him. It's no wonder Alex can't see his true colours. I want to protect him from Max. I need to figure out a way to do it. I don't understand why Max would target Alex like this, but it's definitely not normal. It's all too pointed to be a coincidence.

Maybe I'll talk about it with Alex tonight, warn him. I'll make a nice effort for him, like he made for me a few days ago with the candles and rose petals on the bed. I'll do something sweet and romantic. I'll apologise for slamming the door and we can discuss things calmly like we usually do. I'll express my concerns about Max, and we can sort things out, together, without arguing.

Maybe I'll make one of his favourite meals: lasagne with a nice salad and a bottle of red wine. We can have a romantic evening in and come together, not letting Max drive a wedge between us.

Chapter Nineteen

I find cooking so soothing. There's something uniquely relaxing about following a recipe: the steady rhythm of the kitchen knife as I slice onions and peppers and listen to the sound of them sizzling as I add them to the oil bubbling in my pan. I breathe in the smells that permeate the kitchen as I add each new ingredient. I lose myself in the process, my worries taking a back seat.

I pour a glass of wine as a relaxing playlist flows from my iPhone speakers. I finish preparing the meat mixture and take a dish from the cupboard. then start layering the lasagne, spooning the mixture into the dish and adding the pasta sheets.

Glancing at the clock, I see that Alex won't be back for another hour. I'll leave the salad preparation until later. I pick up my glass of wine as Adele plays in the background. I look out of the kitchen window. It's dark outside now. The light in Max's kitchen suddenly comes on and I flinch, fear cutting through my domestic bubble. I half expect him to be standing there, staring at me with his cold dark eyes, but he's not. All I see is his neat, empty kitchen. It looks surprisingly clean and cosy. There are candles on the dining table and a vase of flowers on the window sill.

Then suddenly Max appears in his kitchen doorway. I stiffen and take a step back from the window. I should close my kitchen blinds and block him out entirely and yet I can't quite bring myself to. I'm curious about him now. I want to make sense of this mysterious stranger.

I stand at the side of the window and watch him as he takes a lighter from a drawer and lights the candles. He doesn't look my way, which surprises me given how much he likes to stare, but it's a relief. He looks busy, lost in his own thoughts. He's dressed smartly – a complete contrast to how he looked this morning in his dirty jogging bottoms and old jumper. He's wearing dark trousers and a black shirt, and his hair is clean and styled. He looks normal, handsome even. He glances around his kitchen as though appraising it and reaches for a cloth, wiping a surface clean. He picks something up from the counter and puts it in the bin. He lights another few candles and then looks around the room one more time before leaving. He's clearly expecting a guest.

The music has changed from Adele to Sam Smith, and I top up my glass of wine. Bizarrely, I'm enjoying myself. It feels like the roles between me and Max are reversing. The spied-upon is becoming the spy. I would never normally be such a nosy neighbour, a snoop, and yet I'm suspicious now. I find myself curious to see who he's having over and what he does at the weekend when he's not blasting out music and annoying his neighbours.

I decide to go ahead with making the salad. I place the chopping board down on the counter and take some tomatoes from the fridge. I start slicing them. I keep looking over at Max's kitchen as I chop, but it's empty. I finish with the tomatoes and transfer them into a salad bowl. I take some lettuce and spring onions from the fridge and start chopping them too. As I'm slicing the head off an iceberg lettuce, Max appears in his kitchen with a woman behind him. Interesting. I take a sip of wine. They're talking and laughing. It looks like a date.

Is she the same woman I saw before? No. She's standing a little stiffly, twirling a lock of long, wavy red hair. She looks shy, nervous, but the other woman seemed like no wallflower. And I'm sure she didn't have the same distinctive scarlet hair.

Max's guest is dressed in quite an over-the-top way, in a short, figure-hugging black dress with platform shoes and bold red lipstick, like she's keen to impress. I can't make her out in too much detail, but she looks attractive, her hair like something from a pre-Raphaelite painting. Max uncorks a bottle of red wine, and she laughs at something he says.

He takes two glasses down from a cupboard and pours the wine. He picks up one of the glasses and hands it to his date. Their eyes meet. She takes a sip, holding Max's gaze for a moment before glancing away, embarrassed. Even from over here, I can sense the chemistry between them. I find myself wondering where Max met her. Was it through a dating app? Through work? The gym? Friends? If he has any. I wonder if he's manipulating her too. Perhaps he's pretending to share all her interests.

They carry on talking as I slice the lettuce. I half watch as Max's date smiles at him, clutching her wine glass, chatting and making flirtatious eye contact from under her lashes. I try to imagine him through her eyes. She must think he's this young, independent, successful professional with a whole house to himself. She probably sees him as a real catch. Little does she realise he's a complete weirdo who stalks his neighbours on social media and inveigles himself into their lives.

By the time I'm done cutting the lettuce, Max and his date have left the room. They're probably going to sit in the living room and chat on the sofa. I feel a little disappointed. I was enjoying watching them.

I finish preparing the salad and check on the lasagne. It's nearly ready. I look at the time. It's almost 8 p.m. Alex should be home soon.

I messaged him earlier, but he hasn't replied. He's probably still annoyed at me.

Ryan hasn't messaged again. I thought he might message me to apologise, but I haven't heard from him. It's probably for the best. Maybe we'll just pretend that Friday night never happened. I'd be fine with that.

Anita has got back to me. She explains that Sam's parents are visiting and suggests we have dinner together on Monday evening to catch up and debrief on the Ryan situation. I smile at the prospect. It's been ages since Anita and I went out for dinner. We used to do it all the time, heading for a meal after work. It's just what I need and I message her back, suggesting an Italian restaurant we used to go to.

As I'm messaging, the front door opens. Alex is back.

I check my reflection in the kitchen window, tucking my hair behind my ear. I've made an effort this evening. Not as much as Max's date next door, but I've put on some make-up and done my hair. I figured it wouldn't hurt to try to look nice. I want to show Alex that I'm trying, that I care.

I head into the hallway. He's kicking off his trainers.

'Hey,' I say.

He looks my way.

'Are you cooking?' he asks.

'Yeah, I thought I'd make lasagne,' I tell him, expecting him to be impressed.

'Oh, right,' he says with a polite smile, before heading into the living room.

Disappointed, I follow him. He's clearly still upset.

'Don't you want any?' I ask.

'I've already eaten,' he says, sitting down on the sofa. 'And I can't drink. Sanjay is off sick and I've agreed to cover his classes for tomorrow.'

123

I feel a flicker of irritation. Why does Alex always have to cover for his workmates? He works long enough hours as it is. It's already difficult to find time to see each other and now he's working on Sunday too.

He picks up the remote and points it at the TV.

He's hardly looked at me, let alone noticed my efforts with my hair and make-up. I feel stupid, deflated. So much for my plans for a romantic evening in. So much for talking, clearing the air.

'Are you sure you don't want some salad or something?' I ask.

'No, I don't,' Alex snaps as the TV comes on.

I feel a pang of hurt. 'Wow, Alex. I thought I'd cook and we could have a chat and a nice evening together, but you're clearly still annoyed at me,' I say.

'I'm not annoyed. You're the one who slammed the door,' Alex reminds me.

'I'm sorry, okay? I was stressed out. Can you just let it go?' I ask imploringly.

'Fine, I'll let it go. Don't worry about it,' Alex says, turning his attention to the TV.

I'm unconvinced. 'You say don't worry about it, but you're clearly still annoyed,' I point out.

'I'm not annoyed, Becky, I'm just tired, okay? I've been working non-stop lately.' He looks over at me and I notice dark shadows under his eyes. He does look tired.

I want to give him a hug. I want to comfort him, but I don't get the feeling he'd appreciate it.

'Okay, I'll leave you to it then,' I say.

Alex smiles weakly and turns to watch the news.

I get up and head back to the kitchen.

I feel completely lost. I was convinced Alex and I were going to have an intimate evening and patch things up, but he seems completely uninterested.

124

I take the lasagne out of the oven. The bechamel sauce has browned just the right amount and it bubbles, piping hot. It looks and smells delicious. It's probably the best lasagne I've made.

I sigh as I serve up one portion for myself. I whisk up a vinaigrette and toss it into the salad. I spoon some on to my plate.

I'm about to sit down and eat when I see movement in Max's kitchen next door. He's back.

He heads over to the fridge, opening it. He takes something out, a tray covered in something – nibbles, sushi perhaps. I can't quite make it out. He peels off a sheet of clingfilm and plucks one of the pieces from the tray, popping it into his mouth. As I watch him, one question keeps looping in my mind. *Who are you?*

'Becky?' Alex says.

I turn to him, startled. I hadn't even heard him coming into the kitchen.

'Hey,' I say.

He eyes me strangely. 'What were you looking at?' he asks, coming over and peering out of the window.

I follow his gaze. Max is now joined by his date. He offers the tray of nibbles to her and she takes one. She looks more relaxed now. Her cheeks are slightly flushed, and I suspect the wine has calmed her nerves.

'Are you spying on him?' Alex demands, turning to me with an accusatory look.

'What? No,' I reply, my voice a little shrill.

'Then why were you standing at the kitchen window peering out of it?' Alex asks wearily. 'You were obviously watching him.'

'Fine!' I admit, holding my hands up, guilty as charged. 'I was watching him. But Max watches me, and you don't seem bothered about that.'

Alex sighs, shaking his head. He takes a glass from the cupboard and fills it with water from the tap.

'I don't know what's going on with you any more,' he grumbles.
He takes his glass of water and heads next door.

I watch him go before looking back out of the window. Max is standing in the doorway of his kitchen. Our eyes meet before he flicks off the light.

Chapter Twenty

I hear a voice. A child's voice. A cry.

'Help!'

My heart races. A cool breeze blows on to my face.

'Help!' The voice echoes in my mind, the walls of the hallway I'm standing in closing around me.

'Becky!'

The walls are closing in on me. My heart is twisting.

'Becky! Wake up!'

I feel hands on me. Dark tentacles.

'Becky!'

I open my eyes, the claustrophobic hall disintegrating like dust.

Alex is standing over me, shaking me awake. I'm drenched in sweat.

'You're having a nightmare,' Alex tells me.

He's dressed in his gym gear. He looks like he's ready to dash out the door.

I blink. I rub the sleep from my eyes, trying to push away the terror in my heart.

I haven't had that dream for a long time.

'I have to go to work,' Alex says. He gives my arm a squeeze and then grabs his gym bag from the bedroom floor. 'I'm running late. I'll see you later.'

I notice, even through my dream-addled fog, that he won't look me in the eyes. He's avoiding my gaze, clearly still annoyed.

'Okay, see you later,' I reply.

He smiles tightly and hitches his bag on to his shoulder, leaving the room. I listen to his footsteps on the stairs and the sound of him letting himself out.

I feel more distant from him than ever. He's avoided me all weekend. He worked all day yesterday. He got home late and all he wanted to do was watch TV on his own like he did on Saturday night. I've tried to speak to him, but it's like he's checked out. He's been so moody and aloof, and I can't quite figure out what's wrong. We may have argued over Max, but Alex's reaction feels disproportionate.

I reach for my phone. It's 7.45 a.m. I need to get ready for work. The nightmare I had and Alex's coldness have got me down. I feel like staying in bed all day, hiding under the covers, but I get up and head to the bathroom. I have a shower and then go downstairs in my dressing gown.

I fill the kettle and switch it on. I look over towards Max's place. His kitchen's empty. It's still neat and tidy like it was on the night of his date, with candles on the dining table and the vase of flowers. I peer up at his upstairs windows, but his curtains are drawn. There's no sign of him and his house has a stillness about it. I didn't see him yesterday either. His car was gone, and I found myself wondering if he and the redhead had headed out for the day. Perhaps she stayed over, and they decided to venture out together, maybe driving out of town for a relaxing walk in the country.

I spoon some coffee into a mug. The kettle boils and I pour in the water, pushing thoughts of Max out of my mind. Maybe Alex is right, and I have become a bit too interested in him, my natural curiosity combined with my passion for true crime lending itself to an unhealthy fixation on my more unconventional neighbours.

I carry my mug upstairs and find a nice dress to wear. I need something conservative, since the last thing I want today is to draw attention to myself around Ryan. I'm dreading seeing him. It would be less awkward if he'd addressed the embarrassing messages he sent on Friday night, but I haven't heard from him. He's not said a word, let alone apologised. No one's heard from him. I spoke to Anita and Lucy yesterday, and even Sophie, but they haven't been in touch with him. He's been quiet on social media too. Perhaps he's just mortified and doesn't know what to say. Hopefully, we can just pretend it never happened and carry on as normal at work.

Sighing, I take a navy long-sleeved dress from my wardrobe and lay it out on the bed. I unwind the towel from my hair and run some serum through it. I blow-dry my hair and pin it back into a neat bun before applying minimal make-up. I put on the dress with a blazer and appraise my reflection. I look a little drab. Hardly dressed to impress. But I'm pleased – it's exactly the effect I'm aiming for.

I grab my bag and head outside. It's a cool morning, with an almost autumnal crispness to the air even though it's only late August. I get into my car and glance over at Max's house once more, but it's deathly still, as before. His car is back though. As I turn my key in the ignition, I find myself wondering when Max leaves for work. I never see him in the mornings. I leave at around 8.30 a.m. and I've never once run into him. I've never seen the lights on in his house in the mornings or seen him getting ready. And his car is always there, parked in its space. It could be that he leaves really early for work, before I'm even up, and takes the Tube. I had a friend who dated a banker once and if I recall correctly, he arrived at work ridiculously early to start in time for foreign markets opening. Perhaps that's the reason I never see Max. Somehow, I'm not convinced.

I sigh, shaking my head. I need to stop obsessing over Max. I pull away and drive to work.

The sky is clear blue with just a few wisps of cloud. I turn the radio on and wind down my window, enjoying the breeze as I listen to the uplifting pop songs on the local radio station. I spent the whole day inside yesterday and as the breeze blows through the car, I feel a twinge of guilt. I usually try to make the most of weekends, but I did nothing yesterday apart from getting odd jobs done around the house and reading a thriller. I finished watching that death row documentary too, knowing Alex was out and wouldn't be able to criticise me for it.

I stop at the traffic lights in front of Alex's gym. I turn to look, not that I'm expecting to see him. There are treadmills lined up by the windows, where usually the fittest and most confident members run, facing the street. One guy, slick with sweat, with a body that could feature on the pages of a fitness magazine, pounds the treadmill, but the rest are empty. I'm about to look away when suddenly I spot Alex, almost but not quite out of sight. He's standing by a weights machine with that woman, Tara. She's instantly recognisable from her long ponytail and perfect physique. My stomach lurches as I see Alex touching her. He places a hand on her back and another on her arm as she pulls down on a weightlifting bar. She looks up at him and he laughs, saying something. My skin prickles with dread. I'm instantly reminded of the way Alex and I were when we first got to know each other during training sessions: laughing, flirting, touching. Has he found someone new? Is he moving on? Is that why he's been quiet and off with me? Or is he getting closer to Tara because he's so annoyed about our arguments over Max?

A car starts honking behind me and I realise the lights have turned green. I steal one more glance at Alex and Tara, still laughing and joking, before I drive off, shaken. I make my way to work on autopilot as anxiety fizzes in my stomach. An affair . . . An affair . . . The thought rattles through my mind. No. Surely not. Alex is the one. He'd never do anything like that. He loves me.

I pull into the office car park and force myself to take a deep breath. I need to calm down. I find a parking space and pull in. I turn off the engine and sit for a moment, gathering my thoughts. Maybe I'm just being insecure? Personal training is hands-on, after all. If Tara were unattractive or a man, would I feel threatened? Unlikely. I'm probably just projecting. It was strange, though, to see Alex looking so relaxed and carefree again. So completely unlike the cold, quiet, reserved version of himself he's been all weekend.

There must be something else going on with him. Even if I do feel a bit uncomfortable over Tara, I can't contemplate that Alex is a cheater. He's just not that sort of person. Despite being good-looking, intelligent and charming, Alex is surprisingly inexperienced with women. I couldn't believe it when we got together and he told me I was only the third woman he'd ever been with. He'd had a girlfriend at school for several years and another at university who he moved to London with after graduating. He was single for a few years after they broke up. There he was, a young, outgoing guy in London, but he didn't play the field. He claimed it never appealed and that he prefers to have a genuine connection with the women he's intimate with. He told me he hadn't found that with anyone since his break-up, so he just stayed single. I found it unusual, but also endearing. It made me feel special and it made me like him even more. I remember joking that I was 'third time lucky', believing we were meant for each other.

A door slams, distracting me. A woman in an apron comes out of the back door of the café next to the office, which shares our car park, and looks over at me curiously before lighting a cigarette. I get out of the car and head to the office, reminding myself once again that Alex isn't a player. He isn't the kind of guy who'd pursue

131

an attractive woman for the sake of it. He wouldn't throw away our relationship. And yet, as I root in my bag for my office pass and swipe it against the sensor, I feel uneasy. I feel like my little world is somehow changing, somehow falling apart.

I try to compose myself as I push open the office door and head inside. I look straight towards Ryan's desk, but he's not in yet. I breathe a sigh of relief. I'm a little bit early and only Wendy, Susan and a few others are here. Susan is standing by Wendy's desk. They're talking, quite intensely by the looks of it, but as I cross the office Susan looks up and spots me, her face suddenly falling. She goes quiet as I approach. I smile, but she doesn't respond. Wordlessly, she slips away and heads to her desk. Odd.

I place my bag down by my keyboard.

'Morning, Becky,' Wendy says as I take off my jacket.

'Morning, Wendy,' I reply. 'Good weekend?' I ask, trying to sound friendly.

'Very nice, thank you,' Wendy replies, giving nothing away as usual before returning her attention to her monitor.

I sit down and turn on my computer.

'Oh, I've been meaning to ask, how are you getting on with the Lake Street property?' Wendy says, turning to me. 'The six-bed.'

'Oh, um . . .' I hesitate, caught off guard.

I feel instant shame at the memory of the last time I was at that house, when I locked myself out. The house has generated hardly any interest since. I've taken the easy route, focusing my attention on flats and smaller houses, places I've thought would be easier to sell.

Wendy regards me coldly, waiting for my response.

'There's not been a huge amount of interest so far, actually, but I'll definitely focus on it this week,' I assure her.

Wendy nods. She pulls her chair closer to my desk. 'Right. It's just that you've been looking after that property for several months now and the sellers are getting impatient. It really needs a more proactive approach, Becky. I'm giving you one more week to sell it and then, if there's no interest, I'm going to have to transfer it over to another member of the team.' She gives me a tight, apologetic smile.

'Oh, okay,' I reply as she turns back to her computer.

One week is hardly any time at all. Flummoxed, I gaze absently across the office and catch Susan looking over at me, clearly having been paying attention to my conversation with Wendy. She quickly looks away, shrinking behind her monitor. Instantly, I suspect – in fact, I know – the Lake Street property will be going to her. That's probably what she and Wendy were discussing as I came into the office. The favouritism is grating, and yet, annoyingly, Wendy does have a point. I've hardly had any viewings, aside from one or two when the property was first listed, and then there was that no-show with that guy Edward the time I got locked out. And he disappeared into thin air, never to be heard from again. It's only natural that the sellers would be getting frustrated at this point. It makes sense that they'd be looking for a new approach.

Now I feel ashamed, embarrassed. I was riding high off selling the Dulwich flat last week, but Wendy's quickly brought me back down to earth. As I log into my inbox, I reason that I have a week. I have a week to try to sell the Lake Street house. It's unlikely that I'll manage to find someone wanting to spend £3m on a six-bedroom mansion in that time, but you never know. It's worth a shot.

I decide to send an email about the house to buyers in my contacts list in the hope that someone might be interested.

As I'm writing the email, trying to make the house sound unmissable, Ryan arrives, and my palms start to sweat. He walks to his desk. He looks how he always looks, slightly windswept and out of breath from having cycled to work, a pair of headphones around his neck, and yet there's a stiffness to his walk. He looks self-conscious.

He takes off his jacket before sitting down. I look over at him, raising an eyebrow at having been so pointedly ignored.

He looks my way. Our eyes meet. His expression is cold and blank, like he's looking through me. He quickly glances away.

I shake my head, scoffing at his immaturity.

I feel hurt, but Ryan's pathetic behaviour isn't my problem. It's not my fault he developed a ridiculous infatuation with me. I try not to think about it and focus on my email instead.

> A rare opportunity has arisen to acquire a stunning six-bedroom town house . . .

I finish the email and go over it a few times, making sure I've left nothing out. I hit 'send', hoping someone is interested. Anita and Lucy arrive and we exchange a bit of chit-chat, but we're all a bit awkward, aware of Ryan, who keeps looking over, clearly listening in.

Determined not to give up on the Lake Street house, I decide to follow up my email by calling everyone in my contacts list who might be interested, but no one bites. One woman snaps at me, telling me she's in a meeting and to remove her from my database 'immediately'. Someone else informs me they're at hospital and 'really don't have the time to speak about this'. I feel like a pest and I'm grateful when lunchtime arrives and I can get out of the office.

Anita is in a meeting and Lucy's out doing viewings, so I head out on my own. I go to the café next door and order a jacket potato, craving some comfort food. Not only am I struggling to drum up any interest in the Lake Street property and having to deal with Ryan being weird, but I'm still thinking about Alex and Tara. His hands on her body. The way she smiled at him.

I carry my tray across the café and take a seat at the back. I check my phone, but Alex hasn't messaged. Alex and I always message in the mornings. Something's definitely up. It's clearly more than just me slamming a door over Max and his music.

I decide to message him. His stubborn silence isn't getting us anywhere.

Alex, what's going on? We really need to talk. X

I hit send.
He appears online instantly and starts typing.

Ok. I have clients until pretty late tonight, but let's talk before bed X

I sigh, feeling second to his clients yet again. I'm beginning to suspect I'd get more attention from him if I registered for training sessions.

Ok. Speak later. x

I feel a little anxious as I put my phone down. Clearly, Alex agrees we need to talk. I really hope the only issue between us is Max and it's nothing more. And yet, I think of Tara and feel another pang of insecurity and jealousy before quickly suppressing it. Alex and I have been together for three years. We're trying for a baby. He's not about to throw in the towel! Hopefully we can have a chat and clear the air and everything will be fine. I take a deep breath and try to relax and focus on my lunch, tucking into my jacket potato. The café's bustling, with almost every table taken and a queue at the counter. The coffee machine churns as the barista makes drinks and a waitress darts around, clearing tables and bringing out meals from the kitchen. The bell on the café door dings and I look up, only to see Ryan coming inside.

I shrink into my seat, cursing myself. Great, just great. Why did I come here? I needed to get away from him. I should have gone somewhere further away. Not to the café right next door to the office. Ryan joins the queue and appraises the specials on the blackboard behind the counter, but no doubt sensing my gaze, he suddenly looks my way.

A darkness enters his eyes, the impassive expression he'd been wearing before vanishing upon seeing me.

He doesn't even look through me this time. In fact, he scowls. He looks menacing, as though he truly hates me. I never knew Ryan had this side to him. So much for being a benign accounting geek. He looks scary, cruel. I glance away, unable to tolerate his cutting gaze. I look blankly back down at my plate, my heart pounding in my chest.

I take another bite of my lunch, but I barely notice the taste. I can feel Ryan watching me. My throat is tight as I swallow. I steal a glance at him and just as I expected, he's glaring at me, as though deliberately trying to intimidate me. I shake my head, exasperated, but he doesn't flinch. He just carries on staring at me with that menacing look.

Irritated, I get up and cross the café, ready to confront him and clear the air.

Ryan eyes me coldly as I approach. His ego is obviously bruised. As I near him, he turns his attention back to the blackboard.

'Ryan,' I say. 'What's going on?'

He doesn't respond, and instead pointedly studies the blackboard.

'Ryan. You can't just ignore me! We work together,' I remind him.

Ryan shrugs, like a petulant teenager.

136

'There's nothing to say,' he responds. 'You led me on and now you're backtracking. It's your problem.'

I laugh, gobsmacked. 'Excuse me?'

Ryan turns to look at me, his eyes cold and disgusted. 'You think it's funny? You think it's funny that you led me on? All the flirting, kissing me, inviting me for drinks, not mentioning your boyfriend, acting like you're single.' He shakes his head. 'Don't pretend you're innocent in all this.'

I gawp at him, staggered by how wrong he's got everything. How can he make out that I've been leading him on? How has he mistaken my casual friendliness for flirting? How has he misinterpreted me being ever so slightly private about Alex as 'acting like I'm single'? The whole thing is absurd.

'I was friendly because I work with you and I thought you were a decent person. I never acted like I was single!' I protest. 'Everyone knows I'm with Alex. And if you really want to know, I invited you for drinks because I thought you and Lucy might hit it off. You've got it all so wrong.'

'Me and Lucy?' Ryan echoes, as though the idea has never crossed his mind.

'Yes,' I admit, even though now I wouldn't want Lucy to touch Ryan with a bargepole.

'I don't believe you,' Ryan says.

'Well, it's the truth.'

'Right, like we never had anything.' Ryan tuts, rolling his eyes. I regard him, taking in his white shirt, navy V-neck, his neatly cut hair. He looks so normal, so ordinary. Like any other office guy, and yet he's off-the-scale delusional. It's unsettling.

'It was three years ago, Ryan! For God's sake!' I plead, losing my cool.

A few people turn to look, and I realise I've raised my voice. I'm making a scene.

Ryan leans forward. 'Don't make out like we don't have a history,' he hisses in my ear. 'It's not like you kiss everyone at work, or do you? Actually, you probably do.'

He pulls back, a smug, twisted smile on his face.

'What's that meant to mean?' I gasp, anger flooding through me.

Ryan shrugs, that smug smile still playing on his lips. He's clearly taking some satisfaction from making out that I get around.

'How dare you?' I spit, my blood boiling, but he doesn't respond.

He looks ahead towards the server, as though he's ready to order. He's clearly done with speaking to me.

'You know, I thought you were a nice guy, Ryan, but I got you so wrong,' I say.

I turn, livid, and head back to my table. I grab my bag and leave my lunch behind.

I march out of the café. I can feel Ryan looking at me, but I ignore him. I don't even glance his way. My heart is slamming in my chest. I walk out of the café and pound the pavement in a daze, tears filling my eyes.

Chapter Twenty-One

'I can't believe what an incel Ryan is,' Anita sighs, shaking her head.

'I know,' I grumble as I take a sip of my wine. 'I can't quite believe it either.'

The Italian restaurant we're in, with its flickering candlelight, ambient music and delicious food, should be calming me down, and yet I'm still rattled, and have been ever since my run-in with Ryan at lunch. I spent the rest of my lunch break sitting in my car, trying to pull myself together. And then I worked quietly all afternoon, doing admin, trying to be inconspicuous, but I still kept catching Ryan scowling at me across the office.

'He seems obsessed with me, Anita,' I sigh. 'One stupid kiss and he's developed a complete fixation.'

Anita pulls a face and shudders. 'Such a creep!' she says.

I look down at the pizza in front of me. A margarita with olives, the same pizza I've ordered every time since Anita and I first started coming to this restaurant years ago. It's always been my go-to, a classic, and yet I can barely bring myself to eat.

'You know you haven't done anything wrong, right?' Anita assures me.

I look up and see her regarding me, a look of genuine concern in her eyes.

I smile weakly. 'I know. I just wish I hadn't invited Ryan out on Friday,' I admit.

All afternoon I've been cursing the state of affairs and wishing I could just go back in time and not have tried to play Cupid. If I hadn't organised drinks, there would be none of this tension.

'You weren't to know what he was like. None of us knew. His weird crush and his terrible behaviour are all on him. Don't blame yourself,' Anita insists with a warm smile.

'Yeah, you're right.' I pick at an olive.

'If he doesn't get over it, we'll go to HR,' Anita states firmly. 'Don't let him bring you down. He's not worth it.'

I nod and cut a piece of my pizza. Anita's words are comforting, but I can't help but worry. What if he takes an embarrassing rejection and turns it into a vicious vendetta? I sigh. I don't want to go on about it and I don't want to be too pessimistic. Maybe Ryan's ego is a bit bruised, but he will get over it.

I reach for my wine. 'Anyway! Enough about Ryan!' I say. 'So, tell me about your weekend.'

While eating her cannelloni, Anita tells me how Sam's parents visited and helped put the final touches on the nursery.

'They're so excited to meet their granddaughter!' she says, her eyes sparkling. 'Sam's mum's been knitting all these tiny little jumpers. They're so adorable. I can't wait to put Flora in them!'

'Flora?' I echo, noting her latest favourite name.

'Oh yeah . . . Flora is in the running.' Anita laughs. 'For now!'

She shows me some photos on her phone of the nursery and the jumpers her mother-in-law has been knitting and I feel the familiar pang of jealousy. I take another few sips of wine, trying to quell it.

Anita scrolls on to some selfies she's taken in her bedroom mirror. She pulls her phone away, embarrassed.

'Oh God, I forgot those were there,' she says, flicking through the pictures out of my eyeline. She flashes one at me.

140

'I look like a fridge, don't I?' She laughs. 'I thought I'd take some pictures just to record what I look like, you know? I never thought my body could get this big!'

'You look great,' I insist, and it's true. I take her phone and peer at the picture. She looks beautiful. She's wearing just her under-wear, exposing her round baby bump, which she holds in one hand while taking the selfie with her other. She looks different to the Anita I see every day at work – the Anita with the shiny bob, make-up and no-nonsense attitude. Instead, she appears soft and peaceful, with a contented smile.

'Thanks! But I can't wait to be back to normal. Although it is quite incredible what your body can do, you know? And when you feel the baby move inside you, there's nothing like it,' Anita says, her eyes misty.

I smile, wishing I could relate. I want to have a cute nursery and tiny knitted baby jumpers. I want to feel a baby kicking inside me and complain about looking like a fridge.

It's been nearly seven months that Alex and I have been trying for a baby. My period's due in a few days and I suspect it's probably coming. Premenstrual tension might be the reason I felt compelled to slam the door at the weekend. Maybe it's even part of the reason I feel so low now. I wonder if I should say something to Anita. Tell her about my struggles getting pregnant, maybe ask for some advice. I'm sure she'd like to help. I kind of want to tell her about Alex and our argument too. Tell her about Max. And yet the Ryan situation is bad enough. How many issues can you offload over one meal?

'Can you pass the garlic bread?' Anita asks, interrupting my thoughts.

'Sure.'

I take the basket of garlic bread next to my plate and hand it to her.

'One thing I will miss is eating for two!' Anita jokes, tearing into a piece.

I laugh and sprinkle some Parmesan over my pizza. Anita changes the subject to the office. She jokes that Susan is Wendy's 'mini-me' and we giggle wickedly. I tell Anita about the Lake Street mansion. Despite emailing my contacts this morning and calling around, it still hasn't had any interest.

'Maybe someone will get back to you this evening,' Anita suggests. 'People are probably busy at work. Give them a chance.'

'I guess. I only have a week though,' I remind her.

'A lot can happen in a week.'

'I suppose . . .' I murmur, not feeling particularly optimistic.

I take my phone from my bag and check my emails as Anita reaches for another piece of garlic bread. The waiter passes our table and Anita stops him and asks for a glass of water. He asks if I'd like another glass of wine, and even though I would, I decline. I've been drinking too much lately and it's probably not helping with everything that's going on. As Anita praises her cannelloni, I quickly open my work inbox.

I scan my emails and funnily enough, a reply has come through. A message from a woman called Elizabeth Jones. I'm not familiar with the name, but she must have enquired about a property at some point to be on my contacts list. I open the message.

Hi there,

Thanks for your email. This house looks beautiful! I'd love to arrange a viewing if possible? How about tomorrow?

Kind Regards,
Elizabeth

'Oh my God!' I exclaim, looking up from my phone as the waiter retreats from our table.

'What?' Anita asks.

'I just got an enquiry,' I tell her, suddenly feeling a lot better. 'Someone wants to view the house!'

'No way!' Anita enthuses. 'See? I knew you could sell it!'

'She wants to view it tomorrow!' I tell her, beaming.

'Brilliant! Good for you, Becks!' Anita holds up her empty glass of orange juice, inspects the melting ice cubes it contains. She shrugs and raises it in a toast. 'Cheers!'

I hold up my near empty wine glass and clink it against hers.

'Cheers!' I say, still holding my phone. 'Do you mind if I reply?'

'Go for it!' Anita says as the waiter returns to our table with her glass of water.

I reply to Elizabeth, suggesting we meet at the property at 11 a.m. tomorrow, and hit send.

I place my phone on the table. Thoughts of Ryan have fallen by the wayside now and my dinner suddenly seems a lot more appealing. Ryan's just a minor irritation that will pass.

As I tuck into another piece of pizza, my phone buzzes.

I reach for it and see that it's Elizabeth. She's replied.

11am is perfect. See you there?

I fire back a reply, confirming the viewing and address of the property.

'Sorry,' I say, putting my phone in my bag.

'Don't worry about it!' Anita replies.

Excitement is bubbling away inside me now. If this viewing goes well, it could be so lucrative. And getting the sale would prove to Wendy that I am capable.

'Do you know the buyer?' Anita asks.

'No,' I admit. 'But she sounds really keen.'

'Excellent,' Anita replies. 'Well, I'm sure it will be fine.'

Our conversation drifts between work and baby stuff as we finish our meals. It starts getting dark outside and I can tell Anita's getting tired. She yawns a few times, trying to hide it.

'I'm knackered!' she admits. 'My bedtime is just gone nine o'clock these days!'

We agree it's time to get the bill. The waiter passes and I ask him to bring it over.

As we're waiting, Anita checks her phone.

'Just messaging Sam,' she says.

I nod and gaze across the restaurant, taking in the couples dining together, friends catching up, an elderly man in the corner eating alone. Traditional Italian folk music plays softly, accompanied by the hum of conversation.

'Weird,' Anita comments.

I look up to see her scrolling. 'What's weird?'

'I just got a Twitter notification . . . People are talking about this woman. She went missing not far from here. She was last seen just around the corner on Saturday night.' Anita has a perturbed expression on her face.

She shows me her phone, open on a tweet from the Met appealing for information over the disappearance of twenty-six-year-old Esme Jenkins.

Can you help us find Esme Jenkins? the tweet reads. Esme is 5'4" with red waist-length hair. She was last seen on Saturday at around 6 p.m. on Silverdale Road. Esme is believed to have been wearing a short black dress, a long dark coat and high-heeled shoes.

The tweet is accompanied by a photo of a very attractive young woman with wide, slightly lost-looking blue eyes, clear, youthful skin and rosebud lips curled into a shy smile. She has long, striking red hair that falls in pre-Raphaelite waves over her shoulders. Red hair I've seen somewhere else before.

No way . . .

The memory of Max's date instantly appears in my mind. She had the same unusual, striking, long wavy red hair. She looks similar too: pale, delicate-featured, pretty. And the woman in Max's kitchen was definitely wearing a short black dress. Could it be the same person? I feel a cold chill sweep through me, my skin prickling. Did I see Esme Jenkins on the night she went missing?

'Are you okay?' Anita asks.

I meet her gaze, flustered.

'Yeah!' I laugh, handing her phone back.

'Are you sure?' Anita presses me, eyeing me warily. 'You look like you've seen a ghost!'

I hesitate, unsure whether to tell her the thoughts racing through my mind, but she's tired and it would sound crazy.

I think my neighbour might have abducted this woman . . .

No. It sounds too outlandish. It can't be true. I must be wrong. I've got to be.

I think back to the first time I saw Max, the day he moved in. I saw a woman carrying items into the house. I assumed she was Max's partner, only to never see her again. Alex pointed out that she was probably just a friend, but what if she wasn't? What if she went missing too?

No. The thought is absurd. Max is odd, but he can't be that odd. He can't be the kind of person who abducts young women. Surely?

'I'm fine!' I insist. 'It's just sad, you know. I hope they find her.'

'I hope so too,' Anita agrees, shaking her head as she scrolls through the tweets.

A silence passes between us. I think of Esme, around the corner from here just a few days ago. Was she on her way to Max's place?

145

The waiter comes back with the bill, placing it down between us. We thank him and Anita checks it, inspecting the total.

'Shall we go fifty-fifty then?' she asks.

'Sure,' I reply, plastering an easy smile on to my face.

I reach into my bag for my wallet, even though all I can think about is Esme Jenkins and the girl I saw on Saturday night in Max's kitchen. I think of the searching look in the blue eyes of the girl in the photograph. I think of how nervous and unsure of herself Max's date seemed. I think of the way she laughed with him, clinking her glass against his.

And I find myself hoping, truly hoping, that the girl I saw isn't the same person.

Chapter Twenty-Two

I feel tense as I arrive home.

I can't stop thinking about Esme. I picture her bound up somewhere in Max's house, terrified and alone. My imagination's running wild. What if Max is hurting her? Abusing her? Perhaps I could have nipped his behaviour in the bud if I'd only called the police before.

Max's car is still parked where it was this morning. I park behind it and look over at his place. It looks completely normal. It looks like it always looks, an unassuming house on an ordinary street. Nothing to see. I'm probably being completely paranoid.

I get out of my car. All the lights are off at mine and Alex is clearly still at work, as usual on Monday evenings. The street is quiet. A neighbour's cat prowls along a garden wall a few houses down, its eyes glinting in the dark. All I can hear is the hum of traffic. No metal music tonight. No cries from captive women.

I linger outside Max's house for a moment. The lights are off at his place too, and despite the presence of his car outside, his house looks unoccupied. The curtains in his front room are open, and I find myself taking a few steps closer. I glance over my shoulder, checking no one's around, and creep up to his garden gate. It creaks in the silence as I open it, triggering a pulse of adrenaline as I slip through and dash across his front garden. Huddling by the bay windows of his front room, I peer inside. For a moment, I imagine Alex arriving home from work right now and catching me in this act. He'd be so unimpressed.

I push the thought out of my mind and focus on the room. It's dark. The only light illuminating it is the faint sepia glow of the street lamps, but I narrow my eyes and see the shape of a sofa, an armchair, the angles of a coffee table, the outline of a flatscreen TV. I don't know what I'm expecting to see. I'm hardly going to spot Esme bound and gagged, but the room before me is completely unremarkable. There are even coasters on the coffee table, a framed photo on the mantelpiece that I can't make out, and a pot plant. Max's front room looks like any other front room. Certainly not like the front room of a psychopath. I give it another scan, wondering if I've missed something, but all I spot is a pair of slippers by the sofa that I hadn't noticed before. There are no clues about Max's dark nature, or Esme's whereabouts.

Deflated, I turn around. Despite Max's front room looking normal, I still feel creeped out. My hairs are standing on end, and I have an odd sensation of being watched even though the street is quiet.

As I hurry back across Max's front garden, I spot a flash of white out of the corner of my eye. I do a double take and see that there's a letter sticking out of his letterbox. It can't have been pushed through properly when it was delivered. Interesting . . .

I hesitate for a moment, but my curiosity gets the better of me and I walk up to Max's front door and gently, noiselessly remove the letter from his letterbox, closing it as quietly as I can.

The screech of a tyre down the road startles me and I stash the letter under my jacket, my heart hammering in my chest. I dash back down Max's drive and through his front gate as a joyrider whizzes past. I rush back towards my house.

I fumble with my keys and let myself in, close the door behind me and breathe a sigh of relief.

I flick on the hallway light and take a look at the letter, noting who it's addressed to.

Max Sidwell.

Finally, I know his name.

I search my memory, but the name doesn't ring any bells, despite me finding Max oddly familiar. I don't think I've ever heard the name Max Sidwell before.

I kick off my shoes and head into the living room. I turn on the light and close the curtains. Sitting down on the sofa with my phone, I type Max's name into Google, desperate to figure out who he really is.

I scroll through the results. The adrenaline I felt outside from fear turns to excitement. I'm gripped by a sense of intrigue. There must be a Facebook profile, a Twitter account, a LinkedIn page, pieces of a jigsaw that will help me figure out who Max is and what I'm dealing with. Maybe there'll be news articles about criminal convictions, clear evidence that he could be dangerous. But as I scroll through the Google results, I find no social media profiles. Not one. And no articles either.

In fact, all that comes up is a memorial page for a Max Sidwell from Nebraska who died ten years ago. There's a page from an archive featuring a 1940 census containing a Max Sidwell, born in 1913, also now dead. And there are a few more results about dead men called Max Sidwell on sites with names like Find A Grave and A Billion Graves. I shudder. What the hell? Has Max stolen a dead man's name? Or is this just some strange coincidence?

I keep scrolling, but there's nothing that could possibly point to a living Max Sidwell. Nothing. No profile on a company website. No random stray reviews left on Google or TripAdvisor. Nothing comes up. Not a single thing. The only other results are for other

Sidwells. I find an article about an Australian hockey player called Michael Sidwell and an Instagram account for a school kid in Kentucky called Jeffrey Sidwell. Deep in the results is a website for a Frank Sidwell, a photographer based in Glasgow, featuring moody, gritty images of the city at night.

I sigh, disappointed, and place my phone down on the armrest. Yet another dead end. Max is still as mysterious as ever. I gaze blankly across the living room. Weirdly, I still have that strange feeling of being watched, even though I'm safe in my house, the curtains drawn.

I get up and close the curtains even tighter. As I turn to sit back down on the sofa, I spot the letter, which I left on the coffee table.

Picking it up once more, I inspect it. It's crisp, white, hefty, like a bill or a bank statement. That sense of illicit excitement returns. I could open it . . . It might give me some more information about Max, clues the internet isn't revealing. I hold it, knowing that all it would take would be a few seconds, a few quick tears. I could find out where he works, where he spends his money. I might find questionable transactions that back up my misgivings about him. And yet opening another person's mail is a line I know I shouldn't cross. It's a serious breach of privacy. I've already stolen Max's mail to try to find out who he is. That's bad enough. But reading his letters too? It seems a step too far. And it seems premature. I place the letter in my handbag. Perhaps if Esme is still missing in a few days and I still believe Max might have been involved then I'll open it. Or perhaps I'll just post it back through his front door and pretend this never happened, leaving the investigation to the police.

The sound of a door slamming shut outside interrupts my thoughts. I pull the curtains aside a little and peer out of the window, but I can't see anyone. Nevertheless, I find myself wondering if it was Max. Perhaps he's been out and he's only just got home, ready to attend to Esme.

I find myself slipping out of the living room and creeping down the corridor in the dark. I head into the kitchen. It's at the back of the house, and it's almost pitch black with no street light filtering in. I know the layout and tread carefully through the shadowy space, feeling my way past the dining table and up to the kitchen window.

I peer out but there's nothing to see. Max's lights are off. I can't see any signs of life. His place still looks completely deserted.

Suddenly, the front door opens, and I startle, jumping out of my skin, but of course it's only Alex.

'Becky?' he says as he walks down the hall.

I rush to flick on the kitchen light, but I'm not quick enough and Alex appears in the doorway. He flicks on the light and catches me standing in the dark.

'What are you doing?' he asks.

He's in his gym uniform and he looks tired from his long day at work. He regards me with a perplexed, concerned look.

'I was just . . . um . . .' I hesitate, not knowing what to say.

What normal reason is there for creeping around in your own kitchen in the dark?

'I heard you yelp, and I thought you might have tripped,' Alex says.

'Oh, I'm fine!' I insist, laughing awkwardly while wracking my brains for an explanation.

'What's going on?' Alex asks, frowning.

'Nothing!'

Alex glances from me to the kitchen window, the penny dropping.

'Were you spying on Max again?' he asks incredulously.

'No!' I protest, but it's futile. Alex isn't stupid.

He rolls his eyes, sighing.

'Becky, you're obsessed with him. It's not healthy.'

'I'm not obsessed. I just . . .' I trail off, not knowing where to start.

'Not obsessed?! If you're not obsessed, why were you googling him the other day? I saw your search history. Max, London. Max, banker. Max, Athletics Gym. You seem pretty obsessed to me,' Alex remarks.

I gawp at him, mortified.

I must have forgotten to close my laptop after I tried to look Max up on Saturday. I must have left it open on the living-room table for Alex to see. I shouldn't have been that sloppy. Alex is right, I have been acting strangely over Max, but even so, does he have to embarrass me like this? He shouldn't be scouring my search history and then using it against me.

I tell him as much.

'Maybe you're obsessed with me,' I suggest moodily. 'It's not normal to trawl through your girlfriend's internet activity.'

'You left your laptop out,' Alex tells me.

He pulls out a dining chair and slumps into it. 'It was hard to miss. Your screen was open with 'Max, London banker' in the search bar. And honestly, I'm getting a bit worried about you.'

'Worried?' I exclaim. 'Why are you so worried, Alex?'

'Isn't it obvious? You've been off lately. I don't know what's going on with you. And then you develop this weird interest in Max, telling me how creepy he is, getting all worked up over him. It's just . . . It's too much.'

'I don't have a weird interest in him! He's the weird one. You can't see it, can you?'

'A lot of people play their music loudly. It doesn't mean they're weird,' Alex snaps.

I sigh, shaking my head. 'You know, I thought I could talk to you. But it's like I can't say a bad word about Max. You're totally blinded by him, aren't you?'

'What do you mean by that?' Alex asks. He looks weary.

'It's just . . .' I begin. 'Don't you think it's a bit strange? The way he likes everything you like. How he was reading that book on Churchill in the gym that time.'

Alex frowns, confused.

'Do you really think he just happens to be into military history and Britpop and the London Marathon? What if Max looked you up? What if he researched you?'

Alex's eyes widen. 'Are you serious?'

'It's too coincidental that he likes everything you like. You tweeted about that Churchill book, and then he was reading it!' I tell him, throwing my hands up in the air, animated with passion, but Alex regards me warily. He clearly thinks I'm the crazy one, not Max.

'And why would Max do that? Why would he research me?' Alex asks, his voice laced with cynicism.

'I don't know!' I reply. 'I don't know! I wish I did! I just know that he's not who he says he is. Something isn't right about him.'

I think of the Google results. Max's complete absence of online presence. The graves. I shudder, yet again. But of course, I can't tell Alex about that. He already thinks it's bad enough that I tried to find Max online the other day. He definitely wouldn't react well if he knew I'd looked up Max's full name after seeing it on a stolen letter.

'Oh, God,' Alex groans. He lowers his head into his hands.

I can tell he thinks I've lost it, but my gut feeling about Max is so strong that I'm undeterred. I pull out a chair, sit down next to him and place my hand on his thigh, but Alex jerks his leg, flicking my touch away. I try to suppress the feeling of hurt.

Alex isn't exactly enjoying this conversation, obviously, and yet I feel the need to share my worries with him. I want to tell him my concerns over Esme, and yet I'm nervous about bringing it up.

Talking about a missing person case will inevitably remind him of Jacob, and I'm scared to go there. Alex is already upset. Our relationship already feels strained. Alex sometimes gets so upset over missing person cases that he'll turn the TV off if one comes on. We were once heading out of London for a day trip when a missing person case came up on the radio. Alex was in a bad mood for the rest of the day. In fact, he barely spoke.

And yet, despite his discomfort, if Max did have something to do with Esme Jenkins' disappearance, then I need to say something. Part of the reason Alex gets so upset is because he feels he could have done more to protect Jacob. Surely he'd want to protect someone else if they were in danger?

I brace myself, deciding to go for it.

'Did you hear about that missing woman?' I ask.

Alex immediately tenses, just like I knew he would.

'What missing woman?'

'Esme Jenkins. Twenty-six years old. A redhead. She was last seen just down the road on Saturday evening.'

Alex eyes me warily. I can see the sadness falling over him like a shadow.

I tap into my phone and show him the Met's tweet.

'This is her.'

Alex takes my phone and inspects the picture.

'I've never seen her before,' he says, handing my phone back to me.

'Well, I think I have,' I venture nervously.

Alex sighs exaggeratedly and shoots me a dark, warning look.

'What do you mean?' he asks.

'I think I saw her, on Saturday night, with Max.' I get up and dart to the kitchen window. 'You know I was here, making dinner, looking over, and I saw a woman, just like the one in that picture.

154

Exactly like her. She was with Max, in his kitchen.' I point across to Max's place before looking back to Alex.

He regards me with a shell-shocked expression, and I can tell my words have gone completely over his head.

'This isn't healthy, Becky,' he says. 'I don't know what's got into you, but your obsession with Max has gone too far. He hasn't kidnapped anyone! That's a crazy accusation.'

'I saw Max with a woman just like Esme!' I insist.

But Alex shakes his head. 'You're seriously doing this? I know you don't like Max, but implicating him in a missing person case . . . Bringing a case like that up when you know how I feel about that kind of thing?' he says with anger in his eyes. 'Are you really doing this?'

'I'm not trying to upset you, Alex. I genuinely think I saw Esme with Max. Don't you think that's important?' I plead, trying to get through to him.

'No.' Alex won't have it. 'You're wrong. Max would never do something like that. He wouldn't kidnap someone. For goodness' sake! There's nothing wrong with him. And he hasn't been research-ing me online. This is so ridiculous! He's a good guy. The way you're behaving right now is not normal.'

I sigh, exasperated. Alex is so convinced Max is a great guy, but he hasn't witnessed the things I've seen Max doing. He has no idea.

'You don't know Max as well as you think you do, Alex,' I say. Alex rolls his eyes, but I ignore him. 'I saw him with this woman one night just after he moved in. They were arguing. She was clearly upset, but Max marched her to his van really aggressively. He shoved her into the back and slammed the doors shut. Then he drove off and that was that, I never saw him with her again. It creeped me out.'

Alex's expression contorts slightly with shock and confusion.

155

'I didn't want to tell you because I knew it would remind you of Jacob. I didn't want to upset you, but it was so disturbing. I almost called the police.'

Alex looks down into his lap, his jaw tense. I can tell the mention of Jacob is troubling him. I'm about to reach out and comfort him in some way, but he looks back up at me, his expression stony.

'What are you talking about? Max wouldn't do that.'

'Yes, he would! I didn't imagine it,' I tell him. 'I should have told you. It was horrible. I kept trying to forget about it and tell myself it wasn't that bad, but it was . . . There's something not right about Max. You should have seen the way he manhandled that woman. God knows what he did with her next.'

'Stop!' Alex snaps. 'Max wouldn't "manhandle" anyone. He's a good guy. I don't know what you saw, Becks, but it can't have been that bad. I've been training Max. I've spent time with him. He gets on with everyone. He's a gentleman. He wouldn't hurt a woman. He's not this predator or abuser you're making him out to be!'

'I saw him,' I reiterate.

'No. You must have got it wrong,' Alex insists, his eyes steely, adamant.

He won't listen. So much for thinking I could talk to him. It's like he's chosen loyalty to Max over me. I feel betrayed. Small and worthless. He's meant to love me. He's meant to be the one person I can share anything with, and yet he's made me feel unhinged, neglected.

'This obsession you have with Max, it's not normal,' Alex says.

'Fine. Then I'm not normal. Forget it.' My eyes well up and I hope he might realise how much this conversation has upset me, but his face fails to soften. His eyes remain cold.

I get up and leave the room, fuming, shaking.

I march upstairs.

I grab my pyjamas from our bedroom, deciding I'll sleep in the spare room. I slip inside and close the door behind me, while picturing Alex downstairs, that cold, disapproving look in his eyes, his harsh words. I lie down on the spare bed and stare at the wall, trying not to cry.

Chapter Twenty-Three

I arrive early for my viewing with Elizabeth Jones.

I clear the junk mail from the hallway and go from room to room, plumping up cushions and turning on lights, making sure the house looks cosy and welcoming.

Elizabeth is still a bit of a mystery. I googled her this morning, but there wasn't a lot to go on. With a name like hers, quite a few profiles came up. Even when I added 'London' into the search bar, there were still lots of results. Quite a few were professional: a solicitor, a model agent, a personal assistant, a software engineer. My Elizabeth Jones could be any of them, or someone else entirely.

I perch at the huge island in the plush modern kitchen, the spotlights glowing on the ceiling, creating a warm atmosphere. It's not the nicest day outside and the sky is cloudy and overcast. A breeze rustles the branches of the trees. I take my phone from my bag. I have no messages. Nothing from Alex. We didn't speak again after our argument. I slept in the spare room and by the time I woke up, he'd gone to work. Our bedroom was empty, the duvet crumpled. There were droplets of water in the shower and his toothbrush left on the side of the sink, but nothing else. No note to make up. Not a word.

My heart feels raw in my chest as I think about last night, the way Alex wrote off my concerns. One of the things I've always loved about my relationship is the way I can talk to Alex about almost anything, but it's like I can't do that right now. I'm being judged. There's this distance, like Max has got between us. I think of how small and stupid he made me feel when I mentioned Esme and I feel even lower. And yet, this could be so much bigger than just a falling-out with Alex. If I'm right and Max does have something to do with Esme's disappearance, then I should be doing something. I should be speaking out. I shouldn't just be sitting in a kitchen worrying about my relationship. But if I'm wrong, Alex would be so upset with me, I can barely even contemplate it. Not only would I have brought back painful memories of Jacob, but I'd have alienated our neighbour and Alex's client by accusing him of kidnap. How would we ever recover from that?

I contemplate calling the police, my fingers hovering over my phone keypad, but just like last time, I can't quite bring myself to. I feel unnerved, my confidence shaken by Alex's reaction to my suspicions. I open up Twitter instead and scroll through the latest on Esme's disappearance. It's trending now. It's turning into a big story. It's been picked up by the national news, with articles appearing on the BBC, *Daily Mail*, *The Guardian*. The publicity is no doubt helped by the fact that Esme is an attractive, striking young woman, who from the sounds of it comes from a nice middle-class family.

The articles state that she met up with two friends for coffee at a café in Soho before taking a train to Sydenham, south London, where she was last seen. Apparently, she'd told her friends she was heading home, and none of her family and friends seem to have any idea why she might have been in Sydenham. If she is the girl who was with Max, then why would she have kept her date secret? Surely she'd have mentioned to someone that she was going over to a guy's house for drinks? And yet none of them seem to have any knowledge of a date at all. Esme's mother described her disappearance as 'completely out of character'.

More pictures of Esme have been shared online and I scroll through them, trying to figure out if she really was the woman I saw with Max. There's a shot of her in academic dress on graduation day, a selfie of her in her bedroom, a picture of her smiling outdoors with a friend who has been cropped out, another selfie. I zoom in on them, but I can't quite tell if Esme is the woman I saw. She looks slightly different in all the pictures and the more I look, the more confused I feel.

I scroll through the latest tweets, under the trending hashtag #FindEsmeJenkins.

A video's been posted featuring an interview with Esme's mother outside her home. She looks in her mid-fifties, pale and tired, wrapped in a cardigan. A man, presumably Esme's father, stands by her side with his arm around her.

'Please help me find my baby,' Esme's mother implores, looking desperately into the camera. Her eyes are puffy and it's clear she's been crying. 'Esme was my first child. She's my baby. She's my treasure, my darling, my love.' Her voice cracks up and her eyes fill with tears. The man standing next to her squeezes her arm and looks fixedly down at the ground, as though trying to contain his own emotions.

Esme's mother flicks the tears from her eyes.

'Please,' she begs with an intensity to her gaze. 'Esme, if you're watching, come home. I love you. We all do. We miss you so much. And please, if anyone knows anything, I urge you to come forward. Please help me find my baby.'

I feel a chill at her words. Her suffering is plain to see, her love for her daughter undeniable. I feel guilty, like I'm somehow involved in Esme's disappearance. If I know something that might be relevant to the case and I stay quiet, then I am complicit. Every hour counts in missing person cases, doesn't it?

I decide I will call the police. Straight after my viewing. I save the tip line to my phone. If Max has had something to do with this poor girl's disappearance, then I have to say something, whether he's my neighbour or not, and whether Alex likes it or not.

The doorbell rings. I try to compose myself and push thoughts of Esme and Max out of my mind.

I put my phone in my bag, feeling stronger, more confident, and head to the front door.

Chapter Twenty-Four

I smile as I pull the door open.

I'm expecting to see a professional middle-aged woman, someone respectable and well dressed, but the woman standing before me is young, probably a few years younger than me. She's scruffy, in a worn old hoodie and leggings. There are dark shadows under her eyes and her hair is greasy, falling around her shoulders in matted clumps. I spot a tattoo on her neck, the initials 'R.B.' in a heart. She catches me looking at it and sweeps her hair over it.

She shoots me a glare. There's a harshness in her eyes. They bore into me. She looks rough, belligerent, almost disdainful.

I realise I've forgotten my script. I'm just standing in the doorway, taking this woman in, rattled. I'm standing between her and the house, practically guarding it.

'Hi,' I say, with forced brightness. 'You must be Elizabeth?'

I'm half hoping she'll turn out to be someone else entirely, someone who's stumbled upon the wrong house, but I know that's unlikely. She doesn't look remotely surprised to see me. Her gaze stretches over my shoulder and she's clearly ready to come in and view the property.

'Yeah, I'm Elizabeth,' she replies lazily, with a tight, fake smile that drops off her face as quickly as it arrives.

'Right. Great!' I say, still standing in the doorway.

I strongly suspect 'Elizabeth' isn't her real name and that she's a time-waster.

I don't want to be judgemental, but you have to use a certain amount of observation and intuition in my line of work, and the woman standing before me does not look like someone who's genuinely interested in buying a £3m property. I can already tell the sale is not going to happen. But the sense of disappointment is overshadowed by a feeling of unease. There's something not quite right about this woman, and it's not just in the way she presents herself. There's something hostile about her. There's a darkness in her eyes, an almost glowering look. She's making me uncomfortable, and yet I can't exactly turn her away.

'I'm Becky,' I say, extending my hand, deciding to go through the motions with as much enthusiasm and professionalism as I can muster.

'Nice to meet you,' she replies, but there's a note of sarcasm in her voice. She shakes my hand. Her palm is sweaty.

'So, let me show you around.' I step aside to allow her into the property.

She smiles weakly and comes inside.

As she passes me, I smell stale cigarettes on her. A thick, cloying scent that makes me want to breathe through my mouth. I notice her bag, a battered holdall. It's large, open at the top. It's the type of bag that would be perfect for pickpockets. One sleight of hand and an item could easily be stashed inside.

I make a mental note to keep a close eye on her. I feel bad for thinking such thoughts and yet I just know something's not right about this.

'So, shall we start in the living room?' I suggest, trying to sound as relaxed and positive as possible.

'Sure,' *Elizabeth* replies.

I lead her into the room and make a few comments about the 'generous bay windows' and 'elegant marble fireplace'. The woman stands in the doorway. She nods and glances around, but doesn't bother to explore.

There are a few antique ornaments on the mantelpiece, which are no doubt quite valuable, but she doesn't go near them. She doesn't even look at them.

'Very nice,' she comments.

'Beautiful, isn't it?' I reply, standing alone in the middle of the room. 'Wait until you see the kitchen. It's stunning,' I gush, leading her down the corridor.

As we enter, I make a few comments about the stainless-steel appliances and AGA oven, but I don't go into too much detail. I don't want to drag the viewing out unnecessarily.

Elizabeth looks around, her expression bored. She doesn't say a thing.

I feel even more perplexed. What's she doing here? She doesn't seem to want to steal anything. Is she scoping out the house for a possible burglary? If that's the case, then she'll see there's not a lot to take. Maybe she's interested in squatting and is sizing the house up.

I feel anxious as she gazes across the room. She still doesn't speak, and the tension feels like it's brewing between us.

'So, have you been looking for a property for long?' I ask.

'A few weeks,' she tells me.

She crosses the kitchen and ventures into the adjoining dining room, not seeming particularly keen to talk. I follow her, deciding to play along with her story.

'And are you just looking in this area?' I ask.

'Yes,' she replies, not bothering to look my way.

She stops at one of the rear windows, overlooking the garden, and gazes out.

'I see. Are you selling at the moment?'

'No,' she replies curtly.

I roll my eyes behind her back. Her one-word answers are so rude. She's clearly lying, and yet I feel like I can't tell her to leave. I can't just draw the viewing to an end now. I can't afford another negative Google review being left about me online. Not after that guy Edward's. Wendy would not be pleased.

As Elizabeth gazes out over the garden, I think about Wendy. I'm already dreading having to tell her that my viewing's been a dud. Naturally, I'll have to admit that I didn't do any checks beforehand. It's not going to be a good conversation. I might even need to suggest we get some extra security installed here. It's probably for the best if this woman does turn out to be a squatter. That's the last thing the sellers need. Not only have I failed to sell their house, but I've managed to actively put it at risk. I feel like the worst estate agent ever.

'Okay, well let's have a look at the rest of the house,' I suggest to Elizabeth, wanting to wrap things up.

I give up on delivering my usual sales spiel. I don't bother mentioning that the jacuzzi has twenty jets or that the bathroom floor is heated. I don't bother stating that the bedrooms have walk-in wardrobes and are newly painted. I just lead her from room to room and watch as she drifts through, eyeing each room with a bored gaze, barely engaging, like she'd rather be somewhere else.

The master bedroom is the only room that she seems remotely interested in. She crosses it, heading straight for the window. She looks out, over the street.

'Nice view, isn't it?' I comment.

The street is on an elevation south of the river, and in the distance you can see the tip of the Shard and the skyscrapers of the City.

I'd usually use someone looking out of a window like that, taking in the area, as a prompt to talk about the local schools, shops and gyms, but I don't bother.

'Very nice,' the woman replies flatly.

Strangely, she does seem taken with the view. She carries on gazing out of the window and almost nods to herself, as though in approval.

She turns back to me.

'It's a nice house,' she declares with a tight smile. 'But I think I've seen enough now. I need to give it some thought.'

'Of course,' I reply, grateful that the viewing is finally over.

We head back downstairs. She walks in front of me, and I notice a hole in the back of her leggings. If she were trying to play the part of a wealthy homebuyer, she could have at least made more of an effort. I feel a twinge of annoyance at her audacity. She hasn't even tried to hide the fact that she's wasting my time.

She stops at the front door.

'You have my number so if you are interested, please do get in touch,' I say weakly as I open it.

'I will,' the woman replies.

We smile blankly at each other, both of us knowing we'll never hear from each other again.

I say goodbye and close the door.

As it clicks shut, I let out a sigh of relief.

She's gone.

Finally.

I shudder as I cross the hallway. I don't believe in energies or auras or anything like that, but if such things do exist, then that woman's was definitely dark. It was definitely bad.

I wander back into the kitchen, feeling a bit dazed.

That whole experience was so far removed from what I was expecting. I gaze out of the window, recalling the drama I had last time I was here when I locked myself out. I don't want to miss out on a huge sale, but part of me will be relieved to see the back of this house. It seems to have brought me nothing but bad luck.

Deflated, I go back through the house, turning off the lights and making sure all the windows and doors are firmly shut. I set the alarm before I leave, double-checking it.

Once I'm satisfied it's set, I open the front door and head outside.

I'm walking across the drive towards my car when I spot something on the bonnet. Something dark. As I approach it, I realise what it is. A bird. A large black crow.

I panic, thinking it might have flown into my windscreen, but as I approach, I see that something else has happened. Something else entirely.

My blood runs cold.

Chapter Twenty-Five

I stand in front of my car, my hand clasped over my mouth, my heart slamming in my chest.

My stomach lurches as I take in the crow's lifeless body, blood pooling around it.

It's been slashed, brutally slashed. Someone has taken a knife and cut all the way down the bird's body. Its guts tumble out from between its black feathers, red and oozing.

I think of Elizabeth. Her glowering, cold eyes, her fake smile, her clear disinterest in the house. Did she do this?

Things were tense between us during the viewing, but what kind of person would gut a bird to make a point? She seemed a bit off, but getting back at me like this would be psychotic.

Could there be someone else here? I scan the front drive, the bushes, the trees. I look up and down the street, but there's no one there. It's quiet. Peaceful.

I look back towards the house. The driveway is deserted. I check the passageways down the sides of the house, where the owner stores old bikes and folded deckchairs, but there's no one there. I scan the trees and bushes along the drive, but I can't see anyone. I'm alone.

And yet someone was here not so long ago. Someone was here and they wanted to scare me.

I head back to my car. Part of me thinks I must have got this wrong. That I must have mistaken what I saw. But no. As I approach, I take the crow in all over again. Its slashed body, its guts, its black, lifeless eyes. Blood drips off my bonnet on to the gravel drive.

I take a step backwards. And another. And another.

I need to get away. I step back once more and crumple on to the driveway, gasping for breath, stunned.

A memory from my university days comes back to me. We studied *Wheatfield with Crows* by Van Gogh. A work he created just a few weeks before he killed himself. Above the wheatfields in the painting is a darkening sky and a flock of crows swooping across it. I remember my lecturer describing the crows as 'harbingers of doom', symbolising Van Gogh's nearing death. I always found that painting eerie, haunting. And I think of it now.

Is this slaughtered crow a symbol of death? Could someone be trying to send me a message? Could this be a death threat?

My skin prickles. Reality feels like it's bending weirdly out of shape. I must be wrong. Surely I'm wrong.

Who would want me dead?

It can't be Elizabeth. I've never met her before in my life. But if not her, then who?

What if Max did this? What if he's heard from Alex that I don't like him and he's trying to spite me? No. That's ridiculous. And how would he even know I'm here?

Could Ryan have done this? He's certainly not who I thought he was, but he wouldn't go this far, would he? He's a bit weird, but he's not that unstable. Is he?

He could have known I was here though. Only people at work and Elizabeth knew I was at this house for the viewing. So maybe it was Ryan.

I think of the way he treated me in the café yesterday and how unsettled he made me feel. He was frightening. Perhaps he is dangerous, after all.

He wouldn't be the first man to kill over rejection. Stories like that are in the news far too often. Maybe Ryan is the latest in a long string of violent men with bruised egos who have tormented women who didn't want to be with them.

My phone rings, interrupting my thoughts. The ringtone feels jarringly normal against the macabre sight before me.

As I reach into my bag, I realise that my hand is shaking.

I pull out my phone and look at the screen: Wendy.

No. I can't speak to her right now. My head is spinning.

I let the phone ring out.

I get up. I so want to have got this wrong. I want there to be a normal, natural explanation for this bird's death, but it's clearly been attacked. The gash across its body is too deep, too deliberate. Nothing natural could have caused this.

I spot something moving out of the corner of my eye and look over. I see the flash of a figure at the end of the driveway. I scramble to my feet.

I run to the street, half terrified and half fixated upon who would be doing this to me. I want to know. But as I reach the street, I look up and down, scanning it, my eyes darting across the driveways and between the cars, and I can't see anyone.

The street is quiet, deserted, just like it was before.

'What did I do?' I cry out. 'What do you want from me?'

I realise I'm crying.

Hot tears fall down my cheeks as the clouds open overhead and it starts to rain. There's no reply. No movement.

The street is deathly still. The rain starts falling heavily, a sudden torrential downpour.

I turn and head back to my car. The rain is mixing with the blood of the crow and streams of watery blood flow off my bonnet.

Crying, I grab a stick from between the nearby trees and use it to flick the crow away. I try not to look directly at it and its bloody entrails as it falls to the ground with a thud. I shudder, throwing the stick back into the shrubbery, and get into my car.

I twist the keys in the ignition and wipe tears from my eyes before pulling away from the house.

My hands shake against the steering wheel. I feel dirty, like my skin is crawling. I need to get away from here. I need to get far, far away from whoever did this to me.

I drive down the street, my eyes peeled, but I can't see anyone suspicious. Just an elderly lady returning from the shops, a woman walking hand in hand with her child. And yet as I reach the end of the road, I glance up into my rear-view mirror and see a dark figure darting furtively from the bushes by the house and across the street.

My hair stands on end. Instinctively, I know that person must have been lurking, hiding, and that whoever it is was probably responsible for killing the crow. And I know they're after me.

But who are they? And what do they want?

Chapter Twenty-Six

I make a lap of the road, and another, trying to spot the dark figure I saw dashing across the street. But whoever it is has disappeared. Whoever is tormenting me has gone. Vanished into thin air.

In a daze I drive away, cutting down street after street, not sure where I'm heading. All I know is that I need to put distance between myself and what just happened.

I'm contemplating calling the police when my phone starts ringing, startling me.

I slow down, drawing to a halt at the side of a residential road. I take my phone from my bag. It's Wendy again. She must be wondering where I've got to.

I answer, still dazed.

'Hi, Wendy,' I say. My voice sounds strange – choked and distant, far removed from my usual self.

'Hi, Becky, how did the viewing go? When are you coming back to the office?' Wendy asks, her tone chipper.

'I . . . um . . .'

My hands are still shaking. I pull down the overhead mirror and look at my reflection. My mascara is smeared from crying. I'm deathly pale. I can't go into the office, not like this.

'Wendy, I think I need to take the afternoon off,' I tell her.

'What? Why?' she asks.

'Something's happened,' I say, my voice tremulous.

'What's happened? What are you talking about?' Wendy presses me, her tone laced with irritation.

I gaze out of my car window. A man crosses the road with a terrier on a lead. It stops to sniff a lamppost as they reach the pavement. A takeaway delivery driver passes by on a moped. The gutted crow bleeding out in my mind feels so unreal in comparison to the normality of everyday life.

'Becky?' Wendy says.

'I, um, I . . .' I stammer. 'I don't know how to explain it. I . . .'

'You haven't locked yourself out again, have you?' Wendy asks wearily.

'No, I haven't,' I snap. I lock myself out once and of course, Wendy thinks I'm going to make it a habit.

'So, what's going on?'

'Something's happened . . . Somebody . . .' The words get stuck in my throat. Somebody gutted a bird and left it for me to find. Somebody is trying to scare me . . .

It sounds too far-fetched, too extreme. Wendy will think I've lost it.

'Becky? What's going on?' Wendy asks impatiently.

'Sorry.' I clear my throat, trying to gather myself. 'I didn't lock myself out. I came out of the house and there was this dead bird. On my car,' I tell her, feeling overwhelmed, light-headed, as the words tumble out of my mouth.

'What? What are you talking about? A dead bird?' Wendy asks.

'Yes. Someone left it on my car.'

A silence passes. I can hear the background noise of the office at the other end of the line.

'I don't know what to say, Becky. Why would someone do that?' Wendy asks eventually.

'I don't know!' I blurt, as fresh tears spring to my eyes.

'I don't understand. You found a dead bird on your car? And you think someone left it for you?' Wendy says, sounding completely bemused.

'Yes, it had been attacked. Someone cut it. It looked like it had been gutted.'

'Stop!' Wendy protests. 'Give me a minute.'

I hear a beep at the end of the line and then the sound of Wendy's heels clicking against the office floor. I picture her marching from her desk to the meeting room, rolling her eyes at colleagues as she passes them, clutching her cordless phone.

A door closes.

'Becky, sorry about that. I wanted some privacy.' Wendy breathes out a sigh of relief. 'I don't know quite how to put this,' she says in a low voice. 'But you've been acting quite out of character lately. You have been for a while. First there were the negative reviews, the complaints, the erratic behaviour at viewings.'

'Erratic?' I interrupt, hurt. 'I wasn't erratic. A few things went wrong but it was just bad luck. It wasn't my fault.' I realise instantly how childish I sound and cringe, knowing exactly how Wendy must see me.

'Look, Becky, I know you believe that none of the incidents were your fault, but we're all in this industry together and nobody else is having the same issues. I think you need to acknowledge that you might not be as in control at the moment as you think. I don't know what's going on, but I think it might be a good idea if you took some time off. Things seem to have been a bit' – she pauses, searching for the right word – 'chaotic lately. I think it's best if you relax, clear your head, and come back into work when you're feeling better.'

'I don't need time off!' I protest.

'Well, you said you wanted to take the afternoon off. I'm agreeing with you. I think time off would be good for you. I think you need to step away for a while. Take your time,' Wendy says. 'As long as you need.'

My stomach fizzes with anxiety.

'But I don't want that,' I tell her, my heart sinking.

Wendy's making out that she's got my best interests at heart, but this doesn't feel like a compassionate move. It feels like an effort to drive me away. Wendy's never liked me, and it's as though she's using everything that's happened lately, all my misfortune, to try to force me not to come into work when the last thing I want is to be stuck at home.

Work has always kept me grounded. It gives me a routine, a reason to get up in the morning. I like having my coffee and getting in my car to head to the office each day. I like chatting with Anita and Lucy. And I like selling properties! My job means a lot to me. It always has. I don't want to be forced to sit around at home all day, my mind wandering. That's the last thing I need.

'I'd really rather not take any time off, Wendy,' I insist. 'I was just trying to explain why I'm running late coming back to the office.'

Wendy sighs dramatically. 'Yes, with stories about gutted birds! Honestly, Becky, I can't deal with this kind of thing any more,' she says, the softness gone from her voice. 'I really think you could do with some time off. It's not a suggestion. It's an order.'

'Right . . .'

'Call me when you're feeling better, okay?' Wendy asks.

'Fine,' I reply.

'I'll speak to you soon,' Wendy finishes.

A thought occurs to me. If Ryan was responsible for leaving that crow on my car, if he was that person creeping around on the street, then he'd be out of the office.

'Wendy, wait,' I say, before she has a chance to hang up. 'Is Ryan in the office right now?'

'Ryan?' Wendy echoes, sounding confused.

'Yes. Is Ryan there?'

'Why? Do you want to speak to him?'

'No, I don't want to speak to him. Is he there?'

'Yes, he's here. Why are you asking?' Wendy quizzes me, clearly baffled. 'Why do you want to know?'

I ignore her question. 'How long has he been there? Has he been in all morning?'

I know Wendy will find my questions strange, but I'm beyond caring what she thinks of me at this point.

'Yes, Ryan's been in all morning.' Wendy sighs. 'I have to go now. I have work to do.'

I wince at her words. They sound pointed, as though she's a busy professional and I'm an unstable woman ranting about slaughtered birds.

'Okay, bye,' I say as the line goes dead.

I hang up and look out of the window, letting Wendy's words sink in. So the person who left the crow wasn't Ryan.

And if it wasn't him, then who was it?

Could it have been Max?

Chapter Twenty-Seven

As I get home, I see Max smoking a cigarette outside his house.

My chest tightens as I take him in. He looks casual, laid-back. He has shadows under his eyes and his hair is dishevelled, but he doesn't look like he's just slaughtered a crow and then rushed back home.

I park my car as he sucks on his cigarette.

I can feel him watching me; my skin's prickling.

I haven't been able to stop thinking about the crow, its slaughtered body, the blood oozing from it. And yet seeing Max again, in front of his house, reminds me of Esme. I was going to call the police after the viewing, but I got distracted by the crow and everything else.

I get out of my car and slam the door behind me. I turn to Max.

I'm so wound up by everything that's going on that I'm beyond fearing him. I'm beyond worrying about neighbourly tensions. I'm beyond caring. We lock eyes. I scowl at him, shaking my head, but he doesn't respond. He just regards me impassively with that smug smile playing on his lips.

'What have you been doing today, Max?' I ask him, my voice harsh, sharp.

He frowns, but doesn't respond. He takes another drag of his cigarette. He's wearing another ratty old jumper, raggedy at the sleeves.

'You don't work in the City, do you?' I say.

He smirks as he exhales. 'Where did you hear that?' he asks.

I roll my eyes. 'From Alex. You know, my boyfriend. That guy you looked up online and decided you'd manipulate,' I state boldly.

Max lets out a derisive laugh. 'I don't know what you're talking about.'

I scoff, unable to believe his audacity. 'You told Alex you were a banker. You told him you run the London Marathon. That you like Britpop. That you read books on Churchill! You're full of shit!' I shriek, feeling a rush of adrenaline flood through me at having dared to confront him.

Max smirks again. He moves to get up. 'I thought I could stand outside my house and have a cigarette in peace. I'm not going to be harassed,' he says, stubbing his cigarette out against his garden wall.

Harassed?

How dare he? How dare he accuse me of harassment as though he's completely innocent? He's the one who marches women into the back of vans. He's been manipulating Alex, blasting his music and staring at me. He might even have slaughtered a bird and left it for me to find, for all I know. If anyone's guilty of harassment, it's him.

He eyes me darkly, and I get a disquieting, foreboding feeling. What if Max is guilty of more? I'm reminded of the first time we properly met, down the street, when my tyres had been slashed. I think of how Max was there that morning, crouching down, telling me I must have run over some broken bottles. I believed him. I accepted that I was to blame, even though I had no recollection of seeing any broken glass on the road when I parked.

What if Max had something to do with that? What if he slashed my tyres? What if he deliberately parked that battered old van in my parking space so my car was out of sight and then slashed my tyres in the middle of the night? It's possible. And it feels very possible now, as I take him in, his mask having slipped. He clearly isn't the person he's claimed to be. There's no trace of him online. So who is he? What's he capable of?

'You slashed my tyres, didn't you?' I spit as he crosses his front garden, heading inside.

I follow him, darting across the pavement and swinging through his garden gate.

'You slashed my tyres and you toyed with my boyfriend. Don't pretend you didn't stalk him online. What do you want from us?' I challenge him, but he opens his front door and pointedly ignores me. 'Who are you, Max?' I ask as he heads inside.

He turns to me, his face stony, before slamming the door shut.

Chapter Twenty-Eight

I'm shaking as I turn my key in my front door.

That's it. I've had enough. I'm calling the police.

I'm done with Max. I'm done with being silent. I'm done with his dark eyes, his manipulation, his rudeness. He's not who he says he is. And I'm done with playing along. He's hiding something. I just know it.

I just hope he isn't hiding Esme Jenkins.

I find the police tip line saved on my phone and call it.

'Becky?'

Alex appears in the hall, startling me. I thought he'd be at work, but he must have nipped home during his break.

I cancel the call.

'You're here,' I state, pointing out the obvious.

'Yes, and I heard you outside,' Alex comments, fixing me with a dour look. 'Laying into Max.'

His cheeks are flushed. His neck is flushed too, and I feel instantly guilty. Alex's neck only ever gets flushed when he's really angry or really upset.

I had no idea he was home. If I had done, I probably would have thought twice about the things I said. Everything came out in an overflow of emotion, and I must have been raising my voice for Alex to have heard.

'I can't believe you,' Alex says, disappointment etched on his face.

'Max lied to you, Alex,' I protest weakly, crossing the hall towards him. 'He doesn't work in the City. He's not who he says he is. He manipulated you. He's—'

'I don't want to hear it, Becky,' Alex says, turning away.

'He's a liar,' I continue. 'Why would he be at home all the time if he works in the City? He's not genuine. There's something not right about him. He's creepy.'

Alex rolls his eyes. 'He has the day off. He's using up his annual leave. He told me this morning. We had a training session and he mentioned that he was taking the afternoon to relax. For God's sake! It's none of your business how Max spends his time.'

His eyes are cold, his words cutting. I feel two inches tall, unsettled. Maybe Alex is right. Maybe I have been poking my nose into Max's business. His lifestyle isn't really my concern. And yet I think of all the weird grave websites online when I googled his name. I think of the redhead I saw in his kitchen on Saturday night. I think of Esme. I think of the gut feeling I get whenever I'm around him. A feeling of fear, danger.

I want to tell him about the crow and how I feel like someone's out to get me, but it'll probably make him think I'm really unhinged. What if he reacts like Wendy did and shuts me out even more?

'There's something not right about Max. I know it.' I sit down at the kitchen table, feeling overwhelmed.

'No,' Alex sighs. 'You're wrong. Max is a good guy. I don't know why you have such a problem with him.'

I gaze into his cold eyes. I want to tell him everything, but I don't know where to start. I groan, lowering my head into my hands.

'What is it with you and him?' Alex presses me, exasperated.

I look down at the grain of the table. I can feel my heart beating in my chest, my palms beading with sweat.

'I told you, I saw him with that missing girl,' I tell him, desperate. 'She was in his kitchen.'

Alex shakes his head. 'No, she wasn't,' he says, his voice cold, harsh.

'Look, Alex, I saw Esme with Max. She had the exact same long red hair. The same short dress. It was her,' I tell him. 'I saw her with him, in his kitchen, the night she went missing. I know you get upset about missing person cases, but I really think Max—'

'Becky, stop!' Alex barks. 'It wasn't her. Esme Jenkins is back home with her family. Haven't you heard? It's all over the news. She went to stay on some farm in Yorkshire with some guy and didn't bother to tell anyone. Nothing happened to her. She's safe and well. Max had nothing to do with her.'

'What?' I utter, my mind reeling.

'The woman you saw wasn't Esme,' Alex reiterates.

My stomach lurches. I'm speechless. I was so convinced the redhead I saw must have been Esme. She looked so similar.

'See? You got that wrong,' Alex says, his arms folded across his chest. 'Just like you've got Max wrong.'

'I thought . . . Is she really back?' I gasp.

'Yes. Check for yourself.' Alex reaches into his pocket and pulls out his phone. He taps in his pin and hands it to me.

I take it and type Esme's name into Google. A whole stream of news articles appears, confirming that she's been found, safe and well. The story of her being in Yorkshire at a farm is included in all the reports, accompanied by an apologetic and embarrassed quote from Esme.

So Alex is right. Max didn't kidnap her. I was wrong. Max just happened to have a date with a redhead the same night Esme went missing. And yet I was so convinced he was responsible. I feel completely shaken. What if he's not this dark, sinister person and I'm just losing the plot? I blink, unable to make sense of it all.

'See? Maybe you shouldn't jump to conclusions about people,' Alex remarks, taking his phone back. 'You probably shouldn't assume people are kidnappers.'

'Sorry, I just . . . I've had a really strange day. I went to a viewing and I saw this crow and . . .' I stop, regretting mentioning it.

Alex frowns. He gives me a strange look and sighs loudly.

'I think I'm going to go and stay with my parents for a few days,' he tells me. 'I need to clear my head. I think we both need some time to think.'

'Really?' I'm rattled, not quite believing that he could want to get away from me. We don't do that. In our three years together, we've hardly ever spent a night apart. We've always been incredibly close.

'This is getting too much for me,' Alex says, gesturing expansively towards me.

I'm getting too much for him.

'I just need a break. We'll talk in a few days.'

'No. Please, Alex.' I get up and go over to him. I eye him searchingly, but he won't meet my gaze. He stares down at the kitchen floor, his jaw tense. I reach for him, wanting to hold him, but he brushes me off.

'Stop!' he says, pulling away. 'I can't do this right now.'

My stomach drops. 'I'll go over and apologise to Max. I'm sorry.'

Alex sighs again. He leans against the fridge, standing a few paces away from me. 'It's not just about Max,' he says, shooting me an angry look. 'I heard about you and that guy from work.'

'What? What guy?' I ask, confused.

'Ryan,' says Alex, his eyes full of hurt.

'Ryan?' I baulk. 'What are you talking about?'

'I know that he was all over you in The Albert on Friday night. And I saw the comments he left on your Instagram pictures. Saying you could do better than me,' Alex recalls. 'Thanks for deleting those.'

My mind races. How could Alex possibly be threatened by Ryan? And how does he even know about Friday night?

'You've got it all wrong! I invited Ryan out for drinks to try to set him up with Lucy, but he started acting weirdly and inappropriately towards me. He was drunk and he put his hand on my leg. I told him where to go.'

'You didn't seem particularly fussed that he left a load of sleazy comments on your Instagram page,' Alex remarks.

'I was. They were disgusting! I went to delete them and then . . .'

'And then what?'

'I forgot, okay? I deleted them the next day.'

'Whatever.' Alex shakes his head. 'It's a bit upsetting that I was at home lighting candles and scattering rose petals over our bed while you were out flirting with another man.'

'I wasn't flirting, Alex! How could you think that?'

I try to approach him, to put my arms around him, but he moves away and avoids my gaze.

'I need to go,' he says.

He leaves the room. He charges down the hall. I follow him as he marches upstairs, my mind racing, panicked.

'I wasn't flirting, Alex. I love you. I'd never flirt with Ryan,' I insist, but Alex doesn't respond.

He just heads into our bedroom. He looks around and grabs a suitcase from on top of the wardrobe.

'Who told you I was flirting?' I ask.

'It doesn't matter,' Alex mutters as he places the suitcase down on the bed and opens it. He opens a drawer and starts packing socks and underwear into his case.

'I can't believe you'd think I'd flirt with Ryan.' I still can't take this in. Here's my boyfriend, who I love, packing a suitcase over Ryan. Ryan!

'You had a thing before though, didn't you?' Alex says, throwing me a cold glance.

'It wasn't a *thing*! We kissed at the office Christmas party years ago. It was nothing!' I insist.

'And yet he had his hand on your leg.'

'Who told you that?'

Anyone who saw me and Ryan on Friday night would have seen me flicking his hand off my thigh, getting up and telling him where to go. They'd have seen us arguing and me leaving him alone in the pub. Why would they lie and act like we were intimate?

'Does it matter?' Alex sneers as he places T-shirts into the suitcase.

I try to think if there was anyone I know at the pub on Friday night, but apart from the people at our table, I don't recall seeing anyone I recognised.

'Look, I don't know what this person said, but they got it wrong. Nothing happened with Ryan. You're everything to me. You've got to believe me.' Tears spring to my eyes and fall down my cheeks. I flick them away and stare at him imploringly, but he's not listening. 'Please don't go, Alex. You've got it completely wrong. Everything was fine between us.'

Alex doesn't respond. He just piles his gym gear into the case.

Another tear drops down my cheek.

'What about . . . What about our plans? What about the baby?' I croak.

Alex looks up at me, his eyes dark, sorrowful, tinged with a touch of sympathy.

'I think we should leave trying for a baby for now,' he says.

I stare at him, horrified. I feel like I've been winded. This can't be happening.

'No. You don't mean that.'

He zips his suitcase closed.

'Sorry,' Alex mumbles. 'I have to go.'

He heaves his suitcase off the bed and I watch as he leaves the room, my world falling apart.

Chapter Twenty-Nine

I get in the car and drive.

I need to get away. I need to get away from everything. From London. From Max. From Ryan, Alex, Wendy, the house, the street. I need to get away from it all. All the confusion, all the stress.

I need to go somewhere I feel safe. Somewhere I feel happy.

Most people, at times like these, would probably go home. They'd do what Alex is doing and go and stay with their parents, or a sibling. They'd turn to someone who loves them. But I can't do that.

I've never really been able to do that. Linda and Alfie are both in their sixties now, but they still have a few foster kids living with them. I can't just show up on their doorstep, lost and alone, feeling like I am now. It wouldn't be fair on them or their kids.

I pull on to the motorway and sigh, pushing my sad thoughts away.

Linda and Alfie were good to me. They're great people and I was lucky, very lucky, to be put in their care and to grow up in a stable, happy home. That's so much more than a lot of people get to say. Most of the time, I feel enormous gratitude for what I had, but I feel that absence of parents at times like these. Times when everything falls apart and you need a hug from someone who loves you unconditionally, no matter what.

My eyes fill with tears, but I blink them away and pick up speed down the motorway.

I don't need parents to go to. Home isn't just people, it's places too.

It's places that bring back happy memories and make you feel safe.

Saltwater Cove has always been that place for me. A beautiful seaside town in Devon, it's where we used to go on holiday every summer during my childhood. Linda grew up not far from there and she used to visit all the time when she was a child. It was sort of like a family tradition that she ended up taking her own kids on holiday there too.

Each year, we'd visit for a few weeks, renting a cottage by the beach. Linda used to count down the days until those trips. In fact, we all did. I loved those holidays. We'd lie on the sand, swim in the sea and go for long country walks. Real life: school, exams, worries, everything used to just fade into the background, replaced by sunshine, the sparkling sea, ice cream, fish and chips and barbeques in the garden as the sun set. It was bliss.

After Alex left yesterday, I spent a night in the house alone, feeling miserable. I couldn't handle sleeping in our bed without him. It felt horrible. I tried to message him and get him to realise how wrong he'd been about Ryan, but he didn't reply. I had a sleepless night. I couldn't stop thinking about work too. The dead crow on my car. Wendy. I called Anita and poured my heart out, which helped. She couldn't believe how unsympathetic Wendy had been and she tried to reassure me that things would be all right with Alex, but I still felt low, inconsolable. I realised I needed to get away. I needed a break. Luckily there was a vacancy at a hotel by Saltwater Cove beach, so I booked a room and packed my things.

I think about Alex as I drive, the sadness returning.

I think of him saying he wants to stop trying for a baby, but the pain of the memory is too acute. I push it out of my mind and put the radio on instead, letting myself get distracted by the chit-chat of the radio presenter and the pop songs playing.

After driving for an hour or so, I start to feel hungry. I decide to take a break at a service station and pull off the motorway a few miles ahead. I find a parking space and get out of my car, heading inside.

I buy myself some comfort food from one of the fast-food joints and sit down, eating fries and sipping lemonade. I check my messages, but there's nothing from Alex.

I'd hoped he might have cooled off today and got in touch, but there's not one word. It's so unlike him. He's never ignored me before. But I think back to how upset he was yesterday, the flush of anxiety on his neck, the hurt in his eyes, the way he packed his suitcase so quickly, as though he couldn't wait to get away from me.

Gazing blankly across the car park, I feel twinges of period pain creeping up on me. So much for getting pregnant. As usual, another month of failed attempts. It's probably for the best that I'm getting my period now though, considering how Alex feels. I thought my dream of parenthood was so close, but now it feels like it's slipping out of my grasp, falling away from me.

I sigh and reach for another fry. I finish the whole pack before scrunching up the wrapper and heading back outside to my car.

As I approach, I notice a van parked a few spaces down. A battered old grey van.

I frown. It's just like the van Max had. The one he bundled that woman into.

It's the exact same size and shade of grey and it's dented and broken down. Could it be the same van? No. Surely not? Why would Max's van be at a service station halfway to Devon? The thought is ridiculous.

I take a few paces closer and try to catch a glimpse of the driver, but there's no one there. The van probably belongs to a complete stranger. And after all, there must be millions of grey vans across the country and a lot of them will be battered and old like this one. And yet I feel weird. I feel a strange snagging feeling, as though I can't quite let this go. I reach into my bag and take out my phone.

I snap a few pictures of the van, feeling oddly on edge and paranoid.

I put my phone back in my bag and shake my head at my crazy thoughts as I turn to get into my car. Is Alex right? Am I obsessed with Max? I'm taking pictures of vans that remind me of his. That's not exactly normal. I feel a surreal, twisting feeling as I turn my key in the ignition. I don't know what to think any more. Maybe Alex is right. Maybe I am losing it.

As I pull out of the car park, I glance at the van in my rear-view mirror, looking out for someone. Looking out for Max.

Chapter Thirty

I arrive at my hotel in the traditional old Victorian seaside resort, and get settled in.

It's late afternoon but it's still sunny and I decide to take a walk along the beach. I walk through the town towards the seafront. I still remember some of the shops from my childhood holidays, the bakery with its red frontage and wrought-iron chairs set out on the street under an awning. I pass antique shops that I have memories of visiting years ago. I can still recall their musty smell. I used to sift through boxes of old postcards and black-and-white photographs, trying to imagine the lives of the people pictured, while Linda and Alfie turned over the price tags of beautiful pieces of antique furniture. I pass the fish and chip shop we used to go to. It's still exactly the same. Someone sits outside, plucking chips from the same blue-and-white striped trays they had years ago. I remember carrying those warm trays towards the beach, where we'd eat our meals on benches overlooking the sea.

I smile at the memories as the sea comes into sight. It's a dazzling blue, glittering into the distance. I feel happier at once. I've always loved being by the sea: the stunning shimmer of it, the sense of endlessness, the rush of the waves.

There's an elderly man sitting on a bench admiring the view and a few dog walkers passing along the cliffs surrounding the cove.

I walk down the steps towards the beach, the sound of the waves growing louder accompanied by the squeals of children playing on the sand.

I kick off my sandals and feel the sand between my toes as I weave between sunbathers. I walk to the edge of the sea, where the waves break, lapping against the shore. The sad, panicky feeling I've been carrying around lately retreats as I take in their steady rhythm, feeling the sea mist on my face. I can taste it on my lips.

I sit down and watch ships pass in the distance. I sit like that for a while, but eventually a chill creeps into the air and clouds appear in the sky. It looks like it's going to rain. I decide to head back into the town.

A sea breeze blows my hair across my face as I reach the main road. I sweep it out of my eyes before crossing the street, when suddenly I spot a van. A battered old grey van. No way. I take my phone from my bag and compare the licence plate before me with the one in my photo. I realise, stomach lurching, that it's the exact same van.

I freeze in my tracks, unable to quite believe what I'm seeing.

Could this be a coincidence? Could the driver simply have been heading the same way along the motorway, to the same place?

It seems unlikely, but I suppose it's not impossible.

The only alternative is that someone – Max – is following me. Fear shoots through me. I picture him grabbing me and bundling me up into the back of the van like he did to that woman. My whole body tenses up. What if I'm next? Perhaps it's my karma for not calling the police the moment I witnessed that incident.

Heart pounding, I look around, scanning the street, half expecting to see Max standing nearby, watching me, but there's no sign of him. I cross the road tentatively, moving stiffly, on high alert for Max.

I approach the van.

The sun glints off its windows, making it difficult to see inside, but I brace myself and walk right up to the windscreen. I peer in. It's empty.

I grab my phone from my bag and take a few pictures of the van here too, with the street sign in the background. If Max is following me, then I want evidence.

I consider calling the police, but what would I say? That there's a van here in Saltwater Cove that I also saw at a service station? That my neighbour gives me the creeps? They wouldn't listen. None of it sounds rational out loud. My suspicions would probably seem outrageous, just like my fears about Esme. I was wrong about her. Perhaps I'm wrong about this too.

I take another few pictures, my palms sweaty, before heading back towards my hotel. I pass the fish and chip shop, the bakery, the antique shops, but they no longer feel the same. That comforting sense of nostalgia has gone. Instead, I feel scared, on edge, watched, just like I felt in London. So much for finding refuge.

I scan the face of every passer-by, looking out for Max, but I don't see anyone I know.

I'm approaching my hotel when I spot someone loitering outside.

A tall man, with dark hair.

There he is.

It's Max.

Chapter Thirty-One

I hesitate, fear shooting through me.

Max is here. I'm not going mad. He's following me. He's out to get me.

Adrenaline courses through me. I don't know whether to run or what to do.

The adrenaline turns to anger as I take him in. What the hell is he doing? Who does he think he is to follow me all this way? What on earth does he want from me?

I decide to confront him. People are coming and going outside the hotel. It's not like he can do anything.

I take a deep breath, gathering myself, and cross the street, dodging a passing car.

'Max,' I call out as I rush up to him. His back is turned to me. 'What are you doing? Why are you following me?' I grab his arm.

He spins around.

And suddenly, I realise with a jolt that the man before me isn't Max at all.

It's someone else entirely. The man before me has the same dark hair as Max, the same build, even the same dress sense, but he's older. His features are completely different, and they're twisted in shock.

He jerks his arm free from my grip.

'God, I'm so sorry,' I say, deeply embarrassed. 'I thought . . . I thought you were someone else.'

The man smiles tightly. He has a kind face, but he looks taken aback, upset. He backs away from me.

'I'm so sorry,' I repeat, cringing.

'It's fine,' he replies curtly.

His partner comes out of the hotel. She looks my way, puzzled, before slipping her arm through his. They walk away, talking quietly and glancing warily back at me.

I slump against the hotel wall, mortified.

Great. So now I'm harassing random men in the street. This is what it's come to. My paranoia is so extreme that I'm mistaking strangers for Max.

Alex is probably right. I must be losing it. I have to be. This is not normal. I'm taking pictures of vans. I'm running up to strangers in the street and grabbing them.

Seeing that battered old van again must have just been a coincidence. Lots of people visit Saltwater Cove. It's a nice place. Seeing the same van here doesn't mean I'm being stalked. It just means that someone else was heading to Saltwater Cove. And yet I brought it back to Max, just like I assumed that the redhead in his kitchen was Esme Jenkins.

It's like Max has got stuck in my brain and I can't quite shake him. I don't know why. It's bizarre. It's like he's always there, a dark shadow in my subconscious, following me. And it makes no sense. Every time I think I'm going to catch him, I embarrass myself. I end up looking and feeling like a fool.

Sighing, I get up from the wall and head into the hotel. I make my way to my room, along the dated corridor with its seventies carpet and framed pictures of seashells and starfish.

As I turn the key in the door, I see a figure out of the corner of my eye, flitting across the hallway.

Another guest, no doubt. Nothing to worry about. It's about time I stopped being so paranoid.

I let myself into my room and close the door.

Chapter Thirty-Two

I wake up to sunlight streaming into my hotel room.

I climb out of bed and open the curtains. It's a beautiful day. From my room, I can see the sea, glittering into the distance underneath the vast blue sky. But as I admire the stunning view, reality creeps back into my consciousness, my sadness returning.

I think of Alex with his parents in Kent. He's still not talking to me.

Jittery after the events of yesterday, I had dinner in the hotel restaurant before returning to my room for a quiet early night. My cramps were in full force. I sat in bed with a hot-water bottle from reception and watched trashy films on TV, trying to distract myself from the sadness.

I messaged Alex, hoping he might be ready to talk, but my messages went unanswered, just like all the others I've sent. I'm getting worried now. Just how long is he planning to ignore me for? I assumed he needed a day or so to cool off, but I'm beginning to wonder if this is a lot more serious than I thought. I'm almost worried that we're over. What if he doesn't want to try for a baby at any point? The thought is too much.

I grab my phone from the bedside table and scroll through all my messages and social media accounts, hoping I might have heard something from him, but there's nothing.

I consider messaging him again, but decide to leave it. If Alex really needs space from me then I should give it to him.

Heading into the bathroom, I have a shower, lathering myself in the hotel's free jasmine-scented shampoo and shower gel. Then I get ready to head to the beach.

I still feel on edge from yesterday, but I was clearly just being paranoid. Too much time spent watching serial killer documentaries and frequenting the true crime forum clearly isn't good for me, just like Alex has always said.

Sighing, I shake my head as I take a novel, a feel-good romance, from a selection on the shelf in my room, and pack it into my beach bag.

Once I'm ready, I head downstairs. I stop for a quick breakfast at the hotel buffet and have a coffee while sitting at the window seat of the dining room, gazing out.

It really is a lovely day, and other holidaymakers are making their way down to the beach, clutching buckets and spades, umbrellas and towels. Once again, I'm reminded of my childhood holidays, the happy times spent in the sunshine. Linda and Alfie would sunbathe while I'd make sandcastles and play with the other children, running into the sea, splashing each other, or exploring the rock pools, trying to find pretty shells and crabs in the water. The memories of those holidays are still so vivid and I smile to myself, despite everything.

I finish my breakfast and head out of the hotel, putting my sunglasses on as I make my way down the street. I pass the battered grey van, still in the same spot as yesterday. I shake my head, thinking of the paranoia I felt upon seeing it. I walk down the steps to the beach and wander across the sand, finding a quiet spot to spread my towel. I strip down to my swimsuit and spritz sunscreen on to my arms and legs before lying down and relaxing under the sun. I open up the romance novel I took from the hotel and lose myself in its easy plot as the waves crash against the shore.

After a while, I start to feel sleepy and close my eyes. I'm snoozing lightly, drifting in and out of a gentle sleep, the waves lapping in the distance, when suddenly I feel a coolness, a darkness, a shadow falling over me, blotting the light out.

I open my eyes, still dreamy, half asleep, and see that someone's standing above me, looking down.

It's Max . . .

I blink. My heart thuds in my chest. I'm not dreaming. It's really him. He's standing there, staring down, his head haloed by the sun, his lips twisting into that smug smile he always wears.

Fear shoots through me. I scoot out from under him and jump to my feet. Standing face to face with him, my mind reels. He's here. He's really here. I was right to be paranoid after all. The van must have been his. I was right to feel uneasy about him. I was being followed.

Max's smile twists as he takes in my panic.

'What are you doing here?' I croak.

A child runs past us with a bucket and spade, kicking up sand, followed by an apologetic parent, as I stand there glaring at Max, waiting for him to respond. To anyone else, he must look like just another beachgoer, in a pair of shorts and flip-flops, and yet he's not just any other beachgoer. He's some kind of stalker. A psychopath. People are relaxing, sunbathing, eating ice cream all around us, and yet I'm looking into Max's dark eyes, unable to unravel what's going on.

'I think you know what I'm doing here,' Max says.

His eye bore into mine, and something shifts inside me. A lurch. A fear, rising to the surface. My skin prickles.

'You know who I am,' Max persists, his eyes insistent. 'You've always known.'

My palms bead with sweat. I look away, unable to hold his intense gaze. I look down at the sand, heart thudding, mind racing. No. He can't be . . .

I look back up and spot a scar – a huge scar – all the way across Max's chest. A deep, mangled scar. I've never seen him exposed like this before. And suddenly, it hits me. I know exactly who he is.

He isn't Max Sidwell. Max Sidwell is a fiction. A fantasy.

The man standing before me is someone I haven't seen for a very, very long time, and as I take in his scar, the jagged old scar tracing down from his breastbone and across his ribs, I have no doubt about who he is. I thought I'd left him in my past. But he's back. He's tracked me down. He's right here, in front of me, inescapable.

Chapter Thirty-Three

'Robbie,' I gasp.

He's no longer Max, the stranger, the man who appeared next door and always gave me a troubled, nervous feeling. He's Robbie. Robbie, who I haven't seen since I was five years old. I knew he was familiar. Now I know why I've felt that strange sense of familiarity, that sense that I knew him from somewhere but couldn't quite figure out where. Now I know. His scar has confirmed it.

'Oh my God, it's you.'

Tears fill my eyes. A tide of emotion floods through me, part fear, part panic and part affection.

'You must have known,' he says.

I shake my head.

No. I didn't know. I knew he made me feel threatened. I knew there was something about him that I couldn't shake. I knew he unnerved me, but I put it all down to that night when I saw him marching that woman to his van. Otherwise, it was just a sense of unease; a constant feeling of tension that he provoked in me. But could it be that the reason I feared him so much was that some-where, deep down, I knew him? I knew him from a long, long time ago.

'You really didn't recognise me?' he asks.

He stands before me. The smug, faintly cruel smile he was wearing before slides off his face and a softer look appears in his eyes. Eyes that are not dissimilar to my own. His are brown too, just like mine, with a dark outline and an amber ring around the pupil that you only see in bright sunlight, like today's. Now I know why he's always looked so familiar – it's because he looks like me.

I look back down towards his scar. Would I have recognised him earlier if I'd seen it? It never struck me as strange before, but he's always been concealed. When he's been out for a run or sunbathing in his garden, his chest has always been covered. I never paid much attention to it, but seeing his scar now exposes him. It connects him to our past. A past I've spent my whole life trying to forget.

He's Robbie. My brother.

My brother who I haven't seen for years, since before I went to live with Alfie and Linda.

'I can't believe it's you,' I croak, thoughts rushing through my mind, chaotic and confused. The world feels like it's spinning. The waves are still crashing against the shore, the sun is shining, children are laughing and playing, but my brother's here. Max is my brother. He's been using a fake name this whole time. He's Robbie, my brother, who I haven't seen since I was five years old. He was my rock. The one person I could cling to when it felt like the world was tipping upside down.

The last memory I have of him flashes through my mind. It's the memory that's been haunting me my entire life. A memory so bad that I shut it out of my waking moments as much as I can, only for it to emerge in my dreams. For years and years, I've pretended, to myself and others, that I don't remember what happened. I've locked the memories away in a box in my mind, buried them, acted like they never existed. They were contained in the two-year window I tried to erase from my past. The two years I hid from

Alex and everyone else. Everyone I know thinks I don't remember my first home, and that my childhood essentially began when I moved in with Linda and Alfie, but that's not the case. I remember my first home far too well, even though I wish I didn't. I remember my parents and I remember my brother.

I wanted to move on. I've tried so hard to reinvent myself and lead a normal life.

I've wanted to forget about Robbie. I've wanted so badly to forget what happened. I've always hoped Robbie had moved on too, but I never wanted anything to do with him. I didn't want to see him, my long-lost brother, my only family. The only link I have to my past. My awful, hideous past. But now he's here.

'Robbie. What . . . Why . . . why are you here?' I ask, stammering.

Coldness floods his eyes, the fleeting look of softness and tenderness gone.

'Nice, Becky . . .' he sneers. 'You haven't changed, have you?'

He turns and starts walking away.

My stomach twists in shame. He hates me. Just like he did all those years ago.

He strides across the beach. I stoop down and grab my things, scooping them up in a handful before following him. My sunscreen falls to the ground as I pace across the sand, my novel tumbling away. But Robbie marches ahead, swiftly, purposefully, cutting between sunbathers, who sense a commotion and eye us curiously.

'Robbie,' I cry out as he charges up the steps leading to the town, his pace fast, faster than I can keep up with.

Alex was right, he is fit. He takes the steps two at a time. I try to keep up, but he gets too far ahead.

'Robbie, come back,' I plead.

I'm half afraid, and half desperate to speak to him. To connect with him. My brother. By the time I reach the top of the steps, panting, he's crossing the road and jumping into his battered old van.

He pulls away from the kerb and drives into the distance.

I watch him go and crumple on to a bench, unable to believe that after all these years, my brother – the only link to my long-hidden past – is back.

And with him, all the darkness returns.

Chapter Thirty-Four

Overwhelmed, I try to marry together the person I thought was Max with my brother Robbie. Memories, long buried, bubble back to the surface as I gaze blankly at the passing cars.

I pretended to Linda and Alfie that I didn't remember the traumatic events of my first home, and they believed me. I was only five years old and I think they happily accepted that I'd forgotten everything because of my trauma. But I hadn't forgotten everything. I remember exactly what happened in my first home. It's a memory I've spent a lifetime trying to forget. It's the most painful memory of them all.

I see it now in my mind's eye. My dad screaming and swearing in the middle of the night in the living room of our tiny terraced house. I found out afterwards that he was drunk, but at the time I didn't quite understand why he was so out of control, so full of rage.

I'd woken up and come downstairs to find him looming over my mother. She was pleading with him to calm down, to stop shouting. But he wouldn't listen. He was fuming. He wasn't hearing a word she said.

Robbie was standing next to Mum. He must have woken up from the shouting too. He was seven years old, and I remember he was wearing Superman pyjamas.

My father spat in my mother's face. He raised his fist and began raining punches on her, clipping the side of her head with his blows. I started crying. I hid behind the legs of our dining table, terrified. Robbie was crying too. Robbie begged our father to stop. Tears were streaming down his face, but our father didn't listen. He just carried on hitting our mother, screaming at her, his rage uncontrollable.

'Stop it, Daddy,' Robbie implored as blood trickled down my mother's temple and my father raised his fist once more.

But my father was unstoppable. He swung at my mother and she cried out in agony. It was like Robbie wasn't even there.

My father raised his fist. My mother cowered on the floor, shielding her face with her hands, shaking, as blood trickled on to the carpet.

'Daddy, don't! Don't!' Robbie screamed, standing in front of my mother, his arms raised wide, trying to protect her.

Finally, my father registered him. But he was undeterred.

His eyes blazed, livid, and he turned and grabbed a fire iron from the fireplace. He spun round, wielding it before Robbie, a murderous look in his eyes. Robbie gasped and tried to run, but he didn't stand a chance. My father swung the fire iron right into Robbie's chest.

Robbie wailed and went flying, his small body tumbling to the ground. My mother cried out in protest and crawled across the floor towards him, but my father raised the fire iron once more and dealt another forceful blow to Robbie's torso. Blood flowed through his pyjama top.

He lay there, lifeless. Knocked out, unconscious. My mother wailed. She screamed at my father, furious, and tried to comfort Robbie, tears and blood dripping from her face.

I hid behind the table legs, shaking. Neither my father nor my mother had seen me yet, but I feared I was next.

206

Something inside me told me to run.

And so I did. I turned and ran out of the room.

I ran down the hall. I reached for the handle of the front door, my heart beating fast, my father screaming and raging in the background.

As I pulled the handle down, I heard a scream that wasn't from my father.

It was Robbie.

'Becky! Help!' he cried out.

He must have come round. And he cried for me. A desperate, plaintive cry.

I stood with the front door open, a cool breeze flowing through.

'Help!' he cried.

My heart fluttered in my chest. I knew I should turn back and go to help him. I'd always loved my big brother. He read me stories at night when I couldn't sleep and he'd even play with my dolls with me. I knew he didn't want to play girly games like that, but he did it anyway, to make me happy. And yet when he called out, crying for my help, I froze. I was paralysed with fear.

I heard my dad scream and groan, and I bolted.

I ran out of the front door on to the cold street. I ran along the pavement, my feet bare. I ran and ran until someone found me. A couple, on their way home from dinner in town. A kind couple, who I was lucky to find. They called the police, and I was rescued. I never had to go home again. I was taken into care, placed with Linda and Alfie.

I found out what happened next. Linda, accompanied by a few kind, gentle police officers, told me one afternoon. My father had killed my mother and then killed himself. Robbie had survived. He'd been placed in care too.

They spared me the details, but of course, over the years, I found out. My father bludgeoned my mother to death using the fire iron he'd hit Robbie with, and then, when he was done, he took a knife from the kitchen and slashed his wrists. He was a deeply troubled man, with a history of violence and domestic abuse.

A neighbour heard the commotion and called the police, who arrived at the scene to find Robbie sitting in the living room in a pool of our father's blood, crying and dazed. Police said he was holding our dead mother's hand. The thought makes me shudder, even now.

For years, I tried telling myself that Robbie couldn't have stayed conscious. I wanted to believe that he passed out again after calling for help, and that he'd been unconscious when our mother was murdered and our father killed himself. I told myself that he couldn't have seen anything. I wanted to believe it so badly, but I don't think Robbie did pass out. I think he saw everything. I could see it in his dark eyes, in the hateful, hurt way he looked at me. He saw unspeakable horrors that night, more than any child should ever have to see. And if I'd gone back for him, maybe he wouldn't have.

I turned my back on him. When I was placed under the care of Linda and Alfie, it was agreed that Robbie and I would be cared for separately. Our social workers didn't try to keep us in contact. Robbie was a lot more traumatised than me and needed greater support, and I think the social workers decided that I'd be better off if I was apart from him. And I accepted that. I tried to forget all about him. I just wanted to move on.

But I was wrong to think I could outrun my past and all my shameful secrets.

Now it's all coming back. It's finally catching up with me.

Robbie's back. And I suspect he wants revenge.

I left him all those years ago, alone and vulnerable. I tried to save myself.

I left him alone to suffer. And now it's my turn to feel that pain.

Chapter Thirty-Five

I head back to my hotel and jump in my car. I drive back to the spot where Robbie had parked his van, but of course, it's still not there. He hasn't returned. I drive around town, down street after street, keeping my eyes peeled for his battered grey van.

He must be here somewhere, and I need to talk to him. I need answers. I need to explain why I ran. I need to apologise. I've carried the guilt of that moment for years. It's one of the reasons I pushed that part of my childhood down. The guilt was too much to bear. I need to let him know how scared I was and how bad I've felt ever since.

I've been a coward. I wanted to move on from our past so badly that I tried to mentally erase it. I tried to blot Robbie out. Memories snag at my mind as I drive through the town.

I think of one occasion when I was about ten years old. A social worker was visiting Linda and Alfie to discuss some of the other children in their care, but as I walked past the living room, I heard my name being mentioned. I hung back and listened in. The social worker was talking about Robbie. She said that he was violent and aggressive and had been falling out with his carers, being moved again and again. At the time, it made me feel scared of him, and I was glad we were apart. A few years later, Linda and Alfie asked me if I'd be interested in seeing Robbie. Apparently, his social worker had been in touch saying he wanted to reconnect, but I refused. They let the social worker know and that was that. It was never mentioned again.

Guilt wracks me again as I think back to those days. All I wanted was a normal life. I left Robbie behind, not caring about his pain and suffering. He saw so much more than I did that fateful night, and yet I showed him no compassion. Not then, when I was a child, nor as an adult either. I've never bothered to look him up or see how he is.

I drive along the seafront. I cut down street after street, driving past hotels, restaurants, pubs, schools, churches, looking for Robbie and his van, but I can't find him. I get further out of town where it's less scenic, and drive through housing estates and past giant supermarkets and petrol stations, but I still can't find Robbie. I spot a few similar vans, but not his.

It's over an hour, maybe even two, before I eventually start to feel tired. I'm ready to give up and am about to head back to my hotel when I spot a grey van out of the corner of my eye, cutting down a side road.

I swerve, taking a sudden turn on to the road. A bus honks behind me. Flustered, I slow down then try to catch up with the van, but as I get closer, I realise it's not Robbie's. It's not battered enough, and it's got a different number plate.

The driver pulls into a front drive at the end of a cul-de-sac. I reach the end of the cul-de-sac and turn around. My heart sinks as I crash into something. Something hard. I reverse and see that I've bashed into a bollard.

Great. Just great. I'm so tired from looking for Robbie that my driving is getting sloppy. I get out of my car to inspect the damage. There's a huge scratch across my bonnet and a deep dent. I sigh, shaking my head. Normally I'd be upset, but a dent on my car is the least of my worries right now.

I'm kneeling down to check the tyre when I spot something on the pavement. It looks like some kind of gadget, a hard drive or some sort of electronic device.

I pick it up. It's about the size of my hand. I turn it over, inspecting it, when suddenly I realise what it is. In small lettering on the underside are the words 'GPS surveillance system'.

A chill sweeps through me.

Robbie must have installed this device. It's heavy. I hold it against my bonnet and it snaps against the metal, clearly containing a strong magnet. It must have been placed underneath my bonnet, magnetically attached to it all this time, and it took me crashing into the bollard to dislodge it.

No wonder Robbie knew where I was this week. He must have tracked me and followed me here. But the question is, how long has he been monitoring me? How long has he been stalking me?

I think back to the argument I had with Alex, with him telling me that someone he knew had seen me in the pub with Ryan, without admitting who it was. Was it Robbie? Did he follow me there? I have a sudden memory of eating cake in the café near work just a few weeks ago and seeing that man wearing sunglasses with his hood up, glaring at me from a bus shelter down the road. I couldn't make him out properly. He was too far away and too concealed. Just a dark figure in the distance. Could that have been Robbie too? Was he trying to scare me? Unsettle me?

Just how long has he been messing with me?

Did he follow me to the viewing I had with Elizabeth Jones and leave that slaughtered crow on my car for me to find? It must have been him.

My hairs stand on end. Could he be watching me now? Right now? As I squat on the pavement in this quiet cul-de-sac, my mind reels. How far is he willing to go to torment me? To get me back for abandoning him so many years ago?

I look around, glancing over my shoulders, taking in the sleepy suburban houses with net curtains and neatly trimmed hedges. I can't see him. But he could be hiding. I wouldn't put much past Robbie at this point.

I take the GPS and carry it over to a nearby bin.

I dump it in and get in my car.

My hands shake against the steering wheel as I drive away.

Chapter Thirty-Six

I drive back to London, panic-stricken. I want to see Alex. I want to tell him everything. And yet I don't know where to begin. If I tell him what's happened with Robbie, or 'Max' as he knows him, then I have to reveal everything. I have to admit to him that I lied about my childhood. I'd have to tell him that I come from a deeply dysfunctional family, a house of horrors.

The thought is too overwhelming. Alex is such a good, wholesome person. He has such a lovely, decent family. Would he want to be with me if he knew the dark secrets of my past? He can barely handle my interest in true crime, let alone my true crime life story.

I try to rehearse the conversation in my head, picturing myself and Alex in the kitchen, wondering how I'd even begin to tell him about my past. I go over it and over it, but the thought of seeing Alex's face contort with shock or fall with disappointment is too much. I can't stand the thought that he might judge me. Or worse, leave me. I turn the radio on and try to drown out my thoughts instead. Pop songs pour out of the speakers. I lower the window and let a warm breeze blow through. I try to lose myself in the music and the summer weather, but it's impossible. My past has finally caught up with me. My long-lost brother is back and the memory of what happened keeps crashing through my mind.

A car honks behind me and I realise I'm driving too slowly, as if wading through the fog of the past. The driver beams his headlights at me. It's irritating and I wince, picking up speed.

As I near London, I wonder whether Alex will be home. Will he have calmed down and returned by now? I still haven't heard from him.

More than anything, I want to feel his arms around me and for him to tell me that it's all going to be okay. The thought, the need, is so overwhelming that it brings tears to my eyes. I blink them back and concentrate on the road.

I arrive on my street and look over at Robbie's place, still not quite able to believe that my estranged brother has been living next door, putting on an act. There's no sign of his van and his house looks empty. He must still be in Saltwater Cove. Perhaps he's at the cul-de-sac now, looking for me, discovering the GPS device I abandoned in the bin.

I let myself into my house, praying that Alex is here, despite my nervousness about seeing him.

'Alex?' I call out as I step into the hallway, but there's no response.

His shoes are still missing from their usual spot. He could just be out, training clients, but the house feels cold and empty and I can tell he hasn't been back.

I place my overnight bag down and scoop up junk mail from the carpet – takeaway flyers and a free local newspaper that arrives a few times a week. I glance at the front page. There's a story about a missing woman. Yet another one. A nineteen-year-old brunette called Kayla Matthews. Her photo looks like it was taken at an outdoor event, a family barbeque perhaps. She's wearing a summer dress and her long dark hair falls in waves around her shoulders. She smiles into the camera with a wide, innocent smile and sparkling eyes. Hopefully, she'll turn up soon like Esme Jenkins did, having dropped off the grid, disappearing harmlessly for a romantic getaway.

As I wander into the kitchen, my suspicions that Alex hasn't been back are confirmed. The kitchen is exactly as I left it. My work lanyard lies abandoned on the table, and a mug of cold tea is still sitting where I left it before I set out.

My heart sinks. I so wanted Alex to be here. I wanted to feel loved and protected, but he clearly still needs distance from me.

I take my phone from my bag. Still no messages from him. This is getting ridiculous. In all our three years together, we've never once gone this long without speaking. I was happy to give him some space, but I'm starting to get worried now. What if something else is going on?

What if something's happened to him? What if Robbie has done something to him?

No, he wouldn't. Surely not?

I look across towards his kitchen, but it's empty. There's nothing to see.

I try calling Alex, but it goes straight to voicemail.

I wait a few moments and try again, but the same thing happens.

'Oh, God,' I fret.

I sit down at the kitchen table. I check my phone once more, and it's only then that I fully register that I have three missed calls from Anita and three texts spanning the course of the day. I've been so preoccupied with everything else that's been going on that they passed me by.

Anita: Hey Becks, are you ok? How are you holding up? Planning the baby shower and getting a bit nervous. Can we chat?

Anita: Becks?

Anita: Trying to call but can't get through. Is everything ok? You are still coming, aren't you?

Oh no. Anita sounds so tense. I should have noticed she'd been contacting me. I know how important her baby shower is to her and now she's worried I'm not even going. I feel bad, because the truth is that I'd completely forgotten about it. I had been looking forward to it, I'd even bought her that beautiful green blanket, and yet with everything else that's going on, it's been the last thing on my mind. My heart sinks at the thought of it. How can I put on a happy face now? I should pick up the phone and call her, but what am I meant to say? That my long-lost brother is back and that he seems to want to hurt me? That my father's a killer and that I left my brother alone to witness our parents' deaths?

No. I can't tell her that. Like everyone else in my life, Anita doesn't know a thing about my real family, my true past.

The rumble of an engine outside interrupts my thoughts and instinctively, I know it's Robbie. He must have figured out that I'd left Saltwater Cove. Got on my tail.

He's back.

And he's coming for me.

Chapter Thirty-Seven

I rush to the front door and peer out through its small frosted window. I see him getting out of his van. He glances over. I shrink back, hoping he can't see me.

I hear him opening his garden gate. It swings on its hinges.

I peer again and see him cross the front drive and head into his house.

Robbie. My brother. The sight of him still doesn't feel quite real.

I stand, hesitating in the hallway, wondering what to do.

Despite everything Robbie has done, stalking me, manipulating Alex and terrorising me at viewings, part of me is still drawn to him. Part of me wants to unlock the front door, go over to his place and talk to him. I think of that fleeting tenderness and softness in his eyes when I saw him at the beach. It didn't last for long, but it was there. And I felt it too. I felt the pull of that sibling bond. I was looking into the eyes of my brother, looking into the eyes of the only person who knows my truth, who really understands my past. The only person I haven't lied to.

I reach for the door chain and contemplate unfastening it. I could unlock the door and be over at Robbie's place in seconds. I could connect with my brother, who I haven't seen in twenty-five years, and yet, as my hand lingers over the lock, my fear returns.

No. I don't know what he's capable of. Despite the tenderness I saw in his eyes, despite the tug I felt towards him, he could be dangerous. He's clearly unstable.

I wander into the living room. It's getting dark outside now, and I pull the curtains closed. I check my phone again, but there's still nothing from Alex.

I don't know what to do with myself. I want to talk to someone, but I can't. I could call the police. It would make sense to. After all, I am potentially in danger. My fears about Robbie no longer seem quite so far-fetched and unfounded. He's no longer just the weird neighbour who gives me the creeps. He's my estranged brother who's been stalking me. The police would surely listen, and yet I'm not quite sure I can bring myself to call them. For months, after what happened in my first home, the police were sniffing around, and speaking to them now feels like opening a door I wanted to keep closed.

My laptop is on the coffee table next to a bottle of wine I left there on Friday night. I could do with a drink. I get a glass from the kitchen, stealing another glance at Robbie's place. His kitchen is still empty, but the light is on. I stand there watching for a moment, but nothing happens. I head back into the living room and pour myself a glass of wine. I take a sip and reach for my laptop.

I've tried to blot out my past, but I've had moments of weakness when I've descended into the dark pits of my memory. I've looked Robbie up from time to time, but I suspect that, like me, he changed his name.

Our family name is Bradshaw, but when Linda and Alfie fostered me, I chose to take on their surname of Nicholls by deed poll. Becky Nicholls. My new name made me undetectable to any ghoulish people interested in what had happened to me. It gave me a fresh start.

I've googled the name Robbie Bradshaw a few times, and nothing's ever come up. I assumed he was untraceable, but I still found myself looking him up now and then, wondering about him. The last time must have been a few years ago. There could be something new now. A news article, a social media profile, something that might help me assess the danger he poses.

I type in my laptop password and check, but there's still nothing. Just Robbie Bradshaws that aren't him. Profiles I've seen before.

I think back to googling his alias, Max Sidwell, and realise that there's one place I forgot to try: the true crime forum. I've searched for Robbie on there before, worried he might have gone down the same path as my dad, but never found anything. I'd hoped my brother had reinvented himself like I had and was leading a quiet life. Clearly, I was wrong.

I sigh and log on. Part of the reason I've spent too much time on the forum over the years was to try to unravel the secrets of my past. To understand why people kill, whether it's nature or nurture. I felt if I read enough about murderers and understood them, then I could avoid ever ending up like my dad.

I type Robbie's name into the search bar in case there's something new to see, but draw a blank. I try typing 'Max Sidwell' and a post appears.

Fraudster and thief released from jail.

There's a mugshot of Robbie.

My palms sweat as I read the post. It's written by one of the most prolific members of the group.

> This is the face of violent fraudster and thief Robbie Brooks, who goes by the names Max Sidwell, Chester Jones and Matthew Adams, amongst others.

> The fraudster was released from Belmarsh Prison where he was serving a three-year sentence for grievous bodily harm after leaving a 38-year-old man with a fractured eye socket and extensive bruising following an affray outside a north London pub.

> Robbie Brooks has previous convictions for robbery and fraud and has been known to use a number of aliases to con his victims.

So I was right. Robbie did change his name. Like me, he kept his first name and changed his surname. He's no longer a Bradshaw. And yes, he is dangerous. Just like our father. The apple didn't fall far from the tree after all.

I sip my wine as I reread the post. No wonder Robbie has been so good at conning me and Alex – this is what he does. I examine his mugshot, zooming in on it.

He looks so much like me. How did I not see it before? He has the same eyes, the same mouth, the exact same hair colour. Looking at his photo is weirdly like looking in the mirror. A mirror where I see my features and what I could have become.

I google the name 'Robbie Brooks' and a few articles appear, confirming Robbie's assault conviction. I'm shuddering as I take them in, when suddenly, my thoughts are interrupted by a scream. A terrified, blood-curdling woman's scream.

And it sounds like it's coming from Robbie's house.

Chapter Thirty-Eight

I jump up from the sofa and rush to the window. I look over at Robbie's place, but there's nothing to see.

I can't hear a thing. No screaming. Nothing. Just the hum of traffic in the distance, the faint sound of a siren.

The scream vanished as quickly as it came, like a firework blasting and then dissipating into the air. I felt a rush of fear at the sound of it, but now that silence has returned, I don't know what to think. Was Robbie listening to his terrible music again? Or watching a film? Surely he's not hurting someone. I thought I was his target. But I think of the post I found about him in the forum, the articles. Of course he could be hurting someone.

I get my phone. I'm not going to turn a blind eye this time.

I dial 999, my hands shaking.

The operator picks up.

I can feel my heart pounding hard in my chest as I explain what happened. I haven't had to deal with the police for years, not since I escaped from my first home, and speaking to them unnerves me. It brings back even more pain from the past. But I plough on regardless. Even though I'm breathing a little heavily and my words are stuttered, all over the place, I explain everything, from Robbie being my long-lost brother, to his convictions for violence, and my fears that he might be hurting someone.

The operator is silent in response. A few moments pass.

'So you heard a scream from the house next door?' he says.

'Yes,' I reply. 'From my brother's house. He has a history of violence.' I stress my words, trying to bring home quite how serious this is.

'I understand,' the operator says. 'But we can't send anyone over to investigate a scream. Did you see anything?'

I pace the room, agitated. 'No, but what if he's hurting someone? I saw him march this woman into the back of a van a few weeks ago,' I say, explaining the incident in full.

'And do you know who this woman was?' the operator asks.

'No . . .' I reply.

'Right. Unfortunately, we won't be able to send anyone over at this stage. But please call back if you see anything,' the operator says, sounding tense, impatient, clearly wanting to end the call.

I feel two inches tall, deflated. I stupidly thought the police would do something.

'Can you not send someone out? Just to check? He has a history of violence,' I reiterate.

'No, we can't. Not unless you saw an incident, we can't send someone over because of a scream.'

I feel foolish, beaten down.

'Okay, fine,' I reply petulantly.

'Thanks for calling. Goodbye.' The operator hangs up.

The line goes dead. Great. I slump on to the sofa, still shaken, my palms sweaty. So much for reaching out.

I sit like that for a while, trying to calm down, listening to the sounds coming from the street outside. I can hear cars coming and going, a few people walking past chatting, a peel of laughter from a passer-by, but no screams.

I get up and head to the front door. I unfasten the chain lock and step outside. I'm only wearing my socks and I can feel the

222

gravel through the fabric. I walk down my drive and turn to get a good look at Robbie's place.

None of his lights are on. I can't see or hear anything untoward.

I stand on the driveway for a while. A few cars pass on the street. But nothing changes.

I head back inside. I lock the door behind me, adding the chain lock, and go to the kitchen. Robbie's kitchen light is off. I can't see anyone. The lights upstairs are off too. Has he gone to bed? What's going on?

I glance at the time on the oven: it's 10.35 p.m. Perhaps he is in bed.

It's almost like I imagined the scream. I can't see any signs of anything going on at his place.

I sigh and my sigh turns into a yawn. I realise how tired I am. I should probably sleep. It's been a long day. I head upstairs and get into bed, still feeling tense and uneasy, but tiredness overwhelms me and I fall into a deep sleep.

I wake hours later, sunlight streaming through the window, to the sound of banging. Violent, aggressive banging.

It sounds like it's coming from downstairs.

Half asleep, I crawl out of bed and wander down to the hallway. Someone's banging, slamming their fist against the front door.

Fear shoots through me. Who could it be? Robbie? The police?

I stand still, gripped by fear, looking towards the front door. The banging continues. Whoever it is, they're banging the door so forcefully it's as though they want to smash through it.

I hurry back to the bedroom, my heart pounding in my chest, my palms sweating.

I close the bedroom door. As I close it, the banging stops.

Has the person gone?

I wait a moment, listening out, expecting the banging to start again, but it doesn't. It's stopped.

I rush over to the bedroom window and pull the curtain aside, peering out, but whoever was banging has gone. I can't see anyone. The neighbour's cat prowls along the garden fence as usual. A car passes by. A lady living a few doors down pops outside to deposit a bin bag in her bin.

Nothing looks awry. If it was Robbie, he's slipped quickly back into his house.

I let the curtain fall.

My heart's still beating fast. It must have been Robbie. He must have gone back into his house. He must be trying to scare me.

And it's working.

Rubbing the sleep from my eyes, I try to gather myself. I should call the police again. Robbie's tormenting me. This can't go on. Where's it going to end?

As I head to the bathroom, I glance down the stairs towards the front door and spot something. Something red. Red ink on the free newspaper that comes a few times a week.

Strange.

I walk downstairs to get a closer look. The newspaper is lying on the doormat. Something's been written across the front page in a thick red scrawl.

I pick it up. The paper is open on an article about the missing girl, Kayla Matthews, with a message scrawled over it:

It's either you or her.

Chapter Thirty-Nine

My hands shake, the newspaper falling to my feet.

I think of the scream I heard last night. Was it Kayla? Does Robbie have her? I sink down to the floor and pick up the paper once more. The scrawled threat has been written right across Kayla's picture, which is accompanied by the headline: 'Search efforts intensify for missing girl'. According to the article, Kayla has been missing for five days now.

It's either you or her.

The threat is haunting, written in bold red marker pen. Robbie must have Kayla. The thought is unreal, and yet she's missing, I heard that scream last night, and I know that he's violent and unstable. And now he's threatening to hurt Kayla unless I step in. Unless I offer myself to him.

This must be the final stage in his plot to get me back for abandoning him years ago. First he ruins my life, and now he wants me dead, just like our parents. I think of my father. The worst memory I have of him flashes through my mind, the way his face twisted with rage as he screamed and punched my mother, how crazed he looked as he attacked Robbie with the fire iron. He was violent, vicious, intent on causing harm. He was completely out of control. It seems like Robbie is just like him.

I try to shake off the memory and turn my attention back to the paper. I take another look at the picture of Kayla. She looks like a nice girl, her smile bright and happy, her eyes hopeful. My palms bead with sweat as I think of how she must be feeling now, what Robbie could be doing to her. She must be terrified. Five days is a long time to be held captive. Was she locked in his house while Robbie followed me to Saltwater Cove? What's he been doing to the poor girl? I read the article in full, having only skimmed it before. She went missing while walking to work, on the way to start an early shift at a supermarket. Robbie must have swiped her off the road and bundled her into his van. The thought is unbearable. I get up and start pacing around. I don't know what to do. Robbie is even more twisted than I thought. This is no longer between me and him. He's roped a poor, innocent young woman into it. Kayla doesn't deserve to be caught up in this mess. She has nothing to do with me and Robbie.

I reach for my phone. I could call the police and tell them everything, but what if they don't believe me? What if they think I'm making this whole thing up? Long-lost brothers, screams in the middle of the night, scrawled messages on newspapers. It sounds far-fetched. What if they don't take me seriously? What if they write me off as crazy, just like everyone else?

And what if it's too late? What if Robbie is tormenting Kayla right now? What if he kills her while I pace the hallway, panicking?

No. I can't call the police. This is on me. If I hadn't abandoned Robbie, if I hadn't treated him like he didn't exist just so I could move on with my life, then he wouldn't be doing this. He wouldn't be this broken. He wouldn't be this hell-bent on getting revenge.

As I continue to pace, I have an overwhelming urge to be with Alex. To feel his strong arms around me, protecting me from the world, keeping me safe from harm. Tears tremble down my cheeks. Our old life suddenly feels so distant, like a fairy tale. Things were so easy, so perfect. All the little pleasures we shared – nights in spent cuddling on the sofa watching box sets, daydreamy conversations about having kids, Sunday afternoon riverside walks. It feels like another world. One far removed from my new reality. My new, warped, horrific reality.

I think of the fleeting softness in Robbie's eyes as I recognised him on the beach, but there's no softness to him. He's wicked. He's dangerous. He's merciless.

I don't want him to hurt me, but I'm awash with guilt, fear.

Kayla's scream last night echoes through my mind as my heart quickens.

It's me or Kayla.

I can't handle having another person's suffering weighing on my conscience. I can't handle another person dying. Not after my mum. I can't handle leaving another broken person behind me.

I take another look at Kayla's picture. Her wide smile. Her bright eyes. I think of her parents. A loving family, fraught with worry, wanting her back more than anything.

I put the newspaper down and pull my trainers on.

I open the front door and step outside.

Chapter Forty

I walk out on to the overcast street, still wearing my pyjamas, and head next door to Robbie's place.

I push open his gate, drizzle spitting on my face as I walk up to his front door. He must have been waiting for me, looking out of a window, because he opens it the moment I reach his doorstep.

I shudder as I take him in, my stomach turning. His face, his features, just like mine, are twisted with dark anger. His eyes are full of fury, a burning, vengeful passion. He reminds me of a ravenous animal ready to devour its prey. He wants to destroy me. He wants to take my life. This is the moment he's been waiting for. A smile plays on his lips, and it's clear he's excited.

He pulls me into the hallway, and I realise I'm shaking as he closes the door behind me. It clicks shut. I want to run. I want to take back this decision and call the police, scream for help, but the door's closed and Robbie is only inches from me, looming over me. I can smell the sour, pungent odour of his sweat. He smells like he hasn't washed for days. His hair is greasy. He appears to have abandoned his well-groomed Max persona entirely. He's a mess. A scowling, cruel mess.

I hear the sound of moaning. It's coming from his kitchen.

'Kayla. Oh my God! What are you doing to her?' I ask, horrified.

He doesn't respond. He just smirks, pleased with himself.

'Shut up, bitch,' a woman's voice says, and I hear the clatter of metal.

A woman? Does he have an accomplice?

'What the hell, Robbie? What's going on? Let her go,' I plead.

I try to barge past him, but Robbie grabs me, gripping my arms. I try to wrench myself free, but his grip is like steel. He's much stronger than me, and he knows it. He regards me with that cold, cruel smirk as the moaning continues. An innocent woman is suffering and he's smirking, like the cat who got the cream. I feel revolted.

The groaning intensifies. I struggle against Robbie's grip once more. He watches me squirm and then suddenly lets me go. I run towards the sound. It's coming from the kitchen.

'Kayla?' I call out as I cross the hall.

Robbie's house has the exact same layout as mine and I run into the kitchen, but the first person I see isn't Kayla, it's Elizabeth. Elizabeth Jones. That strange woman who came to view the Lake Street house last week, just before I found the dead crow. What the hell?

I look from her to the floor, my stomach lurching as I take in the sight before me. Kayla, unmistakably Kayla, the girl from the paper, in a cage. Her wrists and ankles are bound, a gag in her mouth. She fixes me with a look of sheer terror and moans loudly. I gasp, unable to believe what I'm seeing. She's trapped like an abused animal. Tears stream down her face. She's far removed from the happy, smiling version of herself emblazoned across the front page of the paper. She looks exhausted, like she hasn't slept for days. Her eyes are surrounded by dark shadows, her skin pallid, white as a ghost. Her dark hair, which fell in flowing waves over her shoulders in the photograph, hangs in matted, messy clumps around her face. She groans and squirms against her chains, which rattle as she moves. She eyes me imploringly. I rush over, but the cage is thick and heavy, and locked with chains.

'How could you?' I glare at Elizabeth, who watches me with a cold smirk similar to Robbie's.

Kayla groans.

'I said, "Shut up, bitch",' Elizabeth hisses at her, kicking the cage.

'What the hell is wrong with you?' I spit.

She rolls her eyes. 'What the hell is wrong with me? What the hell is wrong with you, Becky? What's wrong with you?' she rages, charging into me, her fingers jabbing into my shoulders.

I stumble backwards, but someone catches me. Robbie. He's standing behind me.

'Who turns their back on their brother?' Elizabeth continues, screaming in my face. 'Who leaves him all alone? He saw your parents die and you abandoned him. You just forgot all about him. Your own flesh and blood. You're sick.'

I cower, turning away, unable to meet her scathing gaze. I look to Kayla. She eyes me desperately, but she seems shocked by Elizabeth's outburst too and whimpers weakly. I feel like the room is spinning. The past that I've spent a lifetime denying is rearing its head in the worst possible way. An ugly, twisted horror show.

Robbie throws me towards Elizabeth, or whatever her name is, and she grabs me. Her fingers are like claws, digging into my arms.

She shoves me against the wall, and I gasp. She grabs me by the throat, her grip iron tight. I look into her hard, dark eyes, and feel the force of her hate. I can feel it in the strength of her clutch around my neck. This isn't the first time she's done this. I want to hide, run away, be far away, and yet I can't help feeling that on some level, she's right. I am to blame. I turned my back on Robbie and look how he's ended up. Look at what's happened.

I splutter, struggling to breathe as Elizabeth grips my throat. I hear footsteps along the hall and it's only then that I realise Robbie's left the room. I glance at Kayla. She's like a ghost in the corner, cowering in fear, curled up in a ball, her eyes wide and afraid.

Robbie charges back into the kitchen. Elizabeth turns to look at him, smiling. I notice her tattoo again. The initials 'R.B.' on her neck in a heart. I saw the tattoo at the viewing, but I didn't think much of it. R.B. are Robbie's initials. She must be his lover, his partner. She must have been in on this whole thing, distracting me with the viewing while Robbie gutted the crow. No wonder she was gazing out of the bedroom window so long during the viewing – she was probably watching Robbie prepare his morbid spectacle.

My hairs stand on end. I feel like defenceless prey, surrounded by predators. Robbie appears before me. He's still smiling that smug, self-satisfied smile, but now he's carrying a fire iron. A huge, dark, heavy fire iron.

The walls feel like they're closing in on me. It's payback time. He's recreating the past.

'Robbie,' I try to say, but Elizabeth still has her hand around my throat and it comes out as a croak. 'Robbie, please . . .' I splutter.

Elizabeth tightens her grip, her nails digging into my flesh. I wince with pain. She's so close that I can smell her. That sour tobacco smell I remember from the viewing. I can feel her breath on my cheek. I can feel my eyes bulging, my cheeks swelling. She smiles. She's enjoying hurting me. She and Robbie have clearly been waiting for this moment for a while.

'Let her speak. I want to hear her plea,' Robbie says, glancing wickedly at Elizabeth.

She smiles and loosens her grip around my neck.

'I'm sorry. I didn't mean to hurt you. I just . . . I wanted to move on after what happened,' I tell him, tears springing to my eyes. 'It was too painful.'

It sounds weak out loud, but it's the truth. I didn't see as much as Robbie saw that night, but I was scared and broken too. I was terrified of our past. I didn't want to confront it, and Robbie made it real. By blotting him out, I was almost able to pretend that it hadn't happened. Without Robbie, I had a chance to feel normal. But it's selfish. Weak.

Robbie scoffs. 'Yeah,' He laughs. 'You just wanted to move on, didn't you? With your nice boyfriend and your nice little house and your normal job. You forgot that I ever existed. You treated me like I was nothing,' he rages, getting right up into my face, his eyes blazing.

I shrink, looking away, unable to face his rage.

'I cried out for you to help me and you ran away,' Robbie growls.

I meet his gaze. His eyes are dark, full of hurt, rage.

'I'm sorry,' I mutter, even though I know it's not enough. Tears fall down my cheeks. I feel overwhelmed with self-loath-ing. As though I deserve everything. I deserve to suffer. I deserve this.

'I watched our father smash our mother's head in. I watched him bludgeon her to death. I heard the sound of her skull caving in. I saw it all. I heard it all. I watched him slash his wrists,'

I wince. His words are like daggers, wounding me one by one. I can't take it. I blink and more tears fall. He's right. I left him alone to witness the most unimaginable of horrors. I turned my back on him then and I've turned my back on him ever since.

No wonder he's angry. No wonder he hates me. He had no one. He's been alone in the world, carrying the most horrific pain, and I did nothing.

'I'm sorry,' I tell him, meaning it.

I am sorry,' I let him down. I chose the easy route. I chose self-preservation over my brother. I chose a normal life over doing the right thing. Robbie's messed up, but so am I. I'm selfish, ruthless. I would never stalk someone, torment someone. I'd never lock someone in a cage, binding them with chains, and gagging them, like Robbie's done to Kayla, but I trapped Robbie in a cage of sorts. I left him alone to deal with his trauma, trapped in a prison of his past. I knew as a child he'd been wanting to see me, and I simply refused. I had a nice life with Linda and Alfie and that was what mattered to me.

'It's too late for sorry,' Robbie says.

He swings the fire iron.

I gasp, shrinking against the wall. I can barely look as the fire iron careers through the air. Robbie's face contorts with fury as it lands on my arm. A searing pain shoots through me and I cry out in agony.

I'm distantly aware of Kayla moaning when Robbie swings again, this time at my head.

I collapse to the ground. The sound of Kayla muffles. My vision darkens.

I hear something in the distance – sirens, banging – but it's faint, barely a whisper. And then everything goes black.

Chapter Forty-One

I sit, my fingers knotted in my lap.

I can feel eyes on me. A man, sitting at a table not far from mine, is staring at me. He has been for a while. He has haunting bloodshot eyes and wispy white hair, but I'm avoiding looking his way. I pick at a cuticle, keep my eyes down.

The room is cold, icy. It's never quite warm enough, and no matter how many times I come here, I never seem to wear enough layers. I glance up, across the meeting room.

The man with the bloodshot eyes has got bored of me. He's staring at someone else now.

I look up at the clock on the wall. A few minutes to go.

I've been here three times before and every time, I've been a nervous wreck. They don't make it easy. It's not like there's anything in this room that might make me feel remotely relaxed. No wall art. No plants. Nothing. Just shabby old tables. Frosted windows with bars across them. A faint smell of bleachy floor cleaner.

I tap my foot against the floor while staring at the clock.

Robbie's always punctual. To the dot. His prison officer makes sure of it.

The hand on the clock creeps towards the hour point. I tap my foot again. A guard smiles at me. A kind smile, like he can tell that I'm nervous. I smile back and take a deep breath, trying to calm down.

Alex thought it was crazy when I told him I wanted to start visiting Robbie. He begged me not to. Not after what Robbie did. He left me, bludgeoned on the kitchen floor, blood pooling around me. Kayla, trapped in the cage, saw everything. I lost consciousness after the first few blows and apparently Robbie staggered backwards and dropped the fire iron, trembling, as I began to bleed. Kayla told the police that Robbie's accomplice 'Elizabeth' had been urging Robbie to 'finish me off', but he lost his nerve. They ended up having a huge argument.

Meanwhile, Alex arrived home. He'd cooled off at his parents' place and was ready to make up with me, but he found the house empty. He heard the commotion next door, shouting, screaming. He saw Robbie, or Max, as he still knew him, storming across the kitchen, raging at Elizabeth, and he recalled what I'd said about Max manhandling a woman into the back of a van. He panicked. And then he heard a scream, from another woman, from Kayla. He called the police and went over. Robbie didn't answer and Alex urged the police to come, hearing screams emanating from the house.

Fortunately, they showed up. Elizabeth fled the house, barging past Alex on the front doorstep just before the police arrived. Alex walked in to find Robbie sitting at the kitchen table, staring into space, white as a ghost, shaking. He found me, passed out, my arm pulverised, and Kayla in her cage. And then the police arrived.

The door opens and there he is.
My brother.
Our eyes lock. A small smile plays on his lips.
I smile back.

He looks better than the last time I visited, a few weeks ago. The shadows under his eyes have gone. His skin is less sallow. He looks brighter.

His guard walks him over.

His handcuffs rattle as he sits down opposite me. The sound makes me flinch.

'Hey,' I say, ignoring the guard, who watches us both like a hawk, standing just a few feet away.

'Hi, Becky,' he replies.

He regards me. Taking me in, like I took him in. Assessing me. He glances at my arm and looks away, clearing his throat.

I know he regrets what he did to me. My arm will never be the same again. I suffered irreparable nerve damage, muscle damage and broken bones. It's mangled. I have physio appointments every week to try to coax movement back into my wrist and fingers, but it's hard. I can't drive. I can't use a knife and fork properly. I can't type. I can't scratch my face if I get an itch. My arm is just there. A painful reminder of what I went through. A karmic backlash.

'How've you been?' Robbie asks, glancing again at my arm.

I can see the guilt in his eyes. They glaze over with tears. He blinks the emotion away.

The first time I came to visit Robbie, we barely spoke. We just sat there, both of us stunned. I was terrified to see him at first. I cried, I trembled. And then he cried. He cried and cried. He sobbed. He apologised. He said 'sorry' over and over, begging me to forgive him. He told me that seeing me bludgeoned on the kitchen floor didn't give him the release he thought it would. In fact, it made everything fall apart for him. He thought hurting me would set him free, but it only brought home his pain even more. He was wracked with guilt. He's had a huge mental shift and feels terrible for everything he's done.

He wouldn't believe it when I told him I didn't hate him. He was convinced I would, but I can't hate him. To me, he's still that little boy in his Superman pyjamas who called out for help that fateful night. He's damaged and broken, but he's still my brother. My brother who I turned my back on once before and refuse to give up on again.

Despite what I said, Robbie clearly hated himself for what he'd done to me, not only the attack but everything else. He admitted that he'd tracked me down online years earlier and had been paying attention to what I was up to through my social media accounts, gathering scraps of information here and there. He planned to strike when I was doing well, when I had enough to lose, so he waited until I was in a loving relationship, had a good job and had settled down in a nice house. He wanted to pierce my happy bubble and destroy my life. It was a stroke of luck for Robbie when my elderly neighbour moved out. He seized the opportunity to move in next door, charming the landlord and paying rent up front in cash with money from one of his various schemes. He moved in with the intention of tormenting me and destroying my life.

It started with the troll comment on my Instagram feed and went from there. He posed as the buyer, Edward, putting on a voice to arrange the viewing where I got locked out of the house. Of course, I didn't get locked out. I walked down the drive, and Robbie, who'd been hiding in the shadows down the side of the house, snuck out and pulled the door closed. He left Edward's scathing Google review about me. And he admitted that he researched Alex online and deliberately befriended him through training sessions, just like I suspected, with the goal of playing us off against each other.

He'd been following me around too. He was the dark figure I saw down the road that time I was at the café near work, having cake. He admitted to installing a GPS device on my car. He knew

237

where I was. He knew I was at the pub the night I tried to set Lucy up with Ryan. He followed me and looked in from outside, watching what was happening. He told Alex that I'd been flirting with Ryan, planting mistrust and paranoia in Alex's mind. He was relentless.

He gutted the crow too, when I had the Lake Street viewing with 'Elizabeth'. Elizabeth was, in fact, Robbie's on-off girlfriend, whose real name is Scarlett. Like Robbie, Scarlett's been in and out of prison her entire life. She knew about Robbie's desire to get revenge on me, which he'd been harbouring for a long time, and she actively encouraged him. Some of his nasty tricks were her idea, like trolling me on Instagram and leaving nasty reviews. It turned out she was the woman I witnessed Robbie bundle into the back of the van that night. They'd been having some crazy argument, both of them high on something.

It was Scarlett's idea to kidnap a young woman and use her to bait and torment me. Robbie had been fantasising about getting back at me for a long time, but Scarlett galvanised him. Together, they took their plan to a new level. Robbie had planned to hold the redhead hostage when he had her over for a date. She was a woman he met online who he thought he could entrap, but in the end, he couldn't bring himself to go through with it and he let her go, much to Scarlett's disappointment. When she found out, she and Robbie got in Scarlett's battered old van, the one I'd seen Robbie use, and went hunting for a victim. They spotted Kayla and snatched her off the street. Just like that. They roped an innocent girl into their sick twisted revenge plot. I can just about forgive Robbie for what he did to me, but I haven't forgiven him for what he did to Kayla. That's going to take some time. She was saved by police and despite being tired and hungry, she had no physical injuries apart from bruising. But she's been left traumatised, suffering from anxiety and PTSD.

The only thing that Robbie refused to take responsibility for was my botched open house. I figured he'd covered the garden with litter to humiliate me. After all, his alias, Edward, was meant to be showing up. But Robbie denied it. At first I didn't believe him, but then strangely enough, Ryan came forward with another side to the story.

He'd been in the office late on a Friday evening and had walked past Susan's desk, only to find her making a note about my viewing and adding it to her calendar. He thought it was a little odd, but he didn't think too much of it. Then the next morning, he was on a run when he spotted Susan outside the property. At first, he didn't recognise her. She was wearing leggings and a hoodie, with the hood pulled up – a far cry from her usual polished office persona. But then he caught sight of her face and realised who she was. He was about to approach her but noticed that she seemed preoccupied, intense. She was wearing gloves, which struck him as odd for the middle of summer. He stood, taking her in, perplexed as he watched her haul a bin bag of rubbish out of the bin before carrying it around to the back of the house.

Ryan ran on, still a bit confused, especially since she was dressed casually and clearly not about to do a viewing. But he let it go, forgetting all about it, until he heard about everything that had happened to me. He realised that it wasn't just Robbie who'd been messing with me. He had a change of heart and realised how badly he'd behaved.

Susan was interviewed by HR at the office with a police officer sitting in, and she crumbled. She admitted that she'd deliberately left rubbish all over the garden of my open house in the hope of ruining it for me. Anita had been right about her. She wasn't to be trusted.

The matter was taken seriously, and Susan was fired.

I started back at work a few months ago. Part-time for now. It's not easy with the pain and lack of mobility in my arm, but I'm getting there. And work is so much better now that Susan has gone. Wendy has moved on too, thankfully, getting a job closer to her family back home. They were getting me down more than I cared to admit.

Robbie is still blinking back tears. He can't forgive himself for what he did to me. We've been getting to know each other, bit by bit, but the scars remain. At times, I have waves of fear of him, flashbacks. I came to see him a month ago, and I had a flashback of him hitting me that was so intense I had to leave. But I came back. I refuse to turn my back on Robbie this time. And as I've got to know him, I've realised that I like him. He's smart. He would never have got away with all his cunning schemes if he weren't. He can be sweet too. He has issues, a lot of issues, but I think his heart is in the right place. He wants to move forward. I think, deep down, he wants a sister as much as I want a brother. Unwittingly, we've both been fixated on our past for years. I was obsessed with creating an idealised future and shutting it away, and Robbie was obsessed with 'fixing' his past by getting revenge on me. Neither of us had moved on. But now, even in this crazy situation, I think we are.

He places his cuffed hands on the table. I want to hold him, and I reach across. He lets me do that. My fingers are cold against his warm palm. He clasps my hand. I feel relief flood through me. Despite everything Robbie's done, I still care about him. I still love him. I look into his eyes, which still surprise me at times given how much it's like looking in a mirror.

We talk. Robbie tells me about the conditions of his detention: the food he's eating, the exercise he's getting, the books he's reading. He's being held in custody until his trial later in the year for assaulting me and kidnapping Kayla. He knows he'll get a substantial sentence. The outcry over what happened to Kayla was huge, and a lot of people want to see him, and Scarlett, go down for a long time. Personally, I don't want to see Robbie stuck in prison for years and years, but what he did to Kayla was wrong, and I still don't feel completely safe around him either. It'll take time. I'll keep visiting him, building up trust. And hopefully in that time, he can work on himself too.

Despite everything, though, things are good. My arm has caused me immense pain, and I've suffered with anxiety too. But Alex saw me through. I told him everything. All the secrets from my childhood that I'd kept hidden came out. I feared for so long that he would fall out of love with me, but it's been the opposite. We're closer than ever. What we went through has brought us together and we're unbreakable now. I no longer have any doubts or worries over our relationship, like I did before. Our bond feels unshakeable.

Life is looking up for me. And yet I feel guilty about that. I've come out the other side of all this feeling positive about the future. And as usual, Robbie is a prisoner of our past.

We talk about the upcoming trial.

'I deserve whatever I get,' Robbie sighs.

I smile awkwardly and look down at the table.

Robbie tells me about a letter he's written to Kayla. 'My lawyer said her family won't speak to me. They don't want to hear a word from me, but I've written the letter anyway. I want to apologise. She doesn't have to open it.'

'Even if you just wrote it for yourself, it's a good thing,' I comment.

'Yeah, you're right,' Robbie smiles.

A silence passes between us.

The prison guard clears his throat. I glance at the clock. We don't have much time left.

'I feel like there's something else,' Robbie says, narrowing his eyes, regarding me intently.

'What do you mean?' I laugh.

'I feel like you have something else going on, like you're holding something back.'

I laugh again, but I know exactly what he's talking about. We may have lost touch for years and years, but Robbie somehow has a way of seeing me, understanding me.

'Okay, I'll tell you.'

I take a deep breath, gathering strength, although my heart flutters in my chest.

I haven't told anyone what I'm about to tell him. Not even Alex.

'I'm . . .' I glance down at the table, gulp. I look back up, into Robbie's familiar eyes. 'I'm pregnant.'

His mouth falls open before breaking into a grin.

'Seriously?'

'Yes!' I admit, grinning back, tears pricking my eyes. 'I did a test last night. Two, in fact. It hasn't sunk in yet.'

'Becky?' Robbie squeezes my hands. 'I would hug you but . . .'

He rolls his eyes down at his cuffs.

I laugh.

'Congratulations,' he says, his eyes tender.

'Thank you,' I reply.

I blink and two tears fall. I flick them away.

Robbie's eyes are wet too. 'You're going to be a great mother,' he says.

I smile, grateful. 'I hope so.'

We smile sadly at each other, the ghosts of our past still present.

'Time's up. We have to go back now,' the prison guard says to Robbie.

242

We both sigh, groaning. We get up and I hug Robbie, even though he can't hug me back. We say goodbye and he congratulates me again, telling me how he can't wait to be an uncle. His cuffs rattle as the guard leads him away.

I make my way out of the prison.

The air outside is cool, wintry. There are no leaves on the trees. They're gnarled, exposed.

As I walk to my car, I burst into tears and my body starts to shake. Once more, Robbie's trapped and I'm the one who's free.

ACKNOWLEDGEMENTS

I would like to thank my editor at Amazon, Leodora Darlington, for her support and incredibly insightful editorial guidance on this novel. I've learnt so much throughout the editorial process and I feel very grateful to have had such a sharp and talented editor. Thanks so much, Leodora.

A huge thanks too to my developmental editor Emily Ruston, whose knowledge and feedback has been invaluable. Again, I have learnt so much from working with Emily. Thank you too to my copyeditor Gill Harvey for her astute and incisive editorial work on this novel, which has been extremely helpful.

I'd also like to thank my brilliant agent, Rukhsana Yasmin at The Good Literary Agency, for her positivity and faith in me. Having the backing of such a great agent and agency has been a real blessing for my career. Thank you so much, Rukhsana!

Thank you as well to my lovely author friend, Sophia Spiers, for all the chats and camaraderie, as well as her fantastic feedback on this book. Thanks, Sophia! And thank you to fellow Thomas & Mercer author Matt Brolly for allowing me to pick his brains on the thriller author experience!

ABOUT THE AUTHOR

Zoe Rosi has a background in journalism and copywriting. She worked as a reporter for local and national newspapers before moving into the fashion industry as a copywriter. Zoe had four romantic comedies published before writing her debut thriller. It was while working as a fashion copywriter that Zoe had the idea for her first thriller, which she describes as '*The Devil Wears Prada* meets *American Psycho*'. *Someone's Watching Me* is Zoe's second thriller.